Anonymous

by Mike Morey

also by Mike Morey:
Uncle Dirty

Anonymous; Copyright ©2009 by Mike Morey. All rights reserved, including the right to reproduce this book or portions thereof in any form whatsoever. For information, contact the author: mmoreywriter@myspace.com

Morey, Mike
Anonymous: a novel / Mike Morey
ISBN 978-0-557-21380-1

Cover design: Cathy Elliott

for Jeannette

Chapter 1

There is a soft knock on the door.

I ignore it, reasoning that it must be a hallucination. Or maybe just the wisp of a fading dream. Was I asleep?

And anyway, who would be knocking? I couldn't remember the last time it had happened. Years, at any rate. I wonder if the sound came from next door. The acoustics in my building are not good, which is part of the charm of these former warehouses, now converted into chic urban living spaces. The word "loft," as everyone knows, is French for "bad acoustics."

Another knock. Definitely my door. A visitor. A friend? I had one once, my friend the writer, but I haven't heard from him in a long time. If I were a real friend, I would go knock on *his* door, make sure he's all right.

There was a time when my door was always open, receiving fashion models, agents, directors, other actors, an endless parade of young students looking for the secret formula that will make them a star. I didn't have the secret formula, not then, but they didn't know that. The secret is that there is no secret. Fame is a virus you catch by touching the wrong handrail, making contact with the wrong person. You go to bed feeling fine, and by morning you're hot, baby, hot! Surrounded by sycophants and wannabe's, staggering under the weight of all that money, sweating from the exertion of satisfying your many and assorted admirers. Somehow you manage.

It's been nearly a decade since my retirement from the stage and screen, twice that since my name was on anybody's list. Anybody that mattered. Five years since the last young acting tyro wrung from me the final few drops of knowledge and wisdom I had to offer. The intervening years have been a sort of purgatory, neither here nor there, but not entirely unpleasant. Just unproductive, professionally.

And now this relentless knocking. As if I have nothing better to do than answer the door. Let me check my schedule. Call my people and we'll set something up, kiss-kiss.

I look myself over, what I can see of me, and it's not pretty. A ragged housecoat that once belonged to my wife, grey hairs poking from the cleavage like weeds coming up through a sidewalk; bare feet, white and reptilian, cold from the cement floor; hands that suffer tremors when given simple tasks. If there really is someone at my door—and I have lingering doubts—do I want them to see me like this? There was a time when it would have mattered to me, how I looked, how I appeared to others, but no longer. If the Mormons have somehow managed to sneak past the building security, they are in for a shock when I open my door and reveal the extent of my decay. I should have installed a peephole years ago.

And then, like a ship emerging from a dense fog, a name drifts into the shallow harbour of my brain: McInnis...McManus. Something like that, scribbled at the bottom of a correspondence I'd recently received.

Recently?

Barney...no, Barry. A name starting with P or L? A writer, but not my friend the writer, a different one, a movie buff, fan of the great Billy Fox, apparently. A biographer, so he claimed. An interview, if I was agreeable. Possibly a series of interviews over a period of time, names and dates, facts and figures, any anecdote I wished to share with my fans. Too kind, sir, too kind.

"You want to write a book about me?"

(This must have been a follow-up telephone call. Where else would this dialogue come from?)

"Well," said the biographer, "not *just* you. More like a compilation. A sort of *Where are they Now?* thing."

Who else, I asked, and he listed some names I'd never heard of.

"I'd open with you, Mister Fox. Chapter one."

He sounded young. I don't trust young people so much, anymore; they have such a capacity for inattention to details. A better subject for a book, I thought, but didn't say.

What I did say was this: "You might need more than one chapter for me. There's a lot to tell."

His silent pause reeked of incredulity. "In any case..."

Now, I suppose this is the biographer at my door, in person. I have no idea what day it is, what the date is, when or even if we had agreed to meet. My mind is not what it once was, which I've discovered is not always a bad thing.

I'm ready for my close-up.

Next thing I know, there is a stranger in my apartment, my acoustically impaired loft, and I can only assume I've let him in. The door is made of steel, with two good locks. One must be careful, in this neighbourhood. He is a young man, as I had guessed, in his thirties, a head taller than me, ectomorphic in structure, delicate for one so tall. The rims of his nostrils look raw, as if he suffers an enduring cold, a permanent drip. His physical weakness makes me a little nervous, I don't want him to collapse on my floor. Actors are sensitive to anyone who might upstage them. Even former actors. Retired.

"What did you say your name was?"

"Peter," he says, folding himself awkwardly onto my leather sofa. "Peter Koenbutt."

Had I made a mistake? I thought I had admitted a McInnis…McManus, and here I am with a Koenbutt. As I settle into a chair, I look severe. "Surely, you don't intend to put that name on the cover of a book?"

His bones shift in their loose sack. "Is there something—"

"Never mind," I say, swatting invisible flies away from my face. "Tell me a little bit about this book, again. Remind me."

I don't really need to be reminded, I'm just nervous. Unexpectedly.

"Your story, Mister Fox. You're going to tell me about your life as an actor." He snaps on a small tape recorder and sets it on the coffee table between us. "You don't have to start at the beginning. Anything that comes to mind, in any order, will be fine. I can rearrange things, later."

"My true Hollywood story," I say.

"I beg your pardon?"

"Here's the thing about a true Hollywood story: it always ends in tragedy. It's a fundamental rule of the universe."

The biographer looks dubious. He's about to say something, but I cut him off.

"Somehow that doesn't discourage the dreamers, can't convince them to stay in school, get into a decent college, pursue that other great American dream: holy matrimony, two snotty brats and a fixed-rate mortgage. These naïve souls borrow bus money and make the pilgrimage to Hollywood, only to get used by a ruthless industry, and then tossed out like so much trash, like the bad takes left on the cutting room floor. Those once-bright-eyed kids, broken souls, rejected, recycled, now drug addicts or petty-thieves or prostitutes. Waiters, if they have any smarts left. If not, fodder for the conmen and pornographers. The lucky ones make it home, back to the farm, get themselves into rehab, enroll in college, better late than never. But most will never get out. The pull of the dream is too powerful, worse than the worst drug they will ever take. Hooked for life. Like I said: *tragedy*."

The biographer folds his legs, rubs the tip of his chin with a finger. He wants to speak, but this is my script.

"As you know, Hollywood loves a happy ending. But it's just a fictional device, it doesn't really exist. Not backstage, not in real life."

"Are you happy?"

Ignoring a direct question like a pro, I suddenly remember my manners. "You must want a beverage. Coffee or tea? I'm afraid I don't have much else in the cupboard." I get up and cross to the kitchen. One advantage of these open living spaces is that our conversation doesn't need to suffer.

"Are you happy, Mister Fox?" my guest persists.

I fill the kettle and plug it in, and then step from behind the counter, extend my arms like Moses. "I'm a feeble old man who hasn't bathed or shaved in days. I'm not allowed to drink and no woman will screw me. My hair has migrated from my head to my back, and I'm wearing a woman's bathrobe."

He looks me over, and his eyes concur.

"At this point," I tell him, "I'm not sure I'm happy to be alive."

Once the water boils, I deliver two mugs of instant coffee. "I think you'll find most of the happiness in my story is bunched up at the beginning. If you feel your readers want a happy ending, I suggest they read it back to front. Don't be shy about reading this way. The Chinese have been doing it for centuries."

He looks at me carefully, trying to decide if I'm serious. I don't even know myself.

"And I should warn you, my story takes place only briefly in the actual town of Hollywood, somewhere in the middle. I don't make the pilgrimage until I'm already relatively famous. By the time my plane lands in Los Angeles, I'm hardly a bright-eyed kid. And I'm pretty sure I'm drunk."

"Do you believe your drinking was…" He is searching for the right words. "Did it contribute to…"

"I'll let you draw your own conclusions."

The biographer nods, continues to rub his chin.

"Did I tell you about my friend the writer?" I say. "He has a charming habit of portraying himself to an unsuspecting public as a seasoned author of countless, unspecified works. But the truth is, he's never had a single word published in even the most obscure journal. He works in a medical laboratory, examining human blood and faeces, and somehow he manages to maintain his sense of optimism. 'I just keep writing and writing, and someday my ship will come in,'" he tells me. Maybe it's the clichés that are doing him in. What do you think?"

The biographer blinks noncommittally.

"Those of us who know the God-awful truth about him, pray for his ultimate success," I say. "But here's the thing. Fame is a fickle lover, and it goes in the same fashion it comes: instantly and without explanation."

We sip our coffee in silence for a moment. And then I say, "I console my friend the writer as best I can for his unrealized dreams. What are friends for? And besides, who better to understand his desolation than I. After all, I was once a somebody, and now I am, Lord help me, anonymous."

Chapter 2

I was once a beautiful boy.

When I stepped in front of the camera, I was an impressive sight. And I was more than just a pretty face. I had pipes, too. In the most dulcet tones, I took the scripted words and made them mine. If you could have seen me then, you would have believed every word I said.

Back when I was a beautiful, rich, famous boy, I lived with a girl named Selena. Naturally, she was a model. I think I can say, with all due modesty, that the camera loved us both, tremendously. We shared a spacious loft, long before such spaces became trendy. (Back in 1978, a loft was commonly referred to by its original name: a derelict warehouse. We were ahead of our time.) We filled our loft with the expensive toys of the rich and famous. After all, we were just a couple of kids with love in our eyes and money in our pockets. When we weren't strutting before the lens, Selena and I, we played with our expensive toys in the *love loft,* and threw lavish parties for our rich and beautiful friends. I was the envy of many colleagues who didn't have a hit television show, and didn't have a loft, and would never get to live with a beautiful model like Selena until they, too, got themselves a hit television show and a loft. Good luck.

Many of those envious colleagues waited tables in the restaurants that Selena and I dined at, and I always spoke encouragingly to them, never made them feel the lesser for having to pay the rent any way they could.

"I have an audition next week for a daily on your show," said Ralph Cummings. He worked at the Rosedale Diner, Selena's favourite restaurant.

Poor Ralph. He gaped at me expectantly, desperately. Ralph didn't work much. I think it was his name. Ralph: another word for puke. And Cummings: the stuff of dirty sex. Either one by itself was bad enough, but together they failed to be taken seriously in a credit roll. I had once wasted an entire evening buying him drinks and trying to convince him to change his name. For some reason, he was attached to both parts. From that I gathered he wasn't serious about acting.

"Look at Bernard Schwartz," I had said to him.

"Who?"

"Tony Curtis, you fool!"

"Who?"

Perhaps I had bought him too many drinks. Shortly after that, he ran to the bathroom and executed his first name over the first available toilet bowl.

"Maybe you can put in a good word for me," said Ralph, hovering over our table. He appeared to be unwilling to take our food order until I promised to help him. He assumed that since I was the star of a hit television show, I could pull strings and get him the part. He was right.

"Sure, sure," I said. I was starving. No doubt, so was Ralph Cummings.

Anyway, I did him the favour and talked to my producer. It turned out Ralph was up for a bit part as a waiter. One scene and two lines. I didn't think he could pull it off, and I said so to my grateful producer. Ralph needed a bit more practice to be a convincing waiter, I knew from experience.

"Thanks anyway for trying," he said to me, the next time I saw him.

What are friends for?

"You shouldn't hang around with those people," Selena said. She meant people like Ralph Cummings, waiters who think they are actors. "They call themselves your friend, but all they really want is help getting work."

"Is that such a bad thing?"

"They're not really your friends, that's all I'm saying. They're just using you. Get yourself some real friends, who aren't in the business."

"What about my friend the writer?" I said.

"God! His fingers always smell like *shit*."

My beloved Selena has a sensitive nose, dear girl.

Selena had many friends, and they were all in the business of modelling. By the ripe age of twenty, she was a veteran of the runway. She had been snatched off the farm, just outside Cut Knife, Saskatchewan, doe-eyed and lithesome, and dropped into Manhattan with a splash. She drenched the fashion world in her glistening beauty, sent awesome ripples around the globe: Rome, Paris, London, Tokyo, Brazil. She made the cover of Cosmopolitan before her sixteenth birthday, got makeup tips from Jerry Hall before her seventeenth birthday, had an abortion before her eighteenth birthday, entered a posh rehab clinic in Berlin before her nineteenth birthday. Clean and sober, and as gorgeous as ever, she met me before her twentieth birthday.

We met at a party. Neither of us knew the host, a wealthy businessman who was not in either the modelling or the film business, but who liked to surround himself with beautiful and exciting people. See and be seen. That's the name of the game. I went, and saw, and was seen by Selena from across the room.

She latched onto my arm as if we were old friends.

"Hi, Maiken. Nice to see you," she purred, throwing me a smile that nearly knocked me off my feet. Maiken was the name of the character I played on my hit television show. She was not the first to make that mistake.

"My name is Billy," I said, without a trace of reproach. "Billy Fox."

"Suit yourself, Billy Fox. I'm Selena." She walked me out the patio door, where the pool shimmered.

"Selena what?"

"Just *Selena*."

"Is that a joke?"

"All the best people only need one name."

I thought about it for a moment. "You mean like Cher?"

"Now you get it," she said, laughing.

"So you're a singer?"

"No, silly! I'm a model. Didn't you know that?"

"Sure," I lied. Did she think I had a subscription to Vogue?

"I've seen your show," she said, tightening her grip on my arm. "You're really good."

When they say they've seen my show, it means they've heard of it, maybe seen a promo. The real fans memorise my dialogue, and then recite it to me on the street, as if I haven't heard it before. I haven't decided which I prefer. In Selena's case, I couldn't have cared less. She was stunning.

"You have great hair," she said. A girl with priorities.

Anyway, it was true, I did have great hair, back then. "You have lovely hair, yourself, Selena." I realized that if I had beaten her to that punch, she probably would have thrown me down and fucked me right there, next to the rich man's pool. As it was, I had to wait a couple of hours, until the party wound down and we slipped back to her hotel room.

Selena's digs at the Sutton Place Hotel were temporary. She was staying there until she could find a more permanent place to live.

"I've had it with New York," she told me. "It's dirty and loud."

"So you're moving to Toronto?" I didn't think she was gaining much.

"Canadian dirt is cleaner. And the noise in Toronto is more polite."

She had me there. "Why don't you move in with me?" I looked over my shoulder to see who had said that, and saw my face reflected in the dressing mirror. Rats! I had no control over my mouth. "I just bought a great loft. There's plenty of room for two."

Selena propped herself up on an elbow, spilling the sheets off herself, seductively. "Loft? What's that?"

"Well," I said, "it's like an apartment, only bigger, and instead of being in a nice clean apartment building with a rooftop Jacuzzi and a gym in the basement, it's in a rundown warehouse in a shady part of town, with rattling steam pipes and no insulation. It's really cool."

The next day, Selena checked out of the Sutton Place Hotel.

Two days after that, she left for a three-week photo shoot in Los Angeles. That helped me adjust to my new situation more easily. Not having her there definitely helped. Anyway, I was back on set, shooting my hit television series, *Maiken Trouble*. I played Joe Maiken, the cynical private eye who relentlessly pursued all manner of villainy in the greater Gotham area, and frequently found himself collecting his fee from the invariably beautiful female clients in a less traditional fashion. What a gig! My shooting hours kept me away from the love loft, except to roll into bed sometime after midnight.

I thought it was working out nicely, living with someone, until Selena returned from her shoot. One night I came home, slightly drunk and very tired, and there she was, in my...*our* bed.

"What the—"

Then I remembered.

"Hello, darling," she cooed sleepily, rolling over languidly to expose her naked, heavily airbrushed, Cosmopolitan body to me.

When I tried to complain to my agent about this new arrangement, he got tremendously excited.

"That's the best news I've heard all week," said Herb Farley. "Ten years ago, the only way to get the press to look at you was to *come out*, but nobody cares who's a fag these days. Nowadays everyone just assumes that *all* actors are gay. These days, the only way to make the cover of People Magazine is to marry a model."

"Jesus, Herb. I'm not marrying her." I didn't like where this conversation was going.

"Doesn't matter, kid. You're living with her. It's all the same to them. Anyway, it's a double-whammy, 'cause you get a second cover story when you get divorced."

"I'm not married!" I shouted.

"This can only be good for you, Billy. Take my word for it. Just make sure you two lovebirds get out in the public eye. Be seen. Get your picture taken together. Pick a fight with her in a public place, if you have to." Herb looked off into space. "Holy cow," he said, finally. "Not only a model, but she only has one name. I don't know how you guys do it."

"Get a loft." He was no help at all.

"The rest of my stuff is coming sometime this week," said Selena.

"The rest?" It was Sunday, my first day off since she returned from the coast, and our first full day together. Alone. As a couple.

"My things. You know, furniture, clothing, that stuff. It's coming up from New York. It'll be here sometime this week. What did you think, Billy? I only came here with a couple of suitcases."

I shrugged. "They were *big* suitcases. I just thought—" I don't know what I thought. It's not like there wasn't room in the loft for her stuff. But what was I going to do if it was all rattan? I hated rattan. I wisely decided it would be un-politic of me to ask about the rattan.

"What do you want to do today?" she asked, hugging me from behind as I hunkered over the counter, hugging my coffee mug.

Do? Now we were supposed to *do* things? Usually, I liked to spend my rare days off lounging on the sofa, reading the paper. After lunch I'd switch from coffee to beer, and try to fit a nap in between relaxing and lounging. If I found I wasn't tired enough to sleep, I'd scan the television for golf; that usually did the trick. "Whatever you want, honey," I said.

Selena slouched onto the stool next to me and cradled her own coffee mug. "Actually, I wouldn't mind just hanging around in my pajamas all day. Maybe have a nap later."

I think that was the moment I fell in love with Selena.

Chapter 3

There was a soft knock on the trailer door.

I ignored it, reasoning that if it was important, whoever it was would *bang* on the door.

There was a *bang* on the trailer door.

"Mister Fox?" called a woman's voice. "Mister Fox? They're ready for you on the set." It was Marcia, the third AD. I had dallied with her fairly frequently during the first season, before I knew the show was going to be a hit. By the time the fifth season began, we both had the decency to forget it had ever happened. We were pros.

I opened the trailer door and looked down on her. "Okay, Marcia, I'm coming. Give me a minute."

"Sure, Mister Fox. I'll wait here."

I closed the door on her. I didn't need the minute. Not really. I didn't have anything particular to do with the minute other than roam around my spacious trailer aimlessly. I wasn't tending to something that couldn't wait until after the scene was shot. It was just something I did—taking this minute, before coming onto the set—to let them (in this case, Marcia) know that I was the sort of person who usually needed a minute to finish some important business. Part of the game. The more important you seem, the more important you are. I looked at my watch. Forty-five seconds. I shuffled around a bit more and then emerged, permitting Marcia to escort me to the set, as if I didn't know the way.

We strolled along, dodging sand bags and grip stands. "How's Floyd?" I asked, casually. Floyd was Marcia's cat. As I was schtupping her during that first season, she had spoken effusively about Floyd. She was devoted to her cat. She carried photographs of him in her wallet. It was good of me to remember.

16

She looked up at me, slowed down a bit. "He's dead," she said. "He was hit by a car three years ago." She looked away and plodded on.

How was I supposed to know? Jesus! She could have mailed out notices, instead of letting the rest of us embarrass ourselves. How insensitive of her, I thought. This was the thanks I got for trying to be friendly.

When the director saw me coming, he waved his hand feverishly. Roland Sanderson was a tightly wound ball of neurosis. He could not stand still. His assistant spent her fourteen-hour workday following Rollie around with a script in one hand and Rollie's folding chair in the other. Whenever he stopped moving for a moment, she would place the chair two steps behind him, and in all the years I worked with Rollie, I never once saw him sit in it.

Marcia stalked off sullenly to round up the extras.

"Billy...Billy," Rollie gasped. "There you are. Where have you been?" He made it sound like I'd been missing for days. He always spoke like that. He was emphatic, by nature.

"It was that third AD, what's her name? Marcia?" I said, conspiratorially. "She's just not with it."

Rollie turned to his assistant and whispered emphatically into her ear. The young assistant, whose name escapes me now, hurried over to the producer's assistant and whispered into *her* ear. Then the producer's assistant went off quickly to fire Marcia. One more problem dealt with. I held great reverence for the efficiency of the proper channels of power.

Of all the directors who worked on my show, Rollie was my favourite. He directed at least half the episodes, and I felt most comfortable with him. He was a real *actor's* director.

"Okay, Billy. Listen." Rollie shifted his weight from foot to foot as he talked to me, like a kid who has to pee. "In this scene, you've just come upon Victoria in the alleyway. She's been shot in the chest and it doesn't look good. You see the thug who shot her running away, down the alley. Now, your instinct is to go after the thug. You *hate* to see him getting away, but you can't just run off and leave Victoria lying there, bleeding. There's going to be a blood pack under her shirt. Be careful not to get the blood anywhere except your hands. If we have to do a second take, I don't want to be waiting for you to change your shirt, Billy. Got it? Good. Anyway, you kneel down and cradle her. Be careful with the blood again, don't get it on your pants. Or your jacket. Especially your jacket. Okay...now, you say your lines. All that *comforting* stuff. You know your lines for that bit? Good, good. So, she will be looking up at you, dying and such, and she's trying to speak, tell you who did this to her. *Dying words* stuff. You know the drill. But you can't understand what she's saying. You put your ear close to her mouth. She's going to have a blood bag in her mouth. Try not to get blood on your ear. Now, I want you to act upset. Do the *upset-acting* thing for me. You're upset not only because Victoria's been shot and the thug who did it is getting away, but also because if she dies you'll never get the chance to pork her. This is powerful stuff, Billy, but I know you can handle it. This scene is high-octane emotion, an emotional overload. There are so many different emotions going through your mind, just try and keep them all straight. Make sure we really know that you're upset about not getting the chance to pork Victoria. That's the most important thing. Everyone knows you're going to get the thug in the end. You always do. What they don't know is whether or not you're going to pork the girl. That's the clincher, Billy. That's the secret ingredient that makes this show a hit. We all want to see you pork the girl. Got it?"

"Yeah, sure," I said. "Watch the blood, do the *upset* thing. Got it." I was sure Rollie was some sort of genius. He could always get the best work out of me.

I took my place in the alley. The wardrobe girl and the makeup artist and the hair stylist and the second AD (who now had twice as much work to do, now that Marcia was gone) all ensured that Victoria, played by the incomparable beauty Jackie Knowlton, was suitably gussied up for her glamorous death scene. Rollie huddled with the cinematographer, while the producer, Donald Duke (another unfortunate name in the credit roll), looked at his watch and frowned. I waited patiently for everyone else to get their act together.

"What's taking so long?" I called out. "Do I have time to make a quick call?"

Nora, the first AD, assured me I did not have time to make a call. What did she know? She was only the first AD. I winked at her, to let her know that I didn't mind waiting, and that she could keep me company at my start position, if she were so inclined. She was a good-looking woman, in a butch, non-model sort of way. The way she glared at me just confirmed my suspicion that she was a lesbian. To each his own is my philosophy. You can't knock a guy for trying. Then I remembered Selena. That was beginning to happen more often. On top of all the other stresses that filled my day, I was suddenly burdened with guilt.

People began to shout, and I heard walkie-talkies chirping all around me.

"Ready, everyone. We're about to roll!" Nora shouted. "Quiet! Quiet, everyone!"

"Roll sound!"

"Speed!"

"Roll camera!"

"Camera has speed!"

"Ready Billy!"

"You bet."

"Action!"

```
MAIKEN TROUBLE
EPISODE #521 -- GOING WHOLE HOG.
EXT. ALLEYWAY. NIGHT.

JOE and VICTORIA have arranged to meet in the
alley behind the Parkview Motel. VICTORIA is
afraid for her life. She is convinced that
someone is trying to kill her.

JOE arrives at the meeting place ten minutes
late. He sees VICTORIA already waiting. She is
not alone. She is having a heated discussion
with an unidentified man.

                    JOE
               (calling out)
          Sorry I'm late,
          Victoria. Too much
          traffic getting out of
          midtown. Hope you
          haven't been waiting
          too long.
```

JOE walks toward the pair and waves
a hand at the unidentified man.
                    JOE (con't)
               Who's the friend? I
               thought you'd be alone.

                    VICTORIA
                    (regards JOE
                    frantically)
               Look out, Joe! He's got
               a gun!

VICTORIA tries to run away, but the man with
the gun grabs her by the arm and fires one shot
into her chest at point-blank range. VICTORIA
crumbles to the ground and the unidentified man
makes a run for it down the alley.

   I ran towards the alley at full speed. I enjoyed those scenes in which I had to run. I was in tremendous shape back then. I could really run, at least for short distances. I looked good when I was running—fit, healthy, sexy, all that. (I cannot run, now. Although I am only in my fifties, running is a fading memory for me. I can barely walk to the corner to buy a newspaper without taking a brief rest at the bus shelter. So it goes.)
   When I saw Victoria lying on the cold pavement, I looked shocked, sad, enraged. I had a broad basket of emotions to draw from. You could see it all on my face. I passed an angry and frustrated glance at the shadow dodging down the other end of the alley. I let the thug go. I would deal with him later. Nothing pissed off Joe Maiken more than bad guys who shot beautiful women—especially ones I hadn't porked yet. I knelt down, cradled Victoria's head in my lap. I was momentarily distracted by suddenly having Jackie Knowlton's head in the exact spot I have longed for it to be for some time. By the look on her face, she must have felt how impressed I was with her. Fortunately for me, it was her turn to speak.
   "Ack!" she said.
   "Don't try to speak, Victoria. Save your strength," I said gently. I noticed the blood on her chest. I put my hands on the blood, ever careful of my jacket and shirt and pants. I tried to rub the blood off her

chest, but there was too much of it. I didn't hold out much hope for poor Victoria. I was devastated. We had passed so many sexual overtures between us, I was certain I would have scored with her. I gave the camera a solid look of disappointment.

"Graghh!" moaned Victoria, still bravely attempting to identify her killer.

"Shh," I whispered. "It's all right. Don't worry Victoria, I'll hunt him down and make him pay. There's nowhere he can run, there's no place he can hide. He's been *makin' trouble* with the wrong guy." They always slipped that in at least once in every show—the "makin' trouble" bit.

My hands were covered with blood, as I rubbed and rubbed Victoria's chest. I tried to subtly shift my legs beneath me. My pleasure was poking uncomfortably in Jackie Knowlton's ear. Unfortunately, that caused me to lose my train of thought. I was pretty sure I had another line, but I couldn't for the life of me remember what it was.

"Sheeshush Chrish!" Victoria suddenly slurred through her bloody lips. What a doll! Jackie was ad-libbing, to cover for me. I concentrated on Victoria, and the great porking I was going to miss, now that she was dying. I hoped they had me in close-up, so they could see how saddened I was by that. Jackie was squirming in my lap. I thought she was really getting into the whole death thing until I realized she was getting up.

"Sheeshush fucking Chrish!" she shouted, throwing my hands off her chest. "Ishn't anyone around here looking at whatsh happening over here? Ish there shomething more intereshting going on in the vishinity that hash dishtracted all you people?" Suddenly, she was on her feet, looking down at me, with my bloody hands and disappointed face. A red trickle slithered out the corner of her mouth.

"Cut!" shouted someone.

"Cut!" shouted someone else.

Walkie-talkies began crackling again.

Rollie came bounding up. "What's the problem, what's wrong? Things were going well. What's happening?" Watching him hop around made me need to urinate.

"Look at thish!" Jackie Knowlton shouted. She indicated her white blouse, stained red from the blood bag. Her mouth was a gruesome sight. That fake blood was very convincing.

Rollie looked at the blouse. "It's blood. You've been shot."

"Look closher," she mumbled, through her fulminating lips. "Shee anyshing odd?"

Then Rollie seemed to see what Jackie saw. "I see, I see."

"The fucking guy wash groping me. He wash feeling me up!" Rollie backed away from the spray of blood erupting from Jackie Knowlton's angry mouth.

Then I saw it, too. Two perfect red imprints of my manly hands, one on each glorious breast.

Donald Duke got off the phone and joined us. "What's the problem?"

"Look at thish!" Jackie Knowlton shouted, again. Another bloody eruption escaped her mouth.

Donald Duke took a long look at her breasts, no doubt pleased to be finally given permission. "What are those hand prints doing there?"

"Thatsh what I'd like to know!" Her cheeks could no longer contain the contents of the burst blood bag. A ghastly crimson wave spilled over her bottom lip, leaving an unsightly stain down her front.

"Listen," I said, getting to my feet. "It was a totally innocent mistake. There was just way more blood than I expected. Besides, it was *Joe Maiken* who groped you, not Billy Fox. That's the sort of guy Maiken is. I'm simply a conduit, a vehicle, you might say, for Joe Maiken. He won't do it again, I promise." I shot her my winning smile.

Jackie Knowlton huffed and stalked off to her trailer to put on a clean shirt, the second AD and wardrobe girl and makeup artist and hair stylist trotting along behind.

"You have time to make your call," said Nora, the surly first AD.

After we wrapped for the night, I visited Jackie Knowlton's trailer to personally apologize for Joe Maiken's behaviour. She was completely receptive to my apology. After all, a guest spot on my hit television show was worth something.

When I walked to my Corvette, later, Marcia was waiting for me, leaning on the hood.

"Hi, Marcia," I said, jingling my keys to let her know that I wouldn't be able to drive her home this time. "Another busy day in the bag, eh?" I jammed the key into the door lock.

She looked sideways at me. For some reason, she did not look happy. "I know what you did, Billy." She walked away slowly, glaring, until she disappeared around the corner. It gave me a chill.

It took me nearly the entire drive home to remember what I "did." It had been a long and busy day, after all. I couldn't be expected to recall every insignificant detail. I suspected she was just upset that her cat had died. Poor Floyd.

With no available parking spaces on my block, I was forced to squeeze my car into a slot two blocks away, thereby blocking vital access to a fire hydrant. Since most of the warehouses in my neighbourhood had been built before fire codes existed, this was perhaps an imprudent move on my part, but I was tired, and I had to park somewhere. There was a party underway when I arrived at the loft. I couldn't find Selena anywhere, so I grabbed some pretty-boy by the arm and asked where she was.

"London," said the pretty-boy.

"London?"

"Or South Africa. I'm not sure." The pretty-boy escaped before I could interrogate him further.

Half a dozen other cities were suggested by others, and although they couldn't agree where she'd gone, they all seemed to agree that Selena had been home at least long enough to open the loft to her friends, before jetting off to wherever. She didn't leave a note. I discovered a strange girl sleeping in my bed, some other model without a last name, no doubt. I ignored her and climbed in. For me, sleeping with a model was no big deal. Anyway, I was up and gone before the unidentified model stirred.

When I got to my Corvette, I discovered all four tires were slashed, and the word ASSHOLE was scratched into the hood. I knew something like that was going to happen. Fucking vandals! Fucking teenagers! Fucking... Then I spotted Marcia. She made no attempt to hide. She stood on the corner, hands on her hips, looking directly at me. She wanted me to see her, wanted me to know that *she* was the fucking vandal who had slashed my tires. Fucking cat-loving third AD! Fucking nutcase! And then she was gone.

She'll never work in this town again.

I arrived on set by cab.

"I need a receipt," I said to the cabbie. He ignored me and sped away. Do any of them understand English? How was I going to get reimbursed for the cab ride without a receipt? I spotted Nora, across the road. "Hey, Nora! Did you see that cab I just got out of?" I thought if I could offer a witness, Donald Duke might not balk at my claim chit. The cheap bastard.

"What?" She looked around. She was out of it, filling her face with a jam-filled donut. "Oh, hi Billy."

"Did you see the cab that just dropped me off?"

"What cab?"

Useless people! I knew what Donald Duke would say: "Don't we pay you enough money that you can't pay for your own taxi?" "That's not the point," I'd say. "It was a business expense. I shouldn't have to pay for it." "Why didn't you get a receipt? If you had got a receipt, I could do something." "I tried to get the fucking receipt, Donald! The guy just drove away. He probably didn't know how to write. Maybe if I were fluent in Jamaican *patois,* I might have made myself understood." "Well, if it were up to me, Billy, I'd push it through, but you know how our accountants are. They're an angry bunch of nitpickers. I can't get reimbursed for a postage stamp, myself, without a receipt. Sorry, chum. By the way, you're looking really great out there. Keep up the good work, Billy." Fuck him.

I caught up with Nora. "Hey, listen. You know that AD named Marcia? She used to work for us?"

Nora looked at me blankly. She had white powdered sugar around her lips. It was not an attractive thing to see so early in the morning. "Sorry, Billy, I don't know who you mean. We don't have an AD named Marcia."

"Not anymore," I said. I needed to find out where the little vandal lived. She was going to pay for those tires, and for the new paint job on my Corvette. "She was let go yesterday. You know, the sort of cute one with blonde hair."

Nora was nodding. "Oh, you mean Leslie."

Rats. Well, at least I remembered her cat's name. I wondered who Marcia was, then? "Leslie. Yes. I don't suppose you know where she lives?"

"Nope. You could try asking Milan. I think he's dating her."

Milan was our cinematographer. He was a talented DOP who had been on the show since the pilot episode. He was responsible for giving the show its dark, brooding look. We had become quite good friends, over the past five years, Milan and I. I was surprised that I didn't know he was dating Marcia—Leslie. Whatever.

I approached a loud huddle taking place at the back of the lighting truck. Rollie was there, and Donald Duke, and a handful of minions. The day hadn't even begun and there already seemed to be an emergency.

"What's the problem?" I asked, coming up behind Rollie.

He spun around. "What in blazes have you done?"

I looked behind me to see who he was shouting at. There was nobody there.

"You! *You!* I'm talking to *you,* Billy Fox!"

"I don't know what you're talking about, Rollie. Why don't you tell me what the problem is, and I'll see if I can help?"

Donald Duke, the calm and reasonable producer, broke in before Rollie could say something regrettable. "The problem is this, Billy..."

Rollie threw up his arms in resignation and went away to pace the sidewalk.

Donald Duke was serene. "I just got a call from Milan. It seems he's not coming back."

"Not coming back? Why? Is he sick?"

"Not exactly. He says he won't step onto the same set with *you.*"

"Me?"

"Apparently," said Donald Duke, "we fired his girlfriend yesterday."

"Marcia?"

"Leslie. The third AD."

I nodded, knowingly. "Yes, yes. I heard about that. Too bad."

"Apparently, you were responsible for getting her fired."

I put my hands up. "Hey, whoa! That's not fair. She wasn't doing her job. Besides, I'm not the big cheese around here. I'm not the one who hires and fires people. That's *your* job."

Donald Duke was blinking very slowly—a sure sign, I knew, that he was working hard to keep his temper in check. One of his cute quirks. "Well, Billy, we're not here to lay blame. The fact remains, Milan won't come back. He's pretty upset."

This was great. I get my tires slashed and get ripped off for a fifteen dollar taxi fare, and now suddenly *I'm* the bad guy. Hell, I was the *victim*. I was the one who should have called in and said I wouldn't be coming to the set until a limousine showed up at my door. I was the fucking star of the show. This was an outrage!

"Give the girl her job back. What's the big deal? She was no worse than any of the other AD's." I probably shouldn't have said that with Nora, the first AD, standing next to me. I could feel her steely gaze bore into the side of my head. She stomped away in search of more powdered relief.

"We tried that. She won't come back, either."

"Well, forget about her. She was useless. You should just offer Milan more money. He has an indoor pool he needs to heat year-round. Throw a few bucks at him, to help pay the gas bill."

Donald Duke looked at me sternly. "And that's why *you're* the actor and *I'm* the producer." He took me by the shoulder and steered me away from the others. "Look, Billy, the season's nearly over. There's only one more episode after this one, and we can't possibly get another DOP up to speed in time to make the schedule. So, I was thinking more along the lines of an apology."

It was my turn to look stern. "I'm going to need more than an apology. I've got four flat tires and a profanity scratched in my hood. Marcia's going to have to pay for that."

"Who's Marcia? Anyway, it's *you* who needs to apologize, Billy. To Leslie and to Milan."

"Me? I've got nothing to be sorry for."

Donald Duke spread his arms in a surrendering gesture. "That may or may not be true, Billy. There are many sides to every story. Why don't you think of it as another acting challenge? If anyone can pull it off, you can. We can have a meeting with Rolland about how to approach this…this apology scene, if I may call it that. You two can discuss what your character's motivation might be for apologizing. I'll tell you this, Billy: if you can pull it off and get Milan back on the set, you will prove to me, once and for all, that I was right about you from the start, that you are a brilliant actor."

How could I refuse? For the good of the show I would do anything. And I pulled it off with flair. I was, in the words of Donald Duke, "brilliant." My effusive blandishments did the job on Milan and he was back on set by ten o'clock. Not bad. We only lost three hours of the shooting day. Marcia didn't come back. She and Milan had apparently had a fight that morning and she left his house in a huff.

Milan arrived by taxi. Marcia had slashed the tires on his Porsche. We consoled each other throughout the day, Milan and I. My old friend.

"I have a meeting next week with the network to talk about next season."

Donald Duke was driving me home, late that night, to spare me further unnecessary travel expenditures. He drove a brand new Mercedes, which was the next best thing to a limousine. "I have every confidence we'll be picked up. The ratings for this season have been very good, as you know. It was a stroke of genius to give Mabel a deadly tropical disease at the end of last season. I find that you have to do that sort of thing, periodically, during the life of a hit show. Bring in some new blood, a change of scenery. It keeps things fresh."

Killing Mabel had been *my* stroke of genius. She was my—Joe Maiken's—ancient and crotchety office secretary. She was the comic relief; she got the laughs. Apart from her, *Maiken Trouble* was a serious drama. But after four years, her caustic repertoire was getting stale. And anyway, at the time, I was sleeping with a pretty little thing who I thought would look great sitting in Mabel's office chair. The Swedish lass Gretchen was sent to Joe Maiken's office by the employment agency after poor Mabel contracted her vile disease. We allowed the old gal to cling to life—unseen, of course—for the first two shows of this season (in part because there was some justified doubt about Gretchen's acting abilities), before she kicked the bucket. That's life, my friends.

"So, there's nothing to be worried about," Donald Duke was saying.

"I'm not worried," I said. "Do I need to be worried?"

"Not at all. There is no need whatsoever to worry about a thing."

"Okay," I said, tentatively. "I won't worry."

"Good, good. Don't worry."

"I'm not."

"Good."

Chapter 4

The pretty-boy had been right the first time. Three days after disappearing, Selena returned from London. She was busy sifting through her new London purchases when I arrived home from the set.

"I thought you were working. When did you have time to go shopping?"

Selena gave me a professional smile. "You'd be surprised how efficient I can be when it comes to shopping. I can spend ten thousand dollars in under fifteen minutes, if I have to."

Who would ever *have* to? Like most men, it wasn't *shopping* to me unless I was buying machinery or electronics. Cars and stereos. Anything else was a chore. Most of my wardrobe came from the show. It was part of my contract.

Not only was Selena there when I got home, her *stuff* had also arrived from New York. I was relieved to see there wasn't a single stick of rattan furniture anywhere, but I was dismayed by how much stuff there was. The love loft suddenly looked crowded. It looked like a furniture showroom. Selena had begun arranging some of her furniture, and there were unopened boxes spread about the space. I spied a stylish pinstriped loveseat in the corner that looked comfortable enough, but it nearly crippled me when I fell casually onto it.

"Holy cow!" I groaned, rubbing my spine. I'd sat on more comfortable park benches.

"It looks great there, don't you think?"

I moved gingerly back to my familiar old leather sofa.

"Anyway," said Selena, "you're not supposed to *sit* on it, silly. It's meant to complement the valances."

I spotted the complementary valances leaning against the wall next to the windows. I supposed I would have to waste my Sunday afternoon hanging them.

Once she had modelled three new gowns and six pairs of shoes for me, Selena deigned to kiss me hello. I grabbed her and carefully peeled the designer gown off. I let her wear the shoes, though. A little spice.

Advice to men: When it comes to women and shoes, it's best to keep your mouth shut. If you say anything disparaging about shoes, or the purchase of shoes, you risk war. If you attempt to say something nice, you risk being accused of being "facetious," which also amounts to war. Unless you enjoy being called a "waggish dipshit," leave the shoes out of it.

Advice to women: same as above, only substitute the word *stereos* for *shoes*.

I had the next day off. They were doing some pick-up shots—one of which was the close-up of Victoria doing her big death scene, for which they had a lucky stand-in to be my groping hands—and also some second unit location shots. One more show, and the fifth successful season of *Maiken Trouble* will be in the can.

Selena made us coffee, stretching the limits of her culinary skills. "Have you thought about selling your car, darling?"

She caught me off guard with that. There could only be one reason why she would want me to sell my two-seater sports car. "Are you trying to tell me you're pregnant?"

"What if I am?" she said, coyly. Twenty-year-old girls must always play these games. *Coy* is a very unattractive quality in a woman, in my view.

"Don't be coy," I said.

"I'm not being coy. I'm just interested in what your reaction would be if I was pregnant." She posed. In only her panties, the pose had a number of sweeping effects on me. "Well?"

"Well what?" I was preoccupied with her posing breasts. I had forgotten the question.

"What if I *am* pregnant?"

I shrugged. I could be coy, too. "It's hard to say how I'd react. I suppose we'll find out once you really *are* pregnant."

"You're spoiling my fun, Billy." She struck another pose. She had no conscious knowledge of what she was doing. She was a modelling machine.

The telephone rang. I let Selena pick it up. It was just as often for her, and I figured if it was for me, having Selena answer it couldn't hurt my reputation. She even *sounded* like a model. I could tell by the tone of her voice that it was Marco. Marco was a model. He and Selena spent a lot of time together. They went shopping for shoes. (There are always exceptions to gender issues, are there not?) I didn't like Marco. The minute he opened his mouth, his appeal fled. He was a ten-year-old mind trapped in a twenty-year-old body. He told extravagant lies with the same zeal as any troublesome ten-year-old. I called him Prince Marco. Why not? He once told me that he was the legitimate heir to the Croatian throne, if only a dastardly pretender had not usurped his glorious ascension. He made it clear to me, with a nudge and a wink, that he was quietly shopping around for an inexpensive triggerman who could clear the path for him to take his rightful place on the throne. It wouldn't have been so amusing if he hadn't been completely serious. "Best of luck, your highness," I had said. He offered me his ring finger to kiss.

Anyway, I dubbed Prince Marco harmless, where Selena was concerned. I assumed he was gay. He didn't know a thing about cars or stereos.

"Marco wants us to go see the new Barbra Streisand movie."

I had to think fast. "Sorry, my love. I'm having lunch with my agent. You two go without me." When Selena stepped into the shower, I quickly called Herb's secretary to make a lunch date. Anyway, Herb had promised to drum up something interesting for me to do during the hiatus. The last time we had spoken, he was utterly confident that scripts for several features were already "in the mail." I had greater appreciation for his optimism when he was right. The rest of the time, it annoyed me. My break was commencing in just under a week. I should have seen these so-called scripts months ago. If I didn't get something soon, it would mean my boyish mug would not be gracing the silver screen during the coming Christmas season, and I'd be stuck doing a few guest spots on someone else's crappy television show.

I shouldn't complain about television. *Maiken Trouble* made me a boodle, and it put me on the celebrity map, thanks in large part to an Emmy nomination, back in '77, for best cinematography. It was a promotional bonanza for the show, and a well-earned nod to my old friend Milan, who stalked out in disgust after he lost. I, at least, remained gracious, even though I had been specifically overlooked for a nomination myself. I, too, would have been a long shot, but it wasn't as if I had just fallen off the back of the tomato truck. I had paid my dues. Alas, nobody ever said the world was a fair place.

The only real problem I had with television was a fundamental one of scale. There was something not quite right about having my likeness *reduced* to fit on the average television screen. For obvious reasons, it made more sense to me that my image should be scaled *up*. I knew I could withstand the closer scrutiny. (Naturally, I have lately revised my view on the subject. These days, the smaller format of television is much kinder to my face, as the horrifying details of my degeneration are lost in the transmission.)

Since I would be permitting Herb to pick up the tab, I selected Cirro's as our meeting place. After Prince Marco came to pick up Selena, I took another damned taxi to the restaurant, and refused to hand over the fare until I was satisfied the driver not only understood what I was asking for, but had begun to pen the receipt. When he finally filled out the slip, we did a mutual exchange, each of us simultaneously snatching the paper from the other's hand, after I had counted down from three. The things one must resort to in this day and age!

Herb was late. As I waited, I gave serious consideration to dropping him as my agent. We had been together since the beginning of my illustrious career and he had, for the most part, served me well. But lately he had become lazy, or distracted, or something else. He was slow returning my calls, and he skilfully dodged my tough questions. And, most significantly, he seemed unable to produce the film scripts that he so earnestly promised. Perhaps I had outgrown him. Maybe he was good at bringing up the new kids, but didn't have the clout to maintain a star like me. I promised myself that I would spend the afternoon making some calls, try to find out who Robert DeNiro's agent was.

As I was nicely dozing off in the booth, there was a thud on the table in front of me.

"Fresh off the presses, Billy." That was tardy Herb, looking pleased with himself. He had dropped a script at my elbow. He noisily settled himself across from me and got the waiter's attention.

"Hi, Billy. Hi, Mister Farley," said our waiter. Les Dodd. Another actor with a stupid name and a thin resume. And speaking of names, should *I* not be the one he referred to as "Mister?" The most unfortunate thing about him was that Les Dodd *was* his stage name. His real name was a truly offensive smattering of foreign consonants that he wisely chose to bury for the sake of his career, but he clearly got some bad advice when he was researching alternatives. He should have asked me. Perhaps if he'd allowed me to re-christen him Vance Logan or Leif Brooke, he might not now be spreading a linen napkin across my lap, drooling at my success.

"Thanks anyway for trying to get me that spot on your show, Billy," said Les. He had been up for a bit part as a victim. All he had to do was die. But I had seen him die a thousand deaths on stage, several years earlier, in a forgettable production of the Scottish play. Leading man Les died the minute he walked on, and it took him three hours to finally fall down and stop moving. It was a painful memory for me. I felt he needed a bit more experience to pull off a convincing death, and I made a point to tell my grateful producer.

"Don't mention it, Les. I'm going to have a Bloody Caesar and the pasta special, hold the sun-dried tomatoes. And have the chef set aside a slice of the cheesecake. He always seems to run out."

"What did I tell you?" said Herb, after Les bunked off to get our drinks. He looked pleased with himself. His eyes flitted between my blank gaze and the script on the table. "Didn't I tell you I'd get you something?"

I looked at the title: *Alpha Force III.* "A sequel?"

"A feature film, Billy. Don't balk."

I thumbed through the pages, not stopping long enough to read any of the dialogue. "Isn't this Lorenzo Larson's gig?" I hadn't seen the first two instalments, other than their respective thirty-second trailers—two of the most egregious displays of gratuitous violence I had ever witnessed.

"He sprained his ankle, so he had to pull out at the last minute. They need someone fast."

"So I'm second banana to Lorenzo Larson?" That didn't thrill me.

"Don't look at it that way, Billy. It's a foot in the door. It's a big screen credit, it's exposure, and believe me, there's plenty of room in Hollywood for another big action hero. It was Lorenzo's idea to have you take his place. He personally recommended you."

I didn't believe that. Any press release that claimed an actor had "sprained an ankle" was just using the standard euphemism for "entered rehab." No doubt the poor kid was so busy fighting off the DTs, he didn't know which way was up, never mind who was going to fill his absent shoes in *Alpha Force III*. "What about the other scripts?"

"Well," said Herb, his smile never wavering, "we've got to look at the offers as they come. We don't put food on the table by pinning our hopes on promises, Billy. We've got the paperwork in front of us and the shooting schedule fits nicely into your break. It's exactly what you were hoping for. It's a feature film, and you get star billing. It's a fantastic opportunity."

I sipped my cocktail and read the first page of the script. It was appalling. "It's appalling," I said.

Herb swirled an olive around his martini. "Of course it is. Listen, nobody's pretending they're remaking *Citizen Kane*, but the first two movies made a neat profit, and they're offering you the same money they were going to pay Larson, minus the points, of course. Not bad for five weeks' work, Billy. You'll be able to move out of that dingy warehouse and get yourself a real home in a nice neighbourhood."

"It's not a warehouse, it's a *loft*." Like I said, I was ahead of my time.

"Once Selena gets pregnant, you'll change your tune," he said, knowingly.

"Christ, Herb. I keep telling you, we're not even fucking married. There's already been too much talk of pregnancy today."

"I'm just trying to help."

"How was Barbra?" I asked.

Selena was reorganizing her shoe cupboard, to accommodate her new purchases. "Barbra?"

"Streisand. The movie."

"Oh, fine." She was a bad liar. They never made it to the movie.

If I hadn't been so engrossed in the script for *Alpha Force III*, I might have wondered more deeply why she would lie about such a trivial thing. I had signed the contract for the movie back in the restaurant, and it changes the way you read a script when you have already committed yourself to the project. If I still had the option of turning it down, I'm certain I would have groaned more. Instead, I scoured the caverns of my brain for a way to save my character from the awful dialogue. There had to be a way.

Selena distracted me briefly by sitting on my lap.

"I've always wanted to do it with a movie star," she said.

I reminded her that this was not my first movie.

"Well, I was just a kid when you made those other ones," she said, innocently, "so they don't count."

Whatever.

"Do you think I'll get to meet Lorenzo Larson?" she asked, riding me.

I suffered a sudden vital loss of circulation.

"What's the matter, darling?" She kissed my neck.

"I can't imagine."

She slinked off to play with her shoes.

Beep..."Hi, Billy. This is Sheila Cohen. I don't know if you remember me...we went to York together. Remember *As You Like It*? Third year? I played Celia? You were Jaques? Gosh, it seems so long ago, now! You were the most wonderful Jaques. You know, we all just knew you were going to become a star. We really did! Anyway, the reason I'm calling is because, I don't know if you know what I've been doing lately, but I've written a play. It's about the war, you know, but from a woman's perspective. It's quite unique, actually. I'm going to be putting it up in the Fringe Festival and I was hoping I could entice you to play the male lead. As you know, working the Fringe ordinarily doesn't pay, but in your case, we could make an exception. By your standards, it may not seem like much, a token amount, really, but it's exposure. Not that *you* need the exposure, Billy. It would certainly be exposure for the play. I don't even know if you do stage work anymore, television is so much more exciting. It's just that when I was writing the piece, I always had you in mind for the lead. It's quite a *meaty* part. So naturally when I got it into the Fringe, I thought: What the heck? I'll ask him. It won't hurt to just ask him. I'm sure you're very busy, doing your television show, but I wondered if you might do it, for old time's sake. By the way, I'll be playing the female lead, if that's any enticement for you. So, give me a call back and let me know what you think. And even if you can't do it, which I will totally understand, Billy, maybe you can make it down to the Fringe to see it. I'd love for you to at least see it, maybe give me some notes. That sort of thing. It's always good to get an expert opinion about these things. As the writer, I can get too close to a project. So, that's my spiel, Billy. It's been great talking to you...well, talking to your machine. Anyway, call me."

It happens all the time. I don't blame them, really. Everyone's looking for an angle, a way through a bigger door, a helping hand to the top, but there isn't room at the top for everybody.

As for Ms. Cohen, neither her name nor her alleged role as Celia, all those years ago at York University, managed to spark my memory banks. Her name meant nothing to me. I did recall that particular *As You Like It* because Herb Farley attended the opening night and singled me out, signed me on the very next day. How could I forget that? I certainly remembered the girl who played Rosalind: Heidi Borland. I couldn't possibly forget her. She was a spectacular beauty, and to my dying day, I will regret that I utterly failed to get anywhere with Heidi. For some reason, I could never make any progress with her, try as I might. She was locked up tighter than a vault. She was impenetrable. She was a mighty fortress of defences against my amorous assaults. After a while, I gave up trying and moved on to better prospects. I thought she was just being a good Mormon, but shortly after I abandoned my education to co-star in my first movie, I heard she became pregnant. She dropped out, so I was told, and married the lecherous fiend who had impregnated her, and hasn't been seen or heard from again. Now *there* was a loss to the stage, as far as I was concerned.

But who the hell was Sheila Cohen? I checked my York yearbook. When I found her photograph, it triggered nothing in my mind except wonder at how I could have erased this person so completely from my brain. She was an utter blank to me. Anyway, since she was so nervous on my answering machine, she failed to leave her telephone number, so I didn't feel too bad about not calling her back.

Alpha Force, the original movie, starring Lorenzo Larson, was like a condom: it had a glossy sheen, a big build-up, and then no payoff whatsoever. By the time you use a condom for the third time, just imagine how awful it is. There's practically no sheen left, there are dangerous holes here and there, and the end is so slack, there is not even the build-up. There is only a messy sort of ooze that causes shame and panic in all those involved. The third time always leads to an abortion.

Was I worried? Not a chance. In a way, I was paying dues all over again. I could do that. If it meant rebuilding a movie career, I could do it. The Hollywood moguls were smart enough to look past the clichés and the cheesy effects and judge my ability to cope with these shortcomings like a pro. I was confident they would see in me a marketable commodity that, given a real script and budget, could pull off a big-time winner at the box office. "Look at it like a two-hour audition," Herb had said to me, and I believed him.

The director of *Alpha Force III* was Blake Dunsmore. This was his third feature film. I was saddened to learn that his other two films had not been either of the other Alpha Force flicks. Apparently, the director of parts one and two had refused to even read the script for *Alpha Force III*. A sensible man. One must have some standards in one's craft. Not only was this Blake Dunsmore's first Alpha Force film, it was his first action flick. His previous films had been of the art house variety; both had been shot in black & white, and had featured handheld camera work that is *de rigueur* with the black turtleneck set. So, not only his first action movie, but his first foray into the wonderful world of Technicolor, and a unique (for him) opportunity to discover the infinite uses of a tripod.

"It'll be a learning process for us both," he said to me, on the first day of shooting, as if I was some wet-eared kid, freshly plucked from the Saskatchewan farm. I bit my tongue. I imagined the only thing I would be learning from this experience was how to direct myself. I didn't have much faith in Blake Dunsmore. Oh, where was Rollie when I needed him?

What makes a movie like *Alpha Force III* worth watching? Well, a futuristic band of highly trained special-ops soldiers blasting their high-tech guns at everything that moves is something. Add some high-speed chases in ultra-mod vehicles, pinched from the rotating podiums of the Futurama exhibit at the most recent World's Fair, and you've come pretty close to capturing the fifteen-to-thirty male audience. Spice it up with a buxom bimbo who simply *must* follow the hero into the most wildly dangerous confrontations with aliens and such, only to have her skimpy wardrobe gradually fall away in tatters as she catches her sleeves on gnarly brambles, and you've nailed it. Formula stuff.

"I could do that," said my beloved Selena. Like all models, she thought that acting was a natural progression in her career. She had no idea.

"You've never acted before," I said, attempting to make it sound like a simple observation, rather than a criticism. "Some of us make it look easy, but it's not. It requires years of training."

"Lots of my friends have done it. It's not so hard."

I refrained from trying to explain the difference between doing it, and doing it well. I was fairly certain the subtle distinction would have been lost on her. Anyway, in *Alpha Force III*, she might have fit in nicely. "I'll see what I can do, but this isn't *Maiken Trouble*. I don't pull the same weight."

"Well," said Selena, "if I can't get in this movie, I'll take a shot at your TV show. That's fine with me."

Me and my big mouth.

I did approach Blake Dunsmore and the producers of *Alpha Force III* with my generous offer of the beautiful and buxom bimbo Selena as my squealing and hysterical sidekick. Alas, they had already cast someone with larger, faker breasts for that all-important role. Selena took the news harder than I expected.

"I'm disappointed in you, Billy. I wonder how hard you really tried."

"I told you I couldn't make any promises. I'm coming into this project late, myself. The casting on this movie was done a year ago. These people are not about to ditch somebody just because *my* girlfriend wants to act. It doesn't work that way. There are contracts that have already been signed. There are legal issues. They could be sued."

"Blah, blah, blah. That's just a lot of double-talk, Billy. You obviously don't love me as much as I thought. I guess I just haven't been supportive enough."

"Don't be ridiculous, Selena."

Advice to men: If there is one word women don't like, it is "ridiculous." Don't ever use it unless you are referring to yourself. Any woman will tell you honestly that only men are ridiculous. The word simply does not apply to women. So, unless you want war, avoid the word at all cost.

More advice to men: If you accidentally, inadvertently, or just plain stupidly use the word "ridiculous" on a woman, there is only one way to correct the mistake: grovel.

I grovelled for two solid days, until I left for my first day of principal shooting of *Alpha Force III*. Then I had other more immediate problems to deal with.

"Okay, Lorrie, you stand over here."

Nobody moved. There were twelve of us standing around in the rain, in full futuristic military gear, photon blasters nestled on our shoulders. It was bloody cold.

"Lorrie!" barked Blake Dunsmore. He looked up from his soggy script for the truant Lorrie. "Where the hell is he?" He squinted at us. In our Johnny Astro helmets and zap-proof vests and war paint, we all looked the same. "*You!*" he shouted, pointing directly at me.

"Yes, Blake?" I was as calm as could be. It's a thing I do when directors get anxious; the louder, more upset they become, the more calm and serene I become. It must be some underlying need I have for balance in the Universe.

"Is your helmet too tight? Can you not hear me clearly?"

"Sure, Blake. I can hear you just fine."

"Then why are you not standing over here?" He pointed at the spot he had assigned to poor missing Lorrie.

I looked at the empty spot, then at Blake. "You were calling someone named Lorrie."

Blake stood perfectly still. He appeared to be counting. "The first goddamned scene and you're already giving me a hard time. Is that how it's going to be?"

"I'm here for you, Blake. One hundred percent."

He was finding inner peace. "Good, okay. Lorrie, this is your spot." He pointed to the magic spot on the ground. Nobody moved. He looked directly at me again. Then he threw his script onto the wet ground and stomped over to the tent where the producers huddled and shivered and bad-mouthed the actors. A heated exchange took place, while we soldiers just shuffled around in the mud, awaiting orders. The cute little script assistant I had been keeping an eye on interrupted Blake's rant. She had retrieved his script from the mud and was pointing something out to him. He stopped ranting. His shoulders dropped.

Blake returned. "*Billy*," he said, with exaggerated flair, "if you would please step over here. This will be your start position."

I gave him my winning smile and complied.

"Thank you," he said.

"You're welcome," said I.

I learned later, from the cute script assistant, that Blake had become accustomed to referring to Lorenzo Larson as "Lorrie," as if they were old friends (they had, in fact, never met), and he had marked the margins of his script with many notes, indicating "Lorrie" does this and "Lorrie" says that, and so on. It was an honest mistake.

We spent three weeks running through the rain-soaked woods of Algonquin Park, blasting the local chipmunk population into oblivion with imaginary photon pulses. It seemed sort of silly as we were doing it, but Blake Dunsmore assured us it would eventually be "cool," once the special effects people painted in the bright orange photon flashes, and the sound effects people mixed in the *thuck-swizzle* that each blast generated. Oh, the magic!

I had a much nicer trailer than the one I'd had on my television show.

"Allo, Meester Fox," said a fruity little man, when I stepped into my luxurious trailer for the first time.

"Who are you?" I asked.

"I weel be assist you, Meester Fox."

I had become quite excited when someone told me that I had a personal assistant named Michel. "I thought you were a girl."

"Mais, non!" He smirked slyly. Wishful thinking on his part, no doubt. Maybe he was saving up for the operation. That was his business.

"What are you doing in my trailer?"

"I weel be stay here wit you, Meester Fox. In case you need anyting."

I started moving around the trailer, shucking my coat, roaming up and down the narrow aisle looking for things. I was trying to occupy the trailer to the utmost, show the little French boy whose place this was. If I had been a dog, I would have pissed on his shoe. I slammed all the cupboards in the galley until I found a tumbler and a bottle of bourbon. I filled the tumbler. I didn't offer my personal assistant a drink. "You're here to fulfil my needs?"

"Oui, monsieur. Whatever you need."

I considered my current needs. "What I need is for you to leave my trailer." He wore a fragrance that offended me.

"But Meester Fox, I have nowhere else, I am assign here, you see? That way to serve you best."

"You can serve me best by finding somewhere else to stay." Jesus! Cheap bastards! They can't even pitch a fucking tent for the minions. Did they think I was the Salvation Army? I detected tears welling up in my little assistant's eyes. "Okay, okay. Don't have a hissy on me. I have an idea."

Fifteen minutes later, it was all settled. Everyone was happy. Well, *I* was happy. I couldn't really speak for the others.

I convinced Michel to have a word with the cute script assistant. Krisha was her name. My personal assistant proved to me that he could at least do his job by convincing Krisha to swap quarters with him. He bunked with the wardrobe girls, which must have suited him better, and Krisha came to my luxurious trailer to stay with me. The only kind of personal assistance I needed in my trailer could not be given by someone like Michel.

"Come in, Krisha," I said. "Don't be shy."

"I'm not shy, Mister Fox." She wore a pair of faded jeans that flattered her lower half, and a tee-shirt that didn't quite reach her waistband. Her shoulder-length hair was tied into two tight braids that made her look like a sophisticated nine-year-old. She had a smattering of faint freckles that completed the illusion.

"How old are you?" I had to ask, for legal reasons.

"Nineteen. Want to see my driver's license?"

"No. I was just curious."

"Uh huh."

She wasn't kidding when she said she wasn't shy. She kept me up half the night, giving me "assistance." I awoke to the smell of frying bacon.

"I bet Selena never does this for you," she said, breaking eggs into a pan. She was already dressed.

"How do you know about Selena?" I wasn't surprised. I just wanted to know where she was getting her information.

"People Magazine," she said. "Congratulations. You got your first cover." She indicated the magazine on the dinette table.

As I settled groggily into the booth and inspected the cover photograph of the happy couple (a corner insert, but the cover nonetheless), Krisha slid my breakfast in front of me.

"Not very good in the kitchen, no doubt," she said, clearly jealous.

"Not when it comes to cooking," I said, somewhat remotely. I was flipping through the magazine, looking for the article. Three pages of small type and a few photos that I didn't know existed. It didn't say much that was deep or interesting, and it completely overlooked my early work with Shakespeare. Failing to mention classical training always makes actors seem less serious. I needed the serious credits to offset the pretty face. I knew how the public's mind worked.

They had interviewed only Selena for the article. "I wonder why Selena didn't mention it,"

"I wonder why they didn't interview you," said Krisha. "They don't say anything about your classical training." She was an impressive girl. "It fixates on Selena's wardrobe, and the fact that she only has one name. It's not very deep, or interesting."

"Well," I said, setting aside the article and fixating on breakfast, "it's free press."

"True enough." She settled in the seat across from me and watched me eat. "I give it six months before your second cover story."

I gave her a hard look that she absorbed easily. "You're not very optimistic. For your information, Selena and I are very much in love. In fact, we were talking just the other day about having children." It wasn't exactly a lie.

"We'll see, Billy. We'll see." We were on a first-name basis now.

The Alpha Force bimbo with the improbable bust was an actress named Jennifer Haimes. She had recently graduated from my old alma mater, York University, and soon discovered that beauty alone would not get her far. After pounding the pavement for months, only to find she wasn't getting the roles she wanted, she chose to exploit other avenues. She took a loan and got a boob job that instantly made her one of the busiest bimbos in town. She had real commitment to her craft. Jennifer arrived on the third day, to shoot her scenes with the hero—me—in the woods.

We were being pursued by unseen aliens, or whatever, over rocky knolls and burbling streams. According to the script, we somehow got separated from the rest of my unit, which left us alone to fend for ourselves and develop the romantic aspects of our relationship. Our two characters openly despised each other. He couldn't tolerate her constant complaining and her inability to keep up with him. She thought he was a boorish ruffian who needed a dose of manners and patience. They were doomed to fall in love.

We weren't breaking new ground with this story.

ALPHA FORCE III
EXT. MISTY WOODS. DAY.

GUS and HOLLY huddle behind a large tree--their only protection from the alien forces that surround them.

          GUS
    (exasperated)
Look, baby, we're sitting ducks, here. If we don't get moving, we're both going to be dead. You have to leave those damned high-heeled shoes behind, or we're never going to get out of here!

         HOLLY
    (frantic)
I can't! I simply *can't!*

         GUS
Look, kid, this is your last chance, otherwise I'm going to leave you behind.

        HOLLY
You wouldn't dare.

                    GUS
          Try me. I don't have
          time to babysit
          helpless strippers.

                   HOLLY
             (shocked)
          I told you that in
          confidence. You
          promised you wouldn't
          tell anyone. I can't
          believe you're bringing
          it up now. You're a
          bastard.

Begins to cry.

                    GUS
          Alright, alright.
          Cripes. Just take off
          the damned shoes, and
          let's get out of here.

                   HOLLY
          I told you, I can't.
          Once I take these shoes
          off, my feet will
          swell, and I'll never
          get them back on again.
          And I'm not leaving
          them behind. I paid
          over two hundred
          dollars for them.

Wipes her tears, readjusts her
shredded dress.

                    GUS
             (resigned)

> Okay, fine, forget it.
> But don't expect me to
> hang around waiting for
> you. You better keep
> up, or I'll leave you
> for the aliens.

                  HOLLY
> (pouting)
> Fine. Don't worry about
> me, buster. I know how
> to take care of myself.

                  GUS
> We'll see about that.

Scans the horizon with his infra-goggles.

> Okay, I'm going to make
> a dash for that fallen
> tree over there. You
> see it?

Hands her his photon blaster.

> Cover me.

Re-arms himself with two hand-held neutron cannons

                  HOLLY
> I don't know how to use
> this thing!

Inadvertently aims it at GUS'S head.

                  GUS
Pushing the muzzle away.

>	Jesus Murphy! It's not any more complicated than a telephone. You know how to use one of those, don't you?
>
>	(HOLLY nods petulantly)
>
>	Good. Just point this end right over there, and every time you want to make a call, pull the trigger with your index finger. Can you remember that?
>
>	(HOLLY nods again)
>
>	Pretend you want to telephone every bad guy you see, okay? Just point the phone at them and say hello with your index finger.

GUS dashes for the fallen tree.

>   *"Cut! Print that one. Check the gate before we break."*

Voices began to murmur throughout the woods. People emerged from the fog. "Okay, everybody. That's lunch. One hour. We're back at two o'clock sharp."

I lined up behind Jennifer at the craft table. "Great work out there," I said. And I meant it, too. "Talk about making a silk purse."

She looked back at me and her grin said it all. "Shakespeare it ain't," she whispered.

"I have food in my trailer," I said.

"Thank God. Let's go."

Krisha caught my eye as Jennifer and I pushed against the flow of hungry crew. She flattened her lips and shook her head slightly. I just shrugged and moved on. She was in no position to criticize me. For all she knew, we were simply looking for a quiet place to have an innocent discussion about back-story.

Michel was in the trailer when we got there.

"*You* again," I said. He had some papers spread out on the dinette, a telephone at his elbow.

"I am your personal assistant, Meester Fox," said the fruit. "Perhaps during the day only. You have call from Donald Duck, but I tink it's a prank." He handed me a slip of paper with a telephone number.

"Duke," I said. "Donald *Duke*. He's a very important man. I hope you weren't rude to him."

Michel looked indignant. "I am sure he say *Duck*. My hearing is twenty-twenty."

"They're serving lunch. Go grab a bite to eat."

"I don't eat lunch."

"Yes you do," I said.

The fruit quickly snatched up his daytimer and skipped off.

Jennifer looked amused. "The downside of celebrity," she said, slipping easily out of what remained of her costume. Her expensive breasts greeted me like a pair of silicon globe lights.

I let go of Donald Duke's telephone number.

After weeks of tramping through the woods, I finally had a day off before we began the intense studio work. As I sped toward the love loft, I discovered I was looking forward to seeing Selena. Apparently I missed her. I was grateful to have had Krisha to console me during my time away from my true love, ditto Jennifer, but I was eager to fall into the luscious arms of my beloved, perfect girlfriend.

"Hello, darling. I'm home!" I was waving the People Magazine over my head. I doubted Selena had seen it. She didn't read. When I heard the shower running, I set the magazine on the kitchen counter and poured myself a drink. Two minutes later, Prince Marco emerged from the bathroom with a towel wrapped around his waist.

"Billy!" He seemed surprised to see me.

"Hey, your majesty." I wasn't in the least surprised to see him. The little *dauphin* was always hanging around the loft.

Selena willowed out of the bathroom behind Marco. Her towel was piled on top of her head. "Billy!" She also seemed surprised to see me.

"Hello, my love," I said, looking her over. If she hadn't already been mine, I would have been envious.

(I know what this must have looked like, I know that alarm bells should have been going off in my brain, but remember: I was absolutely certain that Prince Marco was a fairy. I never would have believed he swung from both vines. And I was deeply, truly, completely in love. The cuckold is always the last to know.)

"What are you doing home?" asked Selena, quickly padding up the stairs to the open bedroom, which overlooked the kitchen and living room. Through the railing, I watched her glide back and forth, looking for something to wear. It was always a pleasure to see her naked. I sipped my bourbon. Marco was picking up his clothes, which were strewn around the living room.

"We start the interior scenes tomorrow. I have the entire day off. Did you see this?" I held up the People Magazine. Selena leaned over the railing, squinting down at the cover. I knew she needed glasses, but she would never admit it. Since she didn't read, I suppose it didn't really matter. "Our first cover," I said, proudly.

"Not your last, I'm sure," said the Prince. I couldn't tell if he was being cynical.

Then I remembered something. "Hey, your highness, there's someone you ought to meet. His name is Michel and he's French. I'll introduce you."

I thought I saw Prince Marco roll his eyes, but I may have imagined it. Anyway, I always enjoyed playing the matchmaker.

Naturally, Selena wanted to spend my day off shopping.

Advice to men: Hang on to that two-seat sports car for as long as possible. It allows you to ditch unwanted hangers-on when you take your girlfriend shopping.

"See ya later, your highness," I called out the window of my Corvette. I left him choking on a cloud of Goodyear vapour. "Why does that guy always have to hang around our place?" I asked.

Selena buffed her nails. The passenger seat of the Corvette was designed specifically for gorgeous women. "He's my friend."

"He doesn't have a shower at his house?" I still wasn't seeing the obvious. Perhaps I needed glasses, myself.

"He stayed over last night. I was lonely."

We were stopped at a light. The car next to me honked. It happened all the time, when my fans recognized me. I looked over and the fat old bastard behind the wheel of the rusty Lada blew a kiss at me. Then I realized he was blowing his kiss at Selena. I gave him the finger and revved the powerful motor at my disposal, to underscore my displeasure. The fat old bastard ignored my threat and flicked his tongue lecherously at my girl. Was he insane? Did he not realize I could crush him like a bug? Did he not notice that he was a fat old bastard who could not possibly interest any woman who was remotely human, never mind a fabulously stunning model with only one name? Sometimes the common man mystified me. When the light changed, I left him far behind.

"Fat fucker!"

"I think it's sweet," said Selena, gently. "You're just in a bad mood, for some reason."

"I'm not in a bad mood!" I shouted, above the roar of my V8.

We had lunch at the Epicure Café, and that cheered me a bit. Three times I got asked for my autograph. I was always glad to do my duty to the fans, even if the men invariably pretended the autograph was for their girlfriends. The place was a hangout for my fellow actors, so I also received a dozen requests for help from my luckless—and in many cases talentless—comrades. Actors are inveterate ass-kissers. If my friend, the writer, could be accused of having shit-smelling fingers, it is only fair to admit that, in the case of the average thespian, it's the proboscis that reeks of doo-doo.

After lunch I took revenge on Selena for dragging me into two-dozen shoe stores by steering her into Bay-Bloor Radio, where I spent more than an hour trading technical lingo with the sales staff. We talked decibels and distortion ratios until Selena was blue in the face. I finally settled on the model I had already decided on before we'd arrived: a sleek and sexy Bang & Olufsen system that I knew would look great in the love loft. It cost as much as a good used car. The salesman was having visions of early retirement from this commission, and I was glad to help. Selena was glad to leave.

When we got home, we made love and had a nap.

Beep..."Hi, love. It's Jackie. I was just thinking about you. I heard you were off shooting a movie, so I'm sure you're tremendously busy, but I wanted to touch base, let you know I was thinking of you. When you get a break, give me a call and maybe we can do the lunch thing. Call me. Five-five-five, six-one-one-four. Ciao."

Beep..."Billy. It's Donald Duke. I know you're on location somewhere. I tried to leave you messages, but you're obviously not getting them. Anyway, we need to talk. Give me a call."

I filed away Jackie Knowlton's number and forgot about Donald Duke; his good news could wait. The next morning, I was back on set, finally out of the rain. We were shooting in a large sound stage in the east end. At least I was in town, and could fall into my own bed at night.

The first interior we shot was the love scene. The end of the movie. If you are new to the movie business, shooting out of sequence can be a confusing experience. Jennifer Haimes seemed to be handling it fine, until Blake Dunsmore told her to take her dress off.

"I'm not doing the scene nude," she said.

Blake put his arms up. "Why not?"

"It isn't in the script. I didn't agree to do a nude scene. I'm not taking my clothes off."

"Of course it's in the script." He jabbed his finger at the pages of his own script.

Jennifer shook her head. "There's a love scene. I read that part. Nowhere does it say that Holly takes her clothes off."

Blake scoured the pages, his face burning crimson. "It says that Holly and Gus make love, right here, on page two-fourteen."

"I'm aware of that passage, Blake, but it doesn't say that I take off my clothes. That's all I'm saying."

"How in blazes do you think Holly and Gus are going to fuck if she doesn't take her clothes off? Tell me that?"

"Shoot around it. Imply it. Martin Scorsese could do it."

Blake threw his script down. Again. He was like a little kid, sometimes. "Well, the next time you're in a Martin Scorsese film—which, at this rate, will be *never*—you can keep your goddamned clothes on. In a Blake Dunsmore film, we fuck with our clothes *off!*"

"Then you can get yourself a new bimbo," said Jennifer. She stalked away to her trailer.

"Oh, that's just fucking great!" shouted Blake. The producers, who had been stuffing their faces with cookies and popcorn at the craft table, came over to see why nothing seemed to be happening.

"I'll go have a word with Jennifer," I said.

I knocked on the door.

"Go away!"

"It's me," I said, gently.

The door opened.

When I stepped inside, Jennifer wheeled around. "I've done Shakespeare, too, you know!"

"I know."

"I was Desdemona!"

"I know."

"I was Portia!"

"I know."

"I was Juliet!"

I would like to have seen that: Jennifer, the silicon marvel, hanging over that balcony. "I know, sweetie."

She fell into a chair and began to massage her temples. "I really thought I could get myself out of the bimbo trap with this movie, you know? I honestly believed that if I brought just a hint of *brains*, just a little *savvy* to the part, I could beat them at their own game. Sure, at first, it would seem as if I was just another brainless twat, running after the big strong man, but I was convinced I could bring a spark of intelligence to the part. I thought if I could do that, I might finally get a serious role. That's all I've ever wanted, to be taken seriously as an actress. Before I got these tits, no one looked twice at me. I've dug a deep hole and filled it with shit and thrown myself into it, and now I can't climb out again. Getting these tits was the biggest mistake of my life."

I begged to differ, but refrained from saying so.

"My mother sold her car to pay for these tits. I'm still paying her back, fifty dollars a month. Isn't that the most pathetic thing you've ever heard?" Tears began to upset the carefully applied makeup beneath her eyes.

"No. The most pathetic thing I've ever heard was the story of a talented actress who had rather ordinary breasts—*nice*, but ordinary—who couldn't get noticed at the auditions. She kept putting herself out there, doing all her best monologues, slugging away at it until, after a while, she just quietly gave up, found herself a useless husband, squeezed out a couple of kids, and spent the rest of her life wondering what might have happened, if only..."

She fucked me.

"You're welcome," I said. "Listen, Jennifer, patience is the name of this game. If your break doesn't happen with this movie, then look forward to the next one. But don't spoil your chance of getting the next one. Don't blow it, just because you're in a temporary rut. Sooner or later, you'll make it."

She did the scene nude, which was a good thing, since Blake Dunsmore didn't have the Scorsese touch. He could never have shot around it. He could not have implied anything. He couldn't get the hang of tripods. He made up for those shortcomings by blowing everything in sight to smithereens.

(As for Jennifer Haimes—she of the boulderous boobs—she later spent thousands of dollars having her silicon implants removed. It was the smartest thing she could have done. She never became the movie star we all dream of becoming, she never made the cover of People Magazine, but she gained a solid reputation as a serious character actress, and to this day remains a ubiquitous presence on the big screen.

I saw her recently, in fact. She had a small but pivotal role in a mega-budget drama as the protagonist's mother. Imagine that. She is well into her forties now and she still looks great, despite a rather ordinary cleavage. Just for fun, I asked the person sitting next to me in the theatre if he knew who that actress was, what her name was? He responded exactly as I predicted he would: "I don't know. I've seen her a million times, but I can't think of her name." Congratulations, Jennifer Haimes. You've made it. You are a serious actress.

What am I, these days? A waiter. If my old arm could stretch that far, I'd pat myself on the back.)

While I was in the midst of shooting *Alpha Force III*, Selena decided she missed New York. She was going to spend the month of April there. "It's not like you're around, anyway. You're doing your *movie*." I could see she was still upset about my failure to get her the part of Holly, the bimbo. "I've got some jobs lined up there, and I need to see my old friends."

"I'll miss you," I said. And I meant it, too.

I talked Krisha into moving in for the month. "I hope it doesn't make you uncomfortable, seeing all of Selena's things lying around," I said, the first time I brought her to the loft.

"Not at all." She made herself right at home. And she made me breakfast every morning. Selena had never made breakfast for herself, let alone for me. And Krisha, also unlike my glamorous girlfriend Selena, devoted one hundred percent of her attention to my comfort and well-being.

"You're everything I could have dreamed a personal assistant could be, Krisha."

She stroked my bare chest. "I'm not your personal assistant. Michel Dumont is your personal assistant. I'm just a script girl who happens to like you."

"Well then, you are everything I could have dreamed a script girl could be."

She laughed.

"Is it too late to ask to see your driver's license?" She really did look young.

When I finally got around to returning Donald Duke's call, he seemed upset. But he could hardly blame me for taking so long. I had a busy career to tend to.

"Can you come to my office this afternoon? We need to talk."

"Sure thing, Donald. No problem."

Toronto film production offices tend to be located in seedy industrial neighbourhoods. It's a trend that I have never understood. For some reason, these million-dollar moguls feel no compunction about giving the appearance of a shabby, fly-by-night operation. Of course, some are, but there's no excuse for the rest. In a business where appearance is everything, it's a wonder to me that they don't look in the mirror more often.

Donald Duke's office was in a shabby building in a seedy industrial neighbourhood. Of course. There were no tufted leather armchairs. There was no well-stocked bar. There was no billiard-size mahogany desk with pearl inlays. There was a small room with tacky wood panelling and a water-stained drop ceiling. There was mashed-down carpeting that was many shades of an unidentifiable colour. There was a small desk with a wood grain finish as phoney as the wood grain walls. There were two squeaky, rickety, rolling chairs.

Every time I tried to lean back into mine, to get out of that upright secretarial posture, I nearly tipped back onto my skull. After several tricky attempts, I found a way to slouch without killing myself.

"What's up, Donald? Did you get the budget for next season? When will I see a preliminary schedule? Herb tells me he hasn't seen a contract yet."

Donald Duke made his fingers into a steeple. The steeple opened. The steeple closed. Opened. Closed. What did the steeple mean? "I have the budget for next season," he said, finally realizing that his sign language meant nothing to me.

"Good. How is it?"

"It's less than I was hoping for."

"Less? Why? How much less?"

"A lot less."

"That's pretty mysterious, Donald. I don't suppose you could be more specific?"

He sighed. "Specifically, it amounts to a one hundred percent reduction in the budget."

"Whoa! That's a lot." Then I thought about it a bit more. "Hey—"

"The show has been cancelled, Billy."

"But—" But what? What came next? What words could follow that *But—*? My brain was fast-forwarding and rewinding, out of control. Then I found the next word: "Why?"

The steeple opened, and stayed that way. "Why indeed, Billy? That was the very question I asked the network. And would you like to hear what they said?"

"No, not really, but I suppose you should tell me anyway."

The steeple closed suddenly, tightly, trapping the congregation within. He read the letter that was on the desk in front of him: "'The ratings are respectable, Donald. *Maiken Trouble* has consistently achieved top-twenty status for five seasons, which is an admirable accomplishment. But, as you know, network television is entering difficult and changing times. Our image is being completely overhauled for this coming September, and part of that overhaul includes a substantially revamped primetime line-up. Let me assure you that *Maiken Trouble* is not the only show that will feel the effects of this change. We are exchanging approximately seventy percent of our programming for brand new shows that are more in keeping with the demands of today's discerning viewers. We are at the dawn of a new decade. The Eighties, we feel, promise a new era of sophistication. Our audience is clamouring for product that is stylish, urbane, and we are dedicated to giving it to them. *Maiken Trouble* is a good show, Donald. You can all be proud of the fine work you've done. Best of luck, and pass on our regards to Billy Fox.'"

"Is that supposed to make me feel better?" I asked.

"I imagine that would be their take on it, yes."

We sat in silence for a minute or two. "Now what do we do?"

The steeple collapsed onto the desk. "We send out resumes, Billy. That's what we do."

When I dialled the New York telephone number Selena had given me, the model who answered told me Selena was no longer staying there. She had, in fact, only spent one night there, before flitting off somewhere else. The model didn't know where. Great. That was just fucking great. Where was Selena when I needed her? Thank God I had Krisha to console me.

I finished *Alpha Force III* and tried not to worry. Herb Farley, my effervescent agent, was typically reassuring.

"Don't worry about a thing, Billy. You've just had a five-year run on a hit television show and you're about to wrap a successful feature film. You've got it made. I already have several irons in the fire. ABC is looking at a new detective series, and they've shown an interest in bringing you in."

"I don't want to do television, Herb. Get me movies."

"Well, let's just see what comes along. Don't thumb your nose at the biggest market available."

"Television makes me small. I want to be *big*."

"You're already a big man on television. Size doesn't matter. Ask anyone."

I asked Krisha. "Of course size matters, Billy. Any woman will tell you that."

During the *Alpha Force III* wrap party, I might have had a few too many vodka martinis. I should have known better. Bourbon is my drink. Vodka makes me crazy, makes me do things I wouldn't ordinarily do. Under the influence of vodka, my mouth works in mysterious ways, saying things that might be better left unsaid, and then it stops working altogether, after it's all too late.

"You pulled it off nicely, Billy," said Blake Dunsmore. "I have to admit, I wasn't sure about you, at first. Naturally, I was looking forward to working with Lorrie. Too bad about his ankle." I suspect Blake Dunsmore was drinking vodka, too. Poor man.

"When this piece of crud flops at the box office," I slurred, "don't come crying to me. You couldn't direct me to the nearest Post Office without tying your ass in a knot. *You* should have played the role of Holly. *You're* the bimbo, Dunsmore. You should take the paycheque from this job and get yourself some fucking breast implants."

That put a damper on the conversation. If he'd had a script in his hand, he would no doubt have flung it to the ground and stamped his feet, the immature prick. The dozen or so people it took to produce the film managed to drag themselves away from the buffet table long enough to separate us before it came to fisticuffs. Lucky for Blake. I was itching for an excuse to put to the test the Judo lessons I had taken in preparation for my role in *Alpha Force III*.

That night, after Krisha put me to bed, the telephone rang. I was too sozzled to answer it, so Krisha picked it up.

"It's for you," she whispered, handing me the extension at the nightstand. "It's Selena."

"Hello, my love," I croaked into the mouthpiece. My jaw had only partially recovered its mobility.

"Who was that who answered the phone, Billy?" Selena's voice was sharp. Since she had not had the decency to contact me in nearly a month, I felt that perhaps I was more entitled to be upset. I was too drunk to be upset.

"My personal assistant," I said.

"What's she doing there so late?"

"Putting me to bed."

"I'll bet."

God! She was jealous.

"What's her name?"

"I forget." That was no lie. "Something French, I think." I was getting my assistants mixed up. "Don't worry. I'm pretty sure she's gay."

"You sound drunk, Billy. Are you drunk?"

"You sound drunk to me," I said, "but that may be due to my ears being so drunk."

"Were you at a party?"

"We wrapped Alpha Farce tonight." Yes, I meant to say *farce*. I was drunk, but not *that* drunk. "When are you coming home, darling? I need you desperately. I think I may be suicidal."

"What's the matter, Billy? Is this just the alcohol talking?"

"They cancelled my show. They ditched me after five good years. They bent me over and shoved a red-hot poker of rejection right up my *ass!*"

"Honestly, Billy, don't talk like that. I know you're upset, but it won't help to worry yourself to death. Everything will work out."

"That's what Herb said, but it's not his ass out on the street with a red-hot poker of rejection shoved up it."

"Billy, I can't talk to you when you're like this. I'm going to hang up now. Get some sleep, and send your little assistant home. I'll be there tomorrow afternoon."

Most of that last bit is guesswork. I passed out right after "Billy…" It was somewhat unfortunate that I didn't catch the part about her coming home the next day, because Krisha was still hanging around in the love loft, nursing me back to sobriety, when Selena crashed through the door with her bursting luggage and a month's worth of shopping bags.

I owe a great deal to my hangover. It prevented me from reacting to Selena's sudden reappearance in any way that suggested I was alive. The only things I could move were my eyeballs, and even they hurt.

"Poor darling," oozed Selena. She dropped her bags and skipped over to my rotting corpse on the sofa, and gave me a welcoming peck on the cheek. She recoiled only slightly from the smell. I thought she handled that fairly well. Of course, Krisha had lain next to that smell all night without complaint, but making a comparison was apples and oranges.

"Hello, love. This is a surprise," I said, showing no sign whatsoever of surprise.

"I told you I was coming, Billy." She began to elaborately remove her jacket and gloves, which she wore not for the weather but for effect. She had one of the gloves off and was pulling at the fingertips of the second when Krisha waltzed out of the bathroom, in much the same fashion as Selena often did: completely nude, except for a towel perched on her head.

"Oh!" said Krisha, when she saw Selena standing over me.

The nude girl caught Selena's eye. Her look of displeasure hardened, turned to granite. "*Je voudrais une couchette inférierure, mademoiselle,*" she said. It was the only French phrase she knew: I would like a lower berth.

"I don't understand," Krisha said, not quite sure what she should do next. In order to retrieve her clothing, she would have to pass close to where Selena stood.

Selena turned to me with an angry look. "French my ass!" she said.

"Are you taking a train?" asked Krisha. "I'm not sure why you're asking me about a lower berth. If you need help making a reservation, I can make a call for you." Was there anything my little assistant couldn't do? Then I remembered she wasn't my assistant. She was only a script girl. My real assistant had been a useless twit.

Selena tipped her head up sharply, as if to accuse God. "I have to get the rest of my things from the taxi, Billy." She dropped her gloves on the coffee table and clicked away on a lovely new pair of shoes.

"Sorry, Billy," said Krisha, skipping up the stairs to quickly dress. She was gone before Selena returned with the rest of her things. I never saw Krisha again. In her haste to vacate the suddenly crowded love loft, she left behind her driver's license. I saw it on the kitchen counter when I shuffled over to get another seltzer. I looked at the birth date, just out of curiosity. She was seventeen. (I still have that young girl's driver's license today. I keep it in my desk drawer, for old times' sake. I never attempted to contact her, I don't know what became of her, but she makes me think of a time in my life before the sky fell in on my head. To me, she is nostalgia, sweet, kind nostalgia.)

Speaking of sweet and kind, here comes my gorgeous Selena, still vibrating with New York energy.

"Is this what I can expect, Billy?" she said, dropping more shopping bags and a makeup case on the floor inside the door. "I leave for a few days and, as I'm walking out the front door, some tramp is climbing in through the window? Is that what our relationship has come to?"

I rubbed my temples, squeezed my eyes. "She got me home last night, like I said. Nothing happened. I passed out." That was all more-or-less true.

"She spent the night. She's walking around here naked. What am I supposed to think about that?"

"She had a shower. Christ, Selena. Prince Marco's always running around here naked."

"Don't bring my good friend into this. We're not discussing Marco."

"I'm sorry, I'm just upset. I can't believe they cancelled my show. I'm completely devastated."

"Of course you are," said Selena, her voice suddenly full of warmth and sympathy. That was better. She settled next to me on the sofa and kissed me a few times on the neck and ear. "Go have a shower, Billy. You smell like a New York sewer rat."

Chapter 5

"CBC is casting a new series. They've put out a call." Herb emptied the fourth packet of sugar into his coffee. A stomach-churning sight.

"Surely, they don't expect me to audition?"

"Well, obviously you're on the short list, but they still want an audition. It's more of a formality, really."

"You can formally tell them to go fuck themselves if they think I'm going to read for some piece of Canadian dreck."

He sipped his coffee and winced. I don't know what he was trying to prove.

"I don't think you're approaching this with the right attitude, Billy. It's not unheard of for actors, even prominent actors like yourself, to audition for roles."

"Get me an audition with Scorsese or Jewison. Where are the movie scripts? I told you I'm not interested in television. I just finished *Alpha Force III*. Find out who else has sprained an ankle recently. I hear Stalone's a clumsy oaf. See what he's got in the works. I'll do *Rocky VII*. I don't care, as long as it's a feature."

Herb tipped another sugar packet into his coffee mug. Was he nuts?

"By the way, MTC is doing *Private Lives*. I talked to the producer this morning, and she wants you. No audition, if that makes you feel better. It'd be good for you to do something funny. You don't want to be pigeonholed. You don't want to be playing tough guys for the rest of your life."

I shut my eyes. I couldn't watch Herb drink his syrup. "You're killing me, Herb," I said, meaning the coffee and the MTC job. "I haven't been on stage in years. Theatre in this country is dead. Why would I go all the way to Winnipeg, just so a couple of fat-assed farm girls can call me Maiken? Who's going to see me out there? How can that possibly help me get movie roles?"

"It'll pay the bills. Some of them. You may think acting is an art, Billy, but it's also a business, and it's your living. No roles, no art, no money, no food on the table. Don't dismiss these jobs just because you have loftier aspirations. You still have to make a living. It's going to be months before *Alpha Force III* is released. We'll see what happens after that. In the meantime, you need the work. No matter what you think of the CBC, the gig is a good one. The money is good. It's high profile work, at least by Canadian standards. As for Winnipeg, I agree that you may very well find the theatre filled with fat-assed farm girls, but the credit will look great on your resume. Trust me. It will demonstrate your diversity as an actor."

"What about the ABC thing? Didn't you say they were doing a new detective series?" If I had to do television, at least this would be an easy transition for me.

"Sorry, kid. That one fell through."

I shrugged. "There are too many detective shows on the air, anyway."

"They're still doing the show. They cast someone else in the lead. They wanted someone younger."

"Younger? Is it the Hardy Boys? I know I'm not exactly a teenager, but I'm not over the hill, yet. Christ, I'm not even thirty."

"Next month," said Herb. He always had the pertinent information at his fingertips.

"Well, now that I'm over the hill, maybe you can get me Willy Loman. *Death of a Salesman* must be playing somewhere within a hundred miles of here."

(A few years back, I had the good fortune to play that choice role in one of the greatest plays of the twentieth century. For three weeks, I roamed the tiny stage in Edmonton, voicing my disillusionment with my life and my family to the polite elderly couples who had come to the Stage West dinner theatre. By that time in my life, I could truly identify with Willy's angst. *Death of an Actor: The Billy Fox Story*. I was magnificent.

How one views life is always a matter of perspective.)

Beep..."Hello, darling. I heard about your show. I hope you're not worrying needlessly. You father and I are a bit surprised we had to hear the news from your sister, though. You should have called us. If you can't rely on your family, who can you rely on? Don't be ashamed just because this acting didn't work out, sweetheart. It's not too late for you to change course. Remember how good your high school accounting grades were? I don't need to remind you that Cameron Faminow is doing quite well in this town as a chartered accountant. I saw him just the other day driving a brand new car. I don't know what kind of car it was, but it was brand new. And I hear he lives in Queensland Heights. I'm not trying to pressure you, Billy. I'm just reminding you that you have options. You still have plenty of time to get yourself on the right track. Maybe now that you have nothing better to do, you'll come out to Calgary for a few weeks. Bring that girl of yours. We're all dying to finally meet her. Jane's doing well. She's the new assistant buyer at Woolco. She's really on her way. We're all very proud of her. Give us a call and let us know when you'll be coming. Your father sends his regards."

My mother wonders why I never come to Calgary to see them. Could it possibly be due to the fact that she constantly talks about those goddamned high school accounting grades? The only reason I passed that course was because I encouraged Lisa Fern's hopeless crush on me, for which she allowed me to copy her stellar work. And Cameron Faminow always has been and will forever remain a boring twerp. I can rely on my family for many things, including making me feel like a loser, even though I have worked steadily for years, and have been more-or-less solely responsible for making *Maiken Trouble* a top-rated hit. I can rely on having an equal measure of guilt and condescension heaped on me by my loving family. I can completely rely on hearing constant comparisons between me, with my dubious lifestyle, and the sensible and mature peers I left behind, to wallow in suburban hell and become BMW-driving accountants. If I remind my father that my car cost almost forty thousand dollars, I can rely on him to say that any sensible and mature man will not drive a Corvette, no matter how much it cost.

To make me feel better, Selena took me on a shopping spree at the hardware store. Spending vast sums of money always made me feel better. With the clarity of hindsight, I see that I might have acted a bit more prudently with my cash. I had money in the bank, but it goes fast when there is no new money flowing in.

"Don't worry about money," said Selena. "I make enough for both of us. Besides, I know you'll be working soon." Her optimism recharged my spirit, invigorated my soul. My beloved safety net. Naturally, I would do the same for her, if she ever found herself in a career crisis. Models are as susceptible as actors to the vagaries of a fickle public. At any moment, Selena could be deemed too tall or too fat or too large-breasted for this month's crop of unhappy housewives. There was no telling when her bubble might burst, when she might have to start using her last name, once again. "Let's go to the Rosedale Diner for lunch."

"Where's Ralph?" I asked the skinny girl who brought our menus. "Who?"

"Ralph. Ralph Cummings. He usually works Saturdays. Is he sick?"

The skinny girl looked nervous, shifty. "I don't know any Ralph, Mister Fox." Aha! Another weepy fan. "I can ask around, if you like."

"Sure, sure." What the hell did I care? I was just curious.

She toddled away without taking our drink order. Bloody incompetence.

Selena looked ravishing in the soft light of our window booth. Her serenity was infectious. For the moment, at least, I was feeling a whole lot better about things.

"I have some news to tell you, Billy." She drilled into me with those diamond-tipped eyes of hers. "I'm pregnant."

If only I had had a drink to splutter all over the table, I wouldn't have looked so foolish coughing and choking on my dry tongue. "Wha—?"

"I hope that coughing fit is just a coincidence. Otherwise, I might think you weren't happy about this."

"I—" More coughing and choking. "I am, darling. It's just that…well, it's a bit of a surprise. I mean, how did this happen?"

"Do I really have to explain it to you, Billy?"

"But you're on the pill. I thought you were on the pill."

"I was. But they were causing me to bloat. Water retention is the number one cause of premature retirement in the modelling business. I couldn't take the risk."

"Jesus, Selena. What do you think is going to happen now that you're pregnant? I'm pretty sure you can expect a bit of *bloating*."

"That's temporary. Anyway, I've been meaning to have a child for some time now. We've talked about it Billy. It's not like I'm dropping this on you unexpectedly."

The only time we had ever talked about it was the last time she told me she was pregnant, which turned out to be a ruse. "Is this another trick? Is this a ruse? You're just trying to find out how I'll react, right? Well, now you know I'll react badly, so you don't have to play these games, anymore."

"I'm not tricking you, Billy. I'm completely serious. This is no joking matter. I've always planned on having children. This should be a wonderful experience for both of us." She thought she was ordering new fabric for the pouf. Parenthood? She had no idea what she was getting in to.

I looked around desperately for the skinny waitress, who had been gone far too long. I needed a drink fairly urgently. "How can you support us if you're pregnant? You won't be able to work."

"Shame on you, Billy. We're going to have a baby and all you can think about is work."

"I'm thinking about our baby living in a gutter."

"You're just being hysterical. Everything will work out fine."

The skinny waitress suddenly appeared. "Mister Fox? I asked around about Ralph Cummings for you." She was chewing her lower lip, a trait that did not instil me with confidence.

"Yes?" I was happy to suddenly have something to distract me from thinking about my faltering career as an actor and my imminent status as a father.

"He quit," she said. "He got offered the lead in a new detective series on ABC."

"Obviously, someone is pulling your leg," I said. But the searing pain in my chest suggested she was telling the truth. Who ever said the good roles go to the best man? I knew how the world worked, and it sucked.

"I've seen all your shows, Mister Fox. I even watch the reruns. It's really a great show."

"Was," I said. "It's cancelled. They're all reruns, now."

"Oh." She disappeared again—again without taking our order. Another actress, I surmised. Now that she knew I couldn't help her, she would ignore us.

63

"I want you to be happy about this, Billy. I really must insist. This is very important to me."

I looked at Selena and knew that if I didn't choose my words carefully, she would cry, or worse.

Advice to men: If a woman wants to have a baby, it is impossible to talk her out of it. Don't even try. Trying will only get you war. You will have a baby *and* war—not a situation conducive to raising a well-adjusted child. Furthermore, twenty-year-old women have a particularly romantic view of motherhood, and will not see reason. Trying to reason with them is a futile and incendiary course. Either their mothers will help them see the light, or you had better start painting the spare room yellow. Suggestion: smile a lot and, if you think it will help, try to think about the hockey playoffs.

"I couldn't be happier, darling. Really." God, I was a great actor!

I made the mistake of waiting until Herb had his coffee mug to his lips before telling him the good news. He had roughly the same reaction I had. I was favoured with a fine mist of extremely sweet java. "Jesus Murphy!" Herb shouted, once he recovered. "I never thought of that. This is great!"

"Are you nuts?" For once, I'd have liked him to see my point of view.

"Wait until I tell People Magazine. They'd be crazy not to jump on this one. What a follow-up! We need a good photo, one where Selena has her hand on her belly. Is she showing, yet?"

"How should I know? She says she's been bloated, lately. How do I tell the difference?"

"When is she due?" Herb asked, ignoring my question.

"I don't know."

"Have you picked names, yet?"

"All that sugar in your coffee is killing your brain cells, Herb."

"We've got to have some details to give the press. Help me out here. Are you sure you're the father?"

"What? Why would you ask me that?"

Herb spread his arms wide. "Come on, Billy. I'm just doing my job. If I don't ask the hard questions, the press will. You mean to tell me you haven't wondered?"

"No," I said, honestly.

"She's a model, for Pete's sake. She flits around the world taking off most of her clothing for photographers and God-knows-who-all. Men must hit her on wherever she goes. Do you think she can sit on an airplane without having the greasy businessman next to her buying her drinks for the entire flight? She just spent a month in New York. Where did she stay? Who did she go out with? Who bought her dinner? Who scrubbed her back in the bathtub?"

I had to interrupt him, before I was forced to cuff his ears. "Why are you putting these images in my head?"

"I have to say, Billy, I really thought you had a handle on this situation."

"What situation? My girlfriend's pregnant and you're trying to convince me it's not my baby. I think I'm missing something."

"You sure are," said Herb. "Let me spell it out for you. We have a famous actor who is living with a gorgeous model with only one name. Get the picture, so far?" He waited for me to nod. "Good. Now, she's twenty and he's thirty—"

"—*barely* thirty."

"Right you are. *Barely* thirty. And now, let me ask you a very important question."

I shrug.

"Why are they together?"

"They're in love."

Herb clapped his hands together. "You see? There's where you're going astray. Now let me tell you the real reason. They are together because it's good for their respective careers."

"No, actually, they're in love."

Herb laughed and laughed. "That's a good one!" He wiped the tears from his cheeks. "Listen, if you were a bus driver and she were a school teacher, you might be in love. That makes sense. People who are nobody fall in love. People who are somebody get libellous articles written about them in tabloids. Why? Because when you are somebody, love means nothing and free press is better than gold."

"That's a pretty cynical outlook, Herb."

"I'm just looking out for your best interests. By the way, I have the script for the CBC thing. It's a period piece—you know, the struggling-pioneers-in-the-old-west thing." He slid the offending script across his desk toward me.

I looked at the cover page. *Heritage Creek*. "Where do they come up with this shit?"

"You haven't even read it."

"The title speaks volumes."

"Read the script. The audition is on Tuesday, at two. Don't give me *that* look. It's just a formality."

"Right."

I arrived at the studio at ten minutes to two. Les Dodd was there. The foyer was teeming with waiters. I took some small comfort in the knowledge that my appearance was strictly a formality, but I felt it was beneath me to be grazing with this herd of lowing cattle.

"Hi, Billy," said Les. He wanted to demonstrate to the others that he knew me personally by speaking too loudly, but he didn't impress anyone. I was acquainted with nearly all the others. Most of them lived off my tips.

"Hi Les," I said, unenthusiastically. I couldn't focus on him. My eyes wandered the foyer, desperately searching for someone more important to stand with. But it was hopeless.

"What are you up for?" asked Les.

"Huh?" I wasn't listening. After all, when did Les Dodd ever have anything interesting to say?

"What role? What are you up for?"

I shrugged. "I don't know. Some guy in cover-alls."

Les laughed. "That's funny, Billy." Then I remembered that all the men in *Heritage Creek* wore cover-alls. Bloody typical. "I'm here for Jud," he said. "Wouldn't it be funny if we were up for the same role?"

I tried to ignore him, but he wouldn't go away.

"What scene are you reading? I'm supposed to do the graveyard scene, but I'm going to segue right into *Hamlet*. I want them to see that I'm a serious actor."

It was his funeral. What did I care? I was planning to read whatever they chose to throw at me. I was a professional; I could do it off the cuff. "Knock yourself out, kid."

By two-forty-five, the crowd in the foyer was thinning. Les had murdered poor Hamlet and split. He had the afternoon shift at Cirro's. At last, my name was called. I was led down a labyrinth of cluttered hallways where pot-bellied men with snide grins loitered, screwing and unscrewing light bulbs in order to look busy. Our tax dollars hard at work. The pot-bellied slob who was guiding me stopped in front of a blue door that was clearly marked *Ladies*.

"I went before I left home," I said.

The slob forced back a smile. His union forbade overt signs of joy. He stalked away, leaving me standing there alone. I shrugged, and entered the ladies' room.

Four tired-looking men sat behind a table at the far end of the chamber. Behind the men, in the corner, another pot-bellied goon stood behind a video camera, buffing his nails. He wore a large, black headset, connected to a microphone. A braid of thick cables wound from the belly of the camera and disappeared into one of the closed toilet stalls.

One of the men at the table began shuffling some papers. "Billy..." said the man, squinting at the top sheet. "Fox," he said, finally.

"That's right," I said, smoothly. "Billy Fox." I smiled, even though I felt I had just been insulted. I came forward and shook hands with the four men. They seemed uncomfortable making physical contact. I concluded that that was because we were in the ladies' room— typically mysterious places that men wanted to know little about. In my peripheral sightline, I thought I saw the cameraman flex. Security fell within the boundaries of his job description, apparently.

"Having your office renovated?" I asked the men, scanning the washroom.

The man on the right flinched. "Who told you that?" The other men glanced his way, shiftily.

"No one," I said. "I was just referring to our presence in this washroom."

They all looked around, as if it was the first time they had noticed the toilet stalls and the rank of sinks along the opposite wall. They didn't seem pleased that I had pointed this out to them. When I looked more closely at the floor, I could see by the dirty spots beneath their shoes that the table had been there a long time. Possibly years. Come to think of it, I hadn't seen a single woman in the place since I'd arrived. They had likely been using the ladies' room to audition for so long, they had completely forgotten what it was originally intended for. It was also evident that at least one of the men at the table was redecorating his office—probably unbeknownst to his superiors, and almost certainly using funds diverted from the screenwriting budget for Heritage Creek. I had only skimmed the script, but what I had seen was glaring evidence of cutbacks in the writing department. I was convinced the pilot had been written by a bored housewife from Grimsby.

"Shall we begin?" asked man number two.

"Wait!" boomed the cameraman, causing me to flinch. "You didn't say to roll tape. We're not rolling, yet."

Man number two sighed. After twenty-three years at the CBC, he was afraid to slit his wrists in case the afterlife was unionized. "Ready camera one, roll tape."

"*Please*," said the cameraman.

Man number two silently counted to ten. "Roll tape...*please*," he said, finally.

"Roll tape!" shouted the cameraman, into his microphone.

"Tape rolling!" shouted a disembodied voice, from within the toilet stall where the cables led.

"Tape is rolling!" shouted the cameraman.

We all waited, in case the cameraman had another grievance.

"You've done some television before?" asked man number one.

There was another shocking silence in the bathroom. Was this a trick question? "*Maiken Trouble*," I said, tentatively. More silence. "NBC," I added. Blank stares. I was going to have to spell it out for them. "For five years, I played the leading role of Joe Maiken in the NBC hit series, *Maiken Trouble*. It was a very successful show. Very popular with the fifteen-to-thirty males. It was nominated for an Emmy."

"And—"

"And then it was cancelled," I said, choking up slightly at the thought.

"If it was such a big hit, why was it cancelled?"

"You'd have to ask NBC about that."

"Is that it?" asked man number three.

"That kept me pretty busy for the last five years, if that's what you mean." Herb was going to pay for this. "I just finished a feature film."

"Title?"

"*Alpha Force III*."

Four pairs of eyes narrowed. "A sequel." They began to whisper amongst themselves. The cameraman scratched something onto a notepad and dropped the paper in front of man number one. Man number one read the note and nodded.

"Stop tape!" shouted the cameraman.

"Tape stopped!" shouted the phantom in toilet stall number three.

Man number one looked up at me. "Thanks for dropping by, Johnny."

"Billy," I said. "Don't you want me to read? Go ahead and pick any scene from the script. I know it's just a formality, but I don't mind. I could even do some Shakespeare, if you like."

"We have to take our break now, Johnny. If you want to wait outside for twenty minutes, we'll hear you read then." Four paper bags suddenly appeared on the table. The quartet noisily unwrapped sandwiches and unscrewed thermoses. The cameraman removed his headset and stalked out of the room. One of the toilets flushed.

Damned if I was going to wait. I turned heel and stepped into the poorly lit corridor, nearly colliding with a woman carrying a stack of papers. She must have been new. She glared at me when she realized I had just emerged from the ladies' room.

"The tampon dispenser is out of order," I said.

The woman muttered something and scurried away.

I kept my head down and made tracks across the foyer toward the exit. As I put my hands up to push the door open, they found themselves pressing into something much softer than the cold glass I was expecting. I looked up. My hands had found Jackie Knowlton's breasts. She was on her way in.

She was so shocked by the sudden appearance of my hands on her breasts, she was as speechless as I was. I took a step back.

"Hello, Billy," she said, recovering.

"Sorry," I said, putting my hands at my side. "I thought you were the door."

"I gathered."

"I got your message. I've been meaning to call you about lunch, but you know how it is. It's been crazy, the past few months. By the way, you look great." I meant it, too. She was a beautiful woman, considering her age. "What are you doing here?"

She plucked at her blonde hair and brushed some imaginary dust off her coat sleeve. "Same thing as you, I imagine. *Heritage Creek*."

"You'll fit right in," I said. "They're holding the auditions in the ladies' room."

For some reason, she found that amusing. "I'm not auditioning, Billy. They offered me Julie-May last week. I'm here for a fitting. Gawd! Who would *audition* for a piece of crap like *Heritage Creek?*"

We both shared a good laugh.

"I'm surprised I didn't hear that they cast you. Did they offer you Jud?"

"Oh, I'm not here for that. I told my agent I'm only interested in doing features from now on. I was just giving my friend Les a lift."

"You mean Les Dodd?"

"Yep."

"I just saw him get on a streetcar."

"Really? That's strange. I wonder why he didn't wait for me?" What an actor I was.

"Well, Billy, it's nice to see you again. We really have to do lunch soon. Give me a call next week."

"Sure, sure. I'll call you."

When Herb called the producers of *Heritage Creek* to check on my status with the show, they seemed to have no recollection of my having been there at all. Needless to say, they didn't make me an offer. I called Jackie Knowlton six times over the next three weeks, and she did not return my calls. I was sure she was busy, as she expected.

Chapter 6

Beep..."Hi, Billy. It's Les Dodd. I just wanted to call and let you know I got the part of Jud on *Heritage Creek*. It's pretty exciting for me, and I'm really looking forward to working with you. I still haven't been able to find out from anyone who you are playing on the show. Maybe it's Clayton. I don't know. If you get a chance, give me a dingle and let me know. We can spend some extra time rehearsing together, something like that. I'm sure I can learn a lot from a master like you. Talk to you later, Billy. Bye-bye."

Fucking goddamned gloating creep.

Selena was splayed out on the sofa beside me. She was apparently suffering from some sort of nausea associated with her pregnancy.

"Can you believe the nerve of that guy?" I was stewing over Les Dodd's message. I was certain he knew I'd been passed over, that he'd got my role in *Heritage Creek*. He was just calling to rub it in.

"Ooh," moaned my sweetheart.

"How are you feeling, darling?"

"Ooh, ooh!"

"You want to hear something funny?" I sipped a bourbon. "The other day, Herb had the nerve to suggest that you and I couldn't possibly be in love, that we were only living together so that we could get free press and advance our careers. Isn't that a laugh?"

"Ooh, ahh!" My poor girl was clearly out of sorts.

"And then he suggested I wasn't the baby's father."

"Aargh! Uhmmh!"

"Personally, I think it's about time for old Herbie to pack it in and move to Florida. His brain's gone soft."

Selena suddenly ran for the bathroom. She could have closed the door, so I wouldn't have to listen to her retch. Well, thank God I loved her.

I had been thinking more and more about this whole baby thing. I knew from hearing other people talk that it was a messy, smelly business. It supposedly changed a person's life. I tried to imagine Billy Junior. In my mind, he was already graduating from high school, a triple-letter valedictorian, about to flee the nest and do us proud at some Ivy League college. Everything leading up to that was an unimaginable blank. I had never touched a real baby.

After she was feeling somewhat better, Selena said to me, "I'm going to Cannes for a couple of weeks."

"What? How can you go, in your condition?"

"One of us has to make a living, Billy."

"Oh, I see. So now it's *my* fault that Coppola's not beating my door down."

"Whose fault is it, then? Mine?"

"I'm not saying that. But what happened to 'Don't worry, Billy, I'll take care of you, Billy, I make enough money for all of us, Billy?'"

Selena's eyes were glassing. She was about to cry. "I meant every word of that. I still do. It's not about money at all. I'm just under a lot of stress, right now."

I held her. "Just tell me what you want, my love."

"I want to go to Cannes."

"Shall I come with you?" Why not? I could use a vacation.

"No! I don't want that. It'll be boring. The weather's not so great there, this time of year. When I come back, maybe we can go somewhere together, lie on a beach, just you and me. Okay, Billy?"

"Sure, honey. Whatever you want."

Two days later, Prince Marco came by to pick her up.

"I can take her to the airport, your highness," I said. "You don't even have a car."

"But I'm going with her," he said.

Selena was upstairs, getting dressed, so she did not witness my jaw hitting the floor. They fled in a taxi before I had time to pick it up.

In my susceptible state, Herb convinced me to take the MTC job. I didn't notice until it was too late that it was slated for January.

Winnipeg in January! I honestly believed I must have done something really bad in a previous life to deserve that.

"If I put the word out that you're available for commercial work, I'm sure I can keep you busy until January, Billy." Herb. On another sugar bender that was evidently scrambling his common sense.

"Do you have a new girlfriend, Herb?" I asked. I knew that that often caused a sort of delirious psychosis in some men. It made them irrational, senseless, stupid.

Herb just looked smug. "As you know, Missus Farley and I have been happily married for twenty-four years."

That doesn't stop most men. "The day I do a commercial is the day I hang myself from the nearest light fixture. Doing commercials is the last bastion for has-beens. It's a safe haven for any actor with a pretty face who could never get the hang of iambic pentameter. Am I a has-been, Herb? Is that what you're trying to tell me?"

"Of course not, but I wouldn't be doing my job if I didn't present you with all the options open to you. If you say no commercials, I'm fine with that. You're the boss. But before you go, let me mention one more thing. Voice-overs."

"Voice-overs?"

"You know, for television commercials."

"Have a shot of bourbon, Herb. It'll clear your head. I thought we just got through discussing this."

"Well," said Herb, "doing the voice-over is a whole different ball of wax. I know it sounds crazy, but advertising agencies love to hire big-name actors to do their voice-overs, and they get some sort of sick thrill paying thousands of dollars for the privilege. Think about it, Billy. You'll slide into a studio, no makeup, no wardrobe, you can wear your slippers if you want, have a coffee and a cigarette, read three lines of copy into a microphone a half-dozen times, just to give them a bit of variety, and an hour later, you're on your way home with a big fat paycheque in your pocket. It's a sweet deal, my friend, and it'll give you something to do in between the real jobs."

"Speaking of which—"

"In the mail, Billy. In the mail."

I figured there would be no harm in doing the odd voice gig, just for a change. I certainly had the pipes for it.

A week later, I was sitting in a recording studio, smoking a cigarette and sipping a coffee. I wore my slippers, just to see if Herb was right. He was. I spied those agency nitwits whispering about my slippers, as if it were the sort of thing that could be expected from a big star like me. I struck them with awe, and impressed them with my eccentricities. Only a celebrity like Billy Fox could get away with wearing his slippers to a recording session.

But I wasn't accustomed to having so many directors. It took some getting used to. Everyone in advertising thinks he is a director. As I sat alone on my stool, separated from the throng by two inches of glass, different voices would chirp over the intercom.

"Billy, could you put the emphasis on the word 'fresh?'"

"Billy, you're raising your inflection at the end of the phrase. Try lowering it, okay?"

"Billy, that was great, but a bit slow. Can you speed it up for me?"

"Billy, can we try it just once more, and this time, think *class,* not *retail*. Know what I mean?"

"Billy, that was great, but a bit fast. Can you slow it down for me?"

"Billy, can you take out the breath between the words *good* and *because?* That should do it."

"Billy, it's a little slick, if you know what I mean. Try and do it *raw*."

"Billy, that was great, but the first part was a bit slow, and the last part was a bit fast. Can you even it out for me?"

And on and on. I let them have their fun. I was mad at Herb for not getting me into this sooner. It was easy work, and I didn't even have to be in the same room as the idiots in charge.

On my second trip to the studio, I wore my pajama tops, along with my slippers, just to get a reaction. There was a ten-year-old grape juice stain down the front. The agency didn't bat an eye. Their clients seemed nervous about me, until I opened my mouth and unleashed my vocal magic upon them. What the heck. Glen Gould was some kind of nutcase, too.

I called the telephone number Selena had left for the hotel she was staying at, in Cannes. The snooty clerk was able to be condescending, even with his faulty English.

"Quelle nom, monsieur?"

"Selena."

"Oui, monsieur. Selena what?"

"Just Selena," I said.

"Monsieur, I cannot find witout secon nom. I must have de secon nom. Dat is how registration work, non?"

"She doesn't have a second name. Just Selena. That's the name she goes by."

"Perhaps you call her Selena, monsieur, but on driver license she have other nom, non?"

"She doesn't have a driver's license. When she wants to go somewhere, *I* drive her."

"In American Corvette, no doubt, monsieur. Vroom vroom."

"Look, Pierre, she's a fucking model. She doesn't need a last name."

"Ooh! Dat Selena! Why you not say before? I know who you ask for now."

"Good. Put me through."

"But I cannot, monsieur."

"Why not?"

"She is not stay here."

"She tell me she stay there," I said. My own language skills were falling apart, talking to this nincompoop.

"Mais, non."

"Is there a better hotel next door I can try?"

For some reason, the line went dead.

Once again, I was left in the dark, wondering where my beloved was, what she was doing, and with whom. Well, I knew that Prince Marco was with her, but who else? And why? Why did she lie about her destination? Did she change the reservation when she got there? How many hotels were there in Cannes? More than I was willing to phone, I surmised, and limited myself to simply wondering.

Out of boredom, I went to the Epicure Café for lunch. The place was crowded, and although many of my friends were there, they were all too wrapped up in their little groups to make room for me. All except Dave Small. He vigorously waved me over to his table, where he sat alone. I joined him, as if I had come to meet him in the first place. To hell with the rest of them.

"Hi, Dave," I said, shaking his hand and slipping into the chair opposite him. "Long time, no see."

"Did you get my message?" he asked, a bit breathlessly. He was excited about having me join him. Ordinarily, I would have nodded and kept moving. "I called a couple of months ago. Maybe you didn't get the message. You were probably busy."

"Right. Something like that."

Dave Small was an earnest and hardworking actor. He learned his lines, and he always showed up on time for rehearsals. He was a positive force in any cast, and he could do a truly impressive Irish accent. The problem was, he had no charisma whatsoever. He did not elicit a sliver of fascination. Your eyes had a tendency to skim right off him, in search of something more interesting. The camera ignored him, and on the stage, he had a way of melting into the background like a prop. He had abandoned a fairly successful career in real estate sales to follow his calling as an actor. He should have stuck to selling homes. And his name...don't get me started.

"Sorry to hear about your show. It didn't deserve to get knocked, like that. I was up for a part as a cab driver. That's why I was calling, you know, just to let you know I was up for the part."

I had a vague recollection of receiving a message from Dave, but I had seen him drive before. Tough luck. "Well, how do you figure those networks?" I said casually, as if I didn't care. "They take a hit show and cancel it, just like that. It doesn't make sense to me, but who am I? Just the star. I mean, I guess they had their reasons. Anyway, I probably would have quit after this season. I'm ready to get back on the big screen. I shot a movie this spring. It should be out for Christmas."

"*Alpha Force III*," said Dave. Those who work the least always know what everyone else is up to. "I heard Lorenzo Larson went into rehab."

I huffed. "I don't know where you've been getting your information, Dave, but I happen to know he sprained his ankle." I didn't need someone like Dave Small bad-mouthing the man who personally recommended me for the role.

"Oh," said Dave. He looked like he was about to say more on the subject, but wisely held his tongue. After an awkward silence, he said, "How are you and Selena enjoying the loft?"

At least we were on a topic that Dave knew something about: real estate. "It's too cold in the winter and too hot in the summer, the ceiling is so thin I can hear my upstairs neighbour flossing, a rat recently made off with a good pair of Italian shoes, there's no Jacuzzi on the roof and no gym in the basement, and the neighbourhood is going to pot," I said. "We love it."

Dave nodded. "You got a great deal, there. Once the idea of living in a loft catches on, your place is going to triple in value. You just wait and see."

(He was right, but it took more than fifteen years to catch on. By that time, I was so thoroughly sodden, and the place was so completely rundown from neglect and an enduring stretch of poverty, the love loft bore a striking resemblance to the grimy warehouse it had once been, and even the shoe-stealing rat had moved up to a better district. In fact, a speculator recently offered me a little less money than what I paid for it, all those years ago. He might have offered triple, if it hadn't required such a massive renovation. I turned down his kind offer, correctly assuming—even in my sodden state—that I would have drunk the money and ended up homeless.)

"So, what's it like," asked Dave, leaning a bit closer into me, "living with a model?"

As was expected of me, I looked bored with the subject. "It's just like living with any woman," I said, "except she looks really great while she nags you about the mess and spends all your money on shoes."

Dave laughed. He thought I was joking. "You're a lucky guy, Billy. I wish it was contagious."

Advice to men: Self-pity is an unbecoming trait. It not only makes you look weak, it makes our entire sex look weak. We men have spent two million years building an image of strength and leadership, so we don't appreciate some mealy-mouthed ninny spoiling all that hard work. Take a cue from the ancient Romans: whenever a corrupt Senator felt the self-pity welling up in himself, he was encouraged to recline in a warm bath, unsheathe his ruby-encrusted dagger and open a vein. Better dead than pathetic.

It is always tricky having a conversation with the little people. The first question out of their mouths (if they haven't already learned the answer from People Magazine) is: What have you been up to? It is a courtesy that should be extended to others who, like Dave, are never up to much. It is a kind act of mutual consolation that keeps the lower order sane while they await their big break. The trouble with having someone like Dave Small ask someone like me that question is that I am obliged to reciprocate: Enough about me, what have *you* been up to? I don't need to read the tabloids to know that Dave has done nothing remotely interesting since he fell of a stage, years ago, during a summer stock run of *Hair*. If I ask him what he's been doing, I will get a prolonged and tedious account of all the auditions he has recently had (to no avail), and describe the play he is "developing" with some other unemployed actor. The play will be dreck, but I will have to hear about it anyway. He and his partner will develop the play for several years, during which they will talk about it, at exhausting length, with people like me. Worse still, he will ask me to read it, give my opinion of the dreck. I will politely decline the generous offer, as would any sensible person, and eventually they will quietly drop the play and begin "developing" a new piece of dreck.

The trouble was, I didn't have anything else to say to Dave. "So, what have you been up to, lately?"

Dave puffed up a bit. "You know Molly Copeman?"

I didn't, but nodded anyway. I assumed the less I knew about her, the better.

"Well, she and I are developing a new play."

"How interesting," I said. He might as well have told me he was a medical lab technician. The faint smell of excrement wafted up from under the table.

"It's an experimental work that explores the underlying correlation between Shakespeare's use of occultism in *Hamlet* and the twentieth century Wicca movement. There's a lot of subtext, you know, it's pretty cerebral stuff. Makes you really think."

Great. Just what the theatre-going public wants: to have to *think*. Why bother? Why not just sit in a pub somewhere with your *cerebral* pals and ponder the deep subtext over a dozen pints of ale? You can impress each other with your powerful intellects without inflicting migraines upon an unsuspecting public. "You know, Dave, I can completely understand the need to explore the deeper side of human nature, and experimental theatre is one of the most powerful tools for that sort of exploration. But my only objection is having to pay for it. When my parents want to go out for a nice evening at the theatre, they want to sit back and relax, and not have to think much. Just ask yourself why *Maiken Trouble* was in the top twenty for five years? Not because it made people think, that's for sure. It seems to me, experimental theatre should be absolutely free. The only people who will spend a *free* evening at the theatre are people who *want* to think. Everyone who pays good money for an evening of entertainment, expects to have their brain spared from over-taxation. If my father ever unwittingly paid fifteen dollars to see an experimental play, he'd cause a scene, and then he'd telephone me long distance, just to shout at me for being associated with this outrageous business. If it was free, he'd hardly have cause to complain, would he?"

My kind suggestion didn't persuade Dave. "I'd like to live in a world where all theatre is free, Billy, but, as you know, actors have to eat. It costs money to put up a play—even an experimental one. We've been fundraising for this play for two years, just to get a small workshop going, but no one wants to invest in experimental work. Everyone wants the same boring, predictable fare. It's a sign of the times that the public doesn't want to see anything different."

I couldn't let him get away with that. It didn't help that I was sipping my fourth vodka martini. "I think if you ask a thousand people at random why they choose to see *Hamlet* over and over again, they will all tell you the same thing, Dave. It's a brilliantly written play that tells us a great deal about the human condition. Isn't that the ultimate goal of theatre?"

But in his condition, Dave was not going to see reason. He'd drunk too many beers. "It may be a brilliant play, but that doesn't mean there isn't room for more brilliant plays. How will we expand our horizons if we don't give new work a chance?"

I nearly choked on the olive as I gulped the dregs of my martini. It was only two in the afternoon and I was already wasted. Fortunately, I was in the mood to be wasted. "I don't see how watching a pair of naked dorks, painted green, rolling around in flour, squealing like stuck sows and waving rubber chickens over their heads will expand anyone's horizon." Clearly, I had hit close to home for Dave. He looked dejected. "If there's a message about the human condition in such a display, I can tell you that I, for one, would not be willing to put the mental effort into deciphering it. I would simply walk out at intermission, go straight home and write a nasty letter to my ombudsman about wasting government grant money on worthless crap."

"As a matter of fact," said Dave, "we're in the process of applying for a grant from the Ontario Arts Council. If we got a nice letter from you, I'm sure we'd get the money." He batted his eyelashes at me. In his drunken condition, he mistook me for a woman.

"Sure," said I. "I'd be glad to help." No matter what I thought of Dave's project, we artists had to stick together, support each other.

Dave pulled a steno pad from his satchel and put it in front of me. He dictated the letter. I was effusive. What the hell. If he ever puts his dreck up, I'm sure I'll be too busy to go see it. I signed the letter and felt good, the way one always feels after making a charitable act.

As I was wallowing in my magnanimity, and my fifth martini, a woman approached our table. She was a stunning beauty. If only all the autograph seekers were this gorgeous, I was thinking, right before she slapped my face.

I was nearly knocked out of my chair by the unexpected assault, but I managed to recover my balance. The trickiest part was when I tried to pretend I wasn't as drunk as I was, and began to sway in the seat as if on rough seas. Often, when I became aware of how intoxicated I was, I studied myself for important details that I could use later, when I needed to *act* drunk. Acting drunk is harder than it looks. If you just stumble around, slurring words and knocking things over, it looks phoney. The trick is, you have to try to act sober. You have to imagine that you are drunk, but are trying to act as if you are not drunk. The trouble with studying my own drunken behaviour was that I usually forgot the important details by the next morning. (In later years, I would master the art of drunken acting by the simple method of actually being drunk. It worked like a charm.)

"You're a bastard, Billy!" she spat.

She hovered over me like a furious goddess, one with snakes for eyes and lightning bolts coming off her fingertips, the sort who is always angry with mortals, for one reason or another. And this goddess had the upper hand, not only because she appeared to be stone sober, but also because, while she appeared to know me (at least she knew my name), I had not the vaguest idea who she was.

"Do I know you?" I asked. Mistake.

Advice to men: Forgetting a woman's name (or, in this case, existence) is roughly equivalent to sitting in your two-seater sports car, trying to talk her out of wanting a baby, after first telling her she looks ridiculous in her new shoes. The word *war* does not begin to describe the conflict.

The goddess wound up and slapped my face again. As that second report cracked through the café, all other conversations stopped, all eyes shifted to our table. In my line of work, any attention is better than no attention. Let them watch. I was Billy Fox, famous actor, loft owner, Corvette driver, model fucker, and I was being slapped around by an exquisitely gorgeous lady, whose identity was, admittedly, a bit fuzzy in my mind. But after this second strike I was nagged by a vague sensation I might have, in fact, once known her. I think it was the violence that was sparking my memory cells. For some reason, I had the feeling this wasn't the first occasion she had hit me.

"What you did was unforgivable!" she shouted. "You are a disgrace to the human race, Billy Fox! Death is too good for you. I hope you rot for a hundred years in obscurity!"

And so, this woman unleashed upon me the most heinous curse an actor could be stricken with: *obscurity*. Back then, two long decades ago, I didn't put much stock in superstition. Unlike many of my performing confederates, I did not rely on Swamis or Tarot card readers to predict my glorious future. I did not interpret omens of any kind. Newspaper horoscopes were for wussies, as far as I was concerned. (For the sake of others, though, I did follow the strict code of theatre ethics and said, "Break a leg.")

Perhaps I was hasty in my dismissal of such wooji-wooji nonsense. Perhaps, like voodoo, these curses exist in the mind, in the soul, an idea planted like an evil seed that takes root and spreads out of control, wreaking havoc, eventually, on reality. Self-fulfilling prophecies, these curses. Did my subconscious mind subvert, and finally destroy, my career? (To be honest, I think it was the booze.)

Thus hexed, I teetered in my chair, stunned and speechless, as the gorgeous myth floated away. I rubbed my sore cheek. The halted conversations around us resumed. The show was over, and now they all had another scandalous chapter for their memoirs.

"Who the hell was that?" I moaned.

Dave looked both embarrassed and proud. If that's possible. No doubt, he was uncomfortable with being so close to such a violent confrontation, yet he must have revelled in the knowledge that his name would be listed in those countless memoirs as having been Billy Fox's companion during that violent episode at the Epicure. I was fairly certain this was the most interesting thing that had happened to Dave since he fell off that stage, all those years earlier. "That's pretty funny, Billy," he said.

I scowled. "There's nothing funny about being assaulted by a stranger."

"Wow! You really don't remember her? I thought you were kidding. Boy, you must be really drunk."

"I'm not drunk," I slurred. The three Daves wavered before my bleary eyes. My hand jerked and knocked the ashtray to the floor.

"That was Tracy," said Dave, quickly, before I caused more drunken damage, attempting to prove how sober I was. "Tracy Ford."

I squinted.

"Tracy. You know, Tracy Ford, your *girlfriend*."

My eyebrows staggered across my face. "My girlfriend is Selena, and she is a beautiful model," I declared. "I'm not as drunk as you think." I might have been sobering up. Certain flashes of memory were coming back to me.

"You dumped Tracy for Selena. Why do you think she was so mad? Jeez, Billy, she helped you pick out the loft. She was all set to move in with you when Selena suddenly showed up."

"She didn't just show up," I said, as if to make my argument. "I invited her."

"Precisely."

I was having more flashbacks, and I had never even tried LSD. "So, what you're saying is, that woman…that gorgeous woman who just slapped my face…twice…and then left…is the woman I dumped for Selena?" Even before I got the whole sentence out, it was coming back to me. And I was also remembering that this was indeed not the first time my face had been struck by that gorgeous woman. Now that the fog was lifting, I recalled it had happened with rather alarming frequency. The face-slapping was, come to think of it, one of the primary reasons I had dumped her. After all, being gorgeous can only gain you so much understanding in a relationship. I have limits, too. "Her hair is different, isn't it?"

Dave shrugged.

"It seems to me," I said, after a moment's reflection, "that I was doing myself a favour, ditching her."

Dave was nodding. "I thought she was going to hit *me,* just for being with you."

Sure, Dave. It's all about you. I did a somewhat poor impression of someone getting to his feet. "Have to be going, chum," I said. I had momentarily forgotten Dave's name.

"I hope you're taking a cab, Billy."

"Yeah, right." I tossed a five-dollar bill on the table to cover my share of what must have been a ninety-dollar tab, then wobbled out of the café, into the blistering afternoon light. Anyway, Dave should have been glad to pay for the privilege of my company. It's not every day one gets to get sozzled with a movie star.

There was a gorgeous woman sitting in the passenger seat of my Corvette. Like Selena, Tracy complemented the Corvette's sleek and sexy styling. All the curves and dips were in the right places.

"How did you get in my car?" I asked. I wasn't sure if I was pleased or not. It depended, I supposed, on the degree of violence I could expect.

Tracy dangled the spare key from her index finger.

I had been wondering what had happened to it.

She dropped the key on the floor. "I suppose going back to your place is out of the question. Your little mannequin will be flitting about."

"She's in France," I slurred. "I think."

Tracy had to help me get my key in the ignition. Somehow we made it to the love loft without causing serious injury or property damage. Of course, those were the days when drunk driving was still fashionable.

As soon as Tracy shed her dress, my full memory flooded back. She had hips that couldn't be ignored, or forgotten. We rolled around the loft like wild animals. Even sex was a violent act for Tracy. Fortunately, I was too intoxicated to feel the pain. The next morning, however, the pain that resulted from my encounter with Tracy Ford was competing with the pain inflicted on me by alcohol.

Tracy did not stay the night. Before she left, she bit my calf—so hard, I had the marks in my flesh for a week—and said, "I just wanted you to know what you're missing, Billy." And then she was gone from my life forever.

I'm pretty sure I knew what I was missing: a fractured skull.

Beep..."Hi, Billy. It's Herb. I just got a call from someone named Sheila Cohen. She says she's an old friend of yours. She's got a show in the Fringe Festival next week and she's offering you a part. Apparently, the guy who was originally going to do it got a film, so he backed out. She said she already talked to you about the project, so you know more than I do. She's willing to pay two hundred for the job. It's not much, but you might think about taking it. You don't have much on your plate until the MTC thing. I'm still trying to get you voice-over work, but if something comes up, I'm sure they can work around your Fringe schedule. I know this isn't what you were hoping for, Billy, but there's no reason to throw work away while we wait for the film scripts to come in. Take the job. It's only five performances over two weeks. It beats sitting around that dingy warehouse all day. Call me back. She needs an answer soon, obviously. You'd only have a week to rehearse."

Beep..."Hi, Herb. It's Billy Fox. You're fired."

Beep..."Hi, Herb. It's Billy Fox again. Tell Sheila Cohen I'll do the job. Then, you're fired."

Two hours later, a courier dropped off the script. Sheila Cohen wasn't wasting any time. There was a note in the package:

> *Billy...I'm so glad you're on board with this project. It is a very dear subject to me. The main character, Gloria, is based on my Grandmother and her experience during World War I. After she died, I just had to write the story, and lo...it became* Waiting for the Smoke to Clear. *Like I told you before, I always had you in mind for the part of George, the war hero, who was my Grandfather. You have always been something of a hero to me. I hope that doesn't make you blush, Billy. Enjoy the script, and I will call later so we can talk about it. We only have six days left before we open, so we will have to make the most of our limited time. I know what a professional you are. I have complete confidence in you. The show has already been blocked. It will just be a matter of getting you into the swing of it. I am really excited to be finally working with you again, Billy. It's like a dream come true. Love, Sheila.*

I opened the script and began to read.

WAITING FOR THE SMOKE TO CLEAR

ACT I. Scene I.

A single shaft of light fades up, stage right, illuminating GLORIA in a pool of light. GLORIA is in her twenties, dressed as a tidy peasant wife. She looks worried, she is wringing her hands.

    GLORIA.   I am a woman...

A timpani drum sounds a single beat; the light fades quickly to black... a three second pause... and the light fades slowly back up, to reveal GLORIA again. She is wringing her hands even more fretfully.

I am a wife and mother...

The timpani drum sounds two heavy beats, synchronized with two flashes of white light... the shaft of light quickly fades to black... a three second pause... and the shaft of light slowly fades up for a third time, revealing GLORIA, who is getting quite frantic.

I am a widow...

The timpani drum strikes three loud beats; in time with three flashes of white light... slowly, very slowly, the shaft of light fades to black.

Scene II

> *A single shaft of light fades up, stage left, illuminating* GEORGE. *He is in his early twenties, dressed in an immaculate uniform: World War I infantryman. He looks stoic.*
>
>   GEORGE.   I am a husband...
>
> *The timpani drum sounds a single beat; the light fades quickly to black... a three second pause... and the light fades slowly back up, to reveal* GEORGE *again. He looks afraid, but he is trying to hide the fear behind his stoic mask.*
>
> I am a father and a soldier...
>
> *The timpani drum sounds two heavy beats, synchronized with two flashes of white light... the shaft of light quickly fades to black... a three second pause... and the shaft of light slowly fades up for a third time, revealing* GEORGE, *who is having trouble disguising his fear.*
>
> I am dead...
>
> *The timpani drum strikes three loud beats; in time with three flashes of white light... slowly, very slowly, the shaft of light fades to black.*

    It was downhill from there. After forcing myself to read to the end, I felt that George was the lucky one. He was dead. Unfortunately, they couldn't let poor dead George rest in peace. They had to keep resurrecting him, propping him up in his crisp, neat uniform, so he could look stoic, and say stoically profound things about being dead, and stoically lament all the things he was missing because he was dead.

As for Gloria, the twenty-one-year-old grieving widow…where to begin? Sheila Cohen was thirty, and she looked thirty-five. If she had been more attractive, she might have had a chance of pulling it off. But her face was a strange mix of parts that didn't really work together. And her figure was as oddly disproportionate as her face, and promised imminent and fulsome expansion. She made me think of the bored housewife in Grimsby that I suspected of writing the pilot episode of *Heritage Creek*. For all I knew, Sheila Cohen *did* write that script. They were both appalling examples of the most trite, amateur drama, full of tired clichés, and lacking in anything remotely interesting.

"How did you like the script?" Sheila asked, when I arrived for rehearsal the next morning.

"Unique," I said.

She ought to have known what I meant by that. Instead, she took it as a compliment. Then she introduced me to the director. "This is Norm."

Norm looked like a grade eight Social Studies teacher. He was tall and thin and stooped, in the manner of teachers who are forever hunched over desks. "It's a privilege to direct someone of your calibre, Mister Fox," he said. He shook my hand limply.

"Norm teaches drama at Eastern Tech," said Sheila. She was the sort of person who was impressed by academics, and assumed that everyone else was, too. I have always been suspicious of anyone who completed a post-secondary education.

"How interesting," I said. I was all smiles. I was planning to make this the easiest gig of my career. I was not going to cause trouble. I was going to do exactly as I was told without complaint. I was going to collect my two hundred dollars and run, knowing that no one of any importance would see the play. The Fringe Festival attracted dilettantes and pasty college students who still dreamed of making the world a better place through anarchy. "What grade do you teach, Norm?"

"Eight," he said, of course. "Actually, I'm the Social Studies teacher. Drama is extracurricular at Eastern. My kids just did *A Midsummer Night's Dream* this spring. I was very proud of them."

I discovered that I coped best when I simply switched my brain off and operated on auto-pilot. I had only a few insipid lines, and I never moved from my circle of light, stage left, so my mind was free to wander. Occasionally, I was snapped out of a daydream when Norm (who, I learned from the bored and cynical stage manager, was Sheila Cohen's husband—a detail they chose to conceal from me) was forced to raise his voice at the sound technician and lighting board operator. They couldn't seem to get themselves synchronized. The lighting girl complained that the sound technician was rushing, that the lighting board couldn't react quickly enough. The sound technician complained that the lighting girl didn't know how to operate the lighting board correctly. Norm complained that he didn't give a hoot who was causing the problem, he just needed them to get themselves in synch, make it work. I drifted off.

It turned out the Cohens were not only amateurs, they were also insane. Once they learned I had accepted their offer, they cashed in their savings bonds in order to pay for half-page ads in the three daily newspapers, promoting my appearance in their production. What were they thinking?

The day before the show opened, Selena returned from Cannes (or wherever).

"Darling," she oozed. "Did you miss me?"

I thought I could detect just the slightest Spanish lisp. "How was France?" I was not about to openly accuse her of anything.

"Trés bella!" She gently kicked aside the pile of shopping bags and skipped over to my stool, where I had been busy balancing my cheque book (the result of which I was not in the best of moods. There were alarmingly few zeros left at the bottom line). She kissed me on the cheeks and forehead, neglecting my expectant lips.

"You look like you've lost weight," I said.

She spun around, as if the shutters were *clicking clicking clicking*. "You really think so?"

"I don't know what it is...you look different." I was squinting at her, wondering if it was just my imagination. After all, I hadn't seen her in two weeks. Then I remembered that, when she left, she was already showing the early signs of her pregnancy. "For some reason, you don't look pregnant anymore."

She looked down at her flat, smooth belly, surprised. "Pregnant?"

I nodded. "You know, that condition unique to women? It usually lasts about nine months, and then there is suddenly a baby in the spare room."

Selena waved her hand in the air. "Oh, that! False alarm. I guess it was just bloating." She distracted herself by unpacking her shopping bags. This time she had bought a lot of hats. She was suddenly on a *hat* kick.

It occurred to me that she was lying. Bloating didn't cause morning sickness. And why would only her tummy bloat? Wouldn't the rest of her body swell if it had been water retention, or whatever? I began to suspect she had flown to Switzerland, not Cannes, and had got herself an abortion. I suppose I could have snuck a peek at her passport to see where she had really gone during those two weeks, but I really didn't care enough. I was glad she was no longer pregnant. If she didn't want to involve me in the process of terminating it, that was fine, too. Prince Marco was more skilled at that sort of female comforting than I was. Better that he held her hand while she got herself scraped clean. One less thing for me to worry about.

I told her about Herb—that I had fired him. And I told her about the Fringe show. "I open tomorrow night. I hope you'll come." In any show, big or small, opening night is very important to an actor. It is a burst of adrenalin and emotions that set the pace for the show's run. It means a lot to have family and friends come to opening night, to get that show of support.

"I don't know, darling. I already promised Marco I'd go to a fashion show with him. His neighbour is in it. I don't see how I can get out of it now, on such short notice."

I was indignant. "Easy. Tell your highness to get another date. Tell him to go without you. For Christ's sake, Selena, you just spent two weeks with the little fucker in France. Give him a night off. It's important to me that you're there. I need you to come."

She smiled her sweetest smile. "That's so sweet."

"Then you'll come?"

"We'll see, Billy. How do you like this one?" She set a wide-brim summer hat on her head, pulled it down over her eyes. She could have tipped a salad bowl on her head and made it look great. What did it matter?

Unbelievably, I was nervous. I hadn't been nervous in a long time. Of course, I hadn't been on a stage in a long time. In live theatre, half the actor's performance comes from the audience. If those polite, stony faces out there in the dark don't respond, don't laugh when they are supposed to, cry when they are supposed to, the dynamics on stage reflect that unbalance. I had almost forgotten what it felt like. Acting for the camera, being disconnected from the audience, is easy by comparison. If someone dried during the shooting of a scene for *Maiken Trouble* (my dear Gretchen comes to mind as a regular culprit), we could rack it back and try again. The moment you step onto the stage—or, in the case of the Rivoli, onto a few sheets of warped plywood balanced on some apple boxes—the show goes forward.

"Look at that," said Norm, the eighth-grade teacher. We were backstage, and Norm was peering around the curtain at the house as it filled with a strange mix of Birkenstocks and black turtlenecks and young women. The sandal-and-turtleneck set were there because they were friends or relatives of the Cohens and were unable to drum up a passable excuse for dodging the event. Small-time theatre works that way: everyone involved agrees to go see everyone else's show, with the understanding that the favour will be returned. In my opinion, stacking the house with their struggling confrères gives them all a misleading impression of how good their work is. The young women were there to see Joe Maiken.

"I knew they'd come," said Sheila, my co-star. She stood behind Norm, looking over his shoulder at my restless and giggling fans as they jostled for a place to stand, along the side and back walls. "Everyone loves you, Billy."

I turned to look at her. It was always a bit shocking whenever I focused on Sheila's face, she was such a strange-looking woman. And it was evident to me, as I regarded her incongruous features, that she included herself—perhaps especially—in the category of "everyone." We all have dreams, baby.

I wasn't interested in Sheila Cohen's crush, nor was I interested in the Birkenstocks or the turtlenecks or the young women who came to see Joe Maiken. I thought only about the shining light of my Selena. I was certain she was out there somewhere. If I had anticipated the success of Sheila Cohen's ambitious advertising campaign, I might have warned Selena that she should arrive early, in order to get a front row seat. I imagined her standing at the back with her arms crossed over her lovely chest, stewing at the prospect of having to stand with the rest of the plebes. No doubt, I would hear about it afterward. I should have reserved a chair for her down front.

I took my mark, stage left. When the spotlight burned the top of my head for the first time (the ceiling was low, my scalp was in danger of igniting), I heard two of Joe Maiken's fans swoon and collapse. I registered their ardour and didn't miss a beat, delivering my line on cue. I tilted my head back and released my poignant words to God—the disembodied voice of God represented by Norm. He was the middleman, between my still-living wife and me. I spoke to God and He spoke to the young widow, on my behalf. Passing messages between a third person was, in my experience, a dubious enterprise, but if you can't trust God to pass on your words without muddling them up, who can you trust? In this case, the message was so pedestrian, He could have translated my lamentations (for what else would a dead soldier/husband/father do other than *lament?*) into Ukrainian and no one would have noticed. The only people who were listening to what was being said were the lighting and sound technicians, who were still struggling with synchronicity. Everyone else sat—or stood—stone-faced and dry-mouthed, plotting the fastest route to the bar that will open as soon as the curtain falls.

The kindest thing I can say about *Waiting for the Smoke to Clear* is that it is only one act. If there had been a second act, we would surely have played it to an empty house. Even my presence on that riser (I refuse to call it a stage) could not have compelled my most ardent fan to endure forty-eight more minutes. I wouldn't have blamed anyone for leaving. Fifteen minutes in, I wanted to discreetly sidle out from beneath my cone of light and make a run for it myself. I stayed only because I didn't want to disappoint Selena. When my heavenly light went out, I squinted into the crowd, searching for my love. She must have arrived at the last minute, and was crammed against the back wall.

Fifteen seconds after the curtain fell, there was a stampede for the bar. The sandals and turtlenecks were seasoned pros, so they got there ahead of the young women—who were clearly torn between the need for a drink and their desire to rush the stage and tear away pieces of my wardrobe, before I disappeared backstage.

Thirty seconds after the curtain fell, the Cohens were eager to rush out to greet their audience. I refused to emerge until at least ten minutes had elapsed (based on my traditional "need for a minute" theory, on a film shoot). Surely our fans would wait ten minutes to congratulate us. The Cohens agreed, reluctantly, to wait.

I doffed my wardrobe—a World War I infantryman's uniform that had belonged to Sheila Cohen's grandfather. It hadn't fit me, and Sheila was adamant about not altering it so that it would. And she was adamant that *it* be used, rather than a costume that might have been tailored to fit me properly. "A good designer might make something that resembles this one," Sheila had said, during dress rehearsal, "but they will not be able to sew into it *authenticity*. Look at the bullet hole in the chest, Billy. That's a *real* bullet hole. That's a *real* bloodstain. That's my grandfather's blood. You can't fake that sort of thing. When the audience sees you in this uniform, they will *know* that it's the real McCoy."

"Sure they will," I responded. "Because it doesn't fit." I could have made more of a fuss. If this had been *Maiken Trouble* or *Alpha Force III*, I surely would have. But I had promised myself that I would make this gig a frictionless event in my life. With my career falling apart before my eyes, I couldn't let this job get to me. "Take the money and run," Herb had said to me, and he was right. I let Sheila Cohen have what she wanted (*almost* everything she wanted), I permitted myself to be directed by an eighth-grade Social Studies teacher and, most impressively, did not make a single pass at the cute (though rhythmically impaired) lighting technician.

As I pulled on my jeans, I could hear the crowd livening up, now that the mind-and-bottom-numbing show was over and the bar was open. My own tongue was tingling for bourbon. It would take more than one, I knew, to purge this experience from my memory banks. The sooner I got to it, the better.

"Okay, let's go."

I was halfway to the bar when I was swarmed by a mob of screaming young women. The Maiken Maidens (as we were fond of calling my young fanlets) hadn't forgotten me. "Joe! Joe! Joe!" they shouted, waving their paper napkins in my face to sign. Several hands groped me, and when I looked over my shoulder, I saw that one of those hands belonged to Sheila Cohen. Poor thing. She looked about to cry. She removed her hand from the seat of my pants and quickly scuttled away to join her husband—who was being congratulated by a smug-looking group of granolas.

As I signed autographs, I peered over the tops of the heads in front of me, looking for Selena. A surprising number of people had drained a fast drink and fled, before they were forced to say something nice to the Cohens about *Waiting for the Smoke to Clear*. There was no sign of my love. She must have really hated it, if she couldn't wait ten minutes—if only to congratulate me for getting through it without losing my mind. I thought, hoped, that she had left quickly because she was preparing a celebration for us, back at the loft.

"Someone get me a drink," I said to the throng that surrounded me. Suddenly, the throng was half the size it had been. Less than a minute later, I had a dozen different drinks thrust at me. Most were undrinkable: rum and coke, gin and seven, white wine. Fucking "girl" drinks. There was one beer, which I took, and drained in two long draughts. Then, to my utter amazement, a bottle of bourbon was floating before me. Knob Creek. Even I only bought that brand for special occasions. I grabbed the bottle, and the girl who was attached to the other end of it. The autograph session was over.

My fans reluctantly dispersed, leaving me alone with a green-eyed doe in a denim smock. She couldn't have been of legal age. "Thanks," I said, unscrewing the cap and slugging back a good sample of KC. "How did you know this was my drink?"

"I know everything about you, Mister Fox," said the doe.

That sent a shiver up my spine. "I hope not." I was joking, but the doe was too nervous to register humour. She seemed hurt that I would suggest she had overlooked something. "That was a joke, honey," I said, putting my free hand on her shoulder.

I offered her the bottle, which she took. She downed four or five good swallows before she came up for air.

"What's your name?"

"Kelly Boyce," she said, handing over the bourbon. She couldn't take her eyes off me, wouldn't even blink, in case she missed something. She had a lovely mouth, with wide, full lips that formed a genuine and endearing smile. Her hair needed the attention of a professional and her wardrobe was hopeless, but otherwise, she was quite attractive. "I'm a virgin," she said, unblinking.

"What?" She could have waited until I swallowed.

"My boyfriend wants to go all the way, he's been pressuring me, you know, but I've been saving myself."

"Really..." I didn't know how to respond to that. This was a bit personal, considering we had just met. She should have been having this discussion with her mother.

"For you," she said. "I dreamed that *you* would be the first."

"Er...well, thanks, but—"

"I don't want to have your baby, Mister Fox," she said, quickly. "I'm not one of those crazy girls who stalks famous people. Really. I wouldn't bring a baby into this world knowing that it's father wouldn't be there for it. That wouldn't be fair. And I wouldn't expect you to marry me, or anything. But I think the first time a girl does it, it should be special. She should remember it forever. I don't want my first time to be a two-minute wrestling match in the back seat of some boy's car. Know what I mean? It should be romantic, sensual, *special*."

"That's a very noble aspiration, Kelly," I said. "You are absolutely right. Your first time should be special."

One minute later, Kelly was sprawled on a table backstage, having the most special two minutes of her life. What else could I have done? My car didn't have a back seat. Once again, I was regretting not having checked a girl's birth certificate.

Halfway through this encore performance, Sheila Cohen arrived backstage. She had an empty wine glass in her hand. "There you—" She stopped short as our eyes met. "Oh, heavens! I—" She didn't know what to do, or say.

"Don't stop, Billy," said Kelly, softly. She stroked my arms, regained my attention. "Don't stop." There were tears in her eyes.

When I looked back, Sheila Cohen was gone.

Fifteen seconds later, the special moment was over. Is there anything I won't do for my fans?

I sped home with the bottle of Knob Creek between my legs. Back in the loft, I found Selena reclined on the sofa in her bathrobe, watching television.

"Hello, darling," she said, when I staggered in. "Where have you been?"

I nearly dropped the empty bottle on my foot. "Where have *I* been? Where have *you* been?"

"I've been here all night. God, I'm so tired! It's been a busy week. It was so nice to just relax, for a change."

"So, you didn't come to my show—" I must have sounded petulant, but, as I said, openings are important to actors.

"What show?"

"Jesus, Selena! *Waiting for the Smoke to Clear!*"

When she shifted on the sofa, one of her lovely breasts fell out of her bathrobe. She knew what she was doing, but I wasn't falling for it, this time.

"You mean that horrible amateur thing you've been complaining about? I thought you said it was dreck." She had picked up some of my lingo, along the way.

"It is dreck. And it's not amateur. I got paid to do it. I said that the *people* who put it up were amateurs. There's a difference."

"Well," said Selena, "it's lost on me."

I stood over her, staring down at her exposed breast. Only Selena could make sloth look glamorous. Even without makeup and fashion to back her up, she was an awe-inspiring sight. She looked up at me. "So, how was it?"

"Dreck," I said. "Pure amateur dreck. Forget about it."

And I fell down upon her.

When you live in a trendy loft with a beautiful model, it's hard to take the rest of life too seriously. But during the quiet moments after making love, I couldn't help fretting about my faltering career.

"It's got to be Herb's fault. That's the only explanation. He just didn't have the contacts to get me the good scripts. I did the right thing by firing him."

"Oh, yeah. Herb phoned tonight. He's got a script for you."

Hell, I couldn't even succeed at firing my agent.

"Whoa, Billy! I thought you were joking," said Herb, the next morning, when I called to remind him of his ex-agent status. "Anyway, drop by this afternoon and pick up the script. I won't describe it to you over the phone, but I know you'll be pleased."

"Is it from the CBC?"

Herb laughed. "No pioneer epic this time, kid. Think *romantic comedy*. Hurry in. This is a hot one." He hung up.

"That's wonderful, honey," said Selena, after I told her the news. "I knew it would work out for you. Didn't I say? Anyway, I'm going out. I need cigarettes." I watched her go. She was wearing high heels and a black dress that was impressively short. She couldn't even buy smokes without looking like a million bucks. After witnessing her fantastic backside swish out the door, I dressed quickly and headed out to Herb's office.

When the Corvette failed to start, I should have taken it as an omen. Not that I cared about making Herb Farley wait. I was more upset about having to subject myself, once again, to the metropolitan taxi service.

Herb puckered his lips when I walked in. He had a mouthful of coffee. He nearly choked on it when he saw me. "Jesus Murphy! What happened to you?"

Like most men, I felt that I knew enough about cars to tinker with their workings. But it's a business best left to the experts. Because I couldn't resist lifting the hood and poking around, myself, I was not only late (and fifteen dollars lighter), but fairly well soiled.

Advice to men: When your car breaks down, do not try to impress your girlfriend—or, as in my case, passers-by—by attempting to fix it yourself. You impress nobody with your loss of temper and your profanity. The probability of fixing the problem will be zero, and that failure with also fail to impress others. If you were mad when the car would not start, you will be in a blue rage after tugging at the confounding cogs under the hood for an hour. And you will soil your shirt cuffs beyond hope. Admitting defeat at the onset is the only way to maintain your sanity and impress others. Leave the dirty work to the professionals. If you must open the hood, do so at your own peril, and know that the odds are against you.

Advice to women: when your boyfriend's car breaks down, don't encourage embarrassing folly with comments such as: "Don't *you* know how to fix this thing?" Nothing good can come of it.

"You look like you were mugged by the Firestone pit crew," said Herb, unhelpfully.

I fell into a chair and glared at him. Herb took the streetcar to work. He didn't own a car. He could speak the patois, so the taxis did not daunt him. I wanted to smack his smug face. "Did I forget to mention that you're fired?"

But the smug bastard just laughed. "Here, take a gander at this." He slid a script across his desk. "It's from your old friend, Donald Duke."

I read the cover page. "*Painting the Cherry*. What the hell is that, a working title?"

"It's a romantic comedy," said Herb, as if to explain. "Starring Eddie Lawson and Jeanette Winters."

"What's the part?"

Herb tilted back in his chair. He had the sort of well-appointed office that I imagined big-shot producers like Donald Duke should have had. He redecorated it once a year, mostly from my commissions. "You would play the part of Joe Ketchum. He's a cynical private eye."

I rolled my eyes. "That's original. I suppose Jeanette Winters is the sexy client I'm porking, and Eddie Lawson is the thug who puts a bullet in her chest. God, Herb! Is everyone allergic to writers, these days?"

"I don't think you get to pork her," said Herb. "I'm pretty sure about that."

"Not much of a romantic comedy if I don't get to pork her."

"Well, I gather porking her is Eddie Lawson's job."

I was momentarily rendered speechless. I gaped at Herb. "The thug?"

"He's not the thug, he's the love interest. I told you it was a romantic comedy. You know the story. The poor boy wants to marry the rich girl, the rich girl's family tries to shut them down. The father hires you to investigate Eddie's background. He wants you to find a reason why his daughter shouldn't marry Eddie. The trouble is, the kid is squeaky clean. He's a good kid. He doesn't even want to marry her for her money. That's where you come in, Billy. If you don't find some dirt on the kid, you don't get your big fat fee from Dad, so you try to throw some dirt on him. None of it sticks, of course. That's what makes the whole thing hilarious. You throw slutty girls at him, but he won't touch them. You try to embroil him in a shady drug deal, but you only manage to get yourself up shit creek. Funny stuff, Billy."

"So, what you are telling me, Herb, is that this is a supporting role."

"What this is, is a guaranteed hit," he said. "And in case you haven't noticed, supporting actors get Oscars, too. They had George Carlin slated for the part, but he got a television series."

"Jesus, Herb! George Carlin? First Lorenzo Larson, and now I'm second banana to George Carlin? Christ, he's not even a fucking actor."

"Neither is Eddie Lawson, if you're going to split hairs, but he's got great teeth and he pulls them in at the box office. This is no time to nitpick. This movie is two big steps up from *Alpha Force III*, and you get to work with two of the hottest young stars in Hollywood. John Travolta offered to do it for half-scale, just to get into the project."

I picked up Herb's empty coffee mug and sniffed it, to see if there was something other than ten sugar cubes in it.

"I think you've got the next line, Billy."

"What?"

"Your next line. You know, the one where you thank me for getting you this one."

"Thanks, Herb." What the hell.

"You're welcome. Now, you'll fly to Los Angeles directly from Winnipeg. The shooting schedule overlaps a bit with the MTC job, but they've agreed to shoot around you for the first week."

"Who's directing?" I'd turn religious if I thought it would help get me a Scorsese film.

"I don't know. I'll find out for you." Herb leaned back and laced his fingers behind his head, looking pleased. "Didn't I tell you not to worry? Things are working out nicely."

When I got home, the loft was empty.

I don't mean to say merely that Selena was not there—which was true—but that her stuff was also not there. The shoes, the hats, the gowns, the Ansel Adams prints, the dried flower arrangements, the ivory end tables, the Osterizer, the battalion of weapons she used to manage her lustrous hair, all gone. There wasn't a fork in the house. Selena had thrown away my mismatched flatware once her stylish stainless steel set had arrived from New York. She even took the welcome mat, which was not hers to take. Perhaps in lieu of the purloined mat, she left behind the pinstriped sofa (the back-breaker) and the complementary valances (which she would have been unqualified to unscrew from the wall).

The other notable thing that was missing was an explanation. She couldn't even be bothered to jot down a quick Dear John letter.

My darling Selena had left me.

Half a bottle of (cheap) bourbon later, I realized that the next day would have been our one-year anniversary. Oh, how sentimental I suddenly became. I'm certain that if Selena had not left me, that important milestone would have passed unnoticed. Now that she was gone, it meant everything to me. One year. One whole year. Once the second half of the bottle of bourbon was gone, I was beyond coherent mourning. I woke up a week later with the worst hangover of my life.

"Jeez, Billy. I was about to call the cops. Where have you been?"

The telephone had roused me, mid-afternoon. It was Herb, frantic with worry.

"Selena left me, Herb. She's gone."

"Gone?"

"Gone."

"Holy cow. Take a cold shower and pull yourself together. I've got to call People Magazine. Think of the publicity."

"I don't give a fuck about the publicity, Herb. Fuck People Magazine. They didn't even mention my classical training."

Herb clucked his tongue. "Did they spell your name correctly?"

"Sure," I said, "*both* of them." Perhaps my anger was slightly misdirected. After all, it was Selena who apparently could no longer tolerate a boyfriend who required two names.

A month after Selena took her flit, I collided with Prince Marco as he was skipping out of a downtown shoe store. After giving his scrawny neck a squeeze, I learned that Selena had fled to Rome, and was currently living with one of Europe's leading screen gods, a swarthy hunk named Livio. That was it: just *Livio!* A few days later, I caught a glimpse of the latest People Magazine at the grocer's. I didn't need to buy the magazine to know that the article about the hottest new celebrity couple would not be very deep or interesting.

Chapter 7

Five minutes of a Winnipeg winter was almost enough to sober me. I choked on the ice crystals that floated in the dry prairie air. My nostrils had stuck together when I took my first breath outside the airport, and they remained stuck until I fell into my room at the Ramada, where I proceeded to empty the mini-bar.

There was a soft knock on the door.

I ignored it, reasoning that if it was important, whoever it was would *bang* on the door.

There was a *bang* on the door.

I rolled over and groaned. When I attempted to open my eyes, I discovered that my eyelids were stuck shut. I managed to pry the left one open with my fingers, but the right was stubborn. Somehow, I got to the door and pulled it open. I was greeted by a middle-age woman in a vast parka, with a wide, lumpy face like some old tea bags carelessly stitched together.

"My God, Mister Fox!"

I tried to speak, but my tongue was stuck to the roof of my mouth. "Sorry," I managed to say, after dislodging my tongue. "I sleep in the nude."

"You're not nude, but you look terrible."

I looked down with my one good eye and saw that I was still wearing yesterday's clothes. They did not look any better for having been slept in.

"Have you been in a fight? What's that smell?" She took a step back.

I'd had a fight with a bottle, and lost. But what I said was this: "Some native asked for a quarter, and wouldn't take *no* for an answer."

Well, it was not so farfetched. The downtown streets of Winnipeg, I had noticed, were teeming with downtrodden natives with their hands stuck in the *out* position. The poor sods. "After beating me up and taking the quarter by force, he poured the remains of his filthy whiskey bottle over my head."

"For heaven's sake, Mister Fox, you should know better. Just give them a quarter and they'll leave you alone. Always remember to keep some quarters in your pockets. I thought everyone knew that."

"Live and learn," I said, philosophically.

"Anyway, I'm Sylvia Parker. We spoke on the phone. I'm the executive producer at MTC. I'm here to bring you to the theatre. Rehearsal began an hour ago, so we must hurry. It's not far."

"Give me a minute," I said, closing the door on her. This time, I needed the minute.

By the time I got to the theatre, my body had come fully unstuck. I could once again see and smell and talk with only moderate difficulty. I was further heartened to discover a nearly full bottle of vodka in a drawer in my dressing room. Some sodden lout had left it behind after the previous run. Lucky me. I was fairly well oiled by the time I sat down to the first read-through.

Diane Frankin, the director, gave a nice little speech to us all about her take on Noel Coward in general and *Private Lives* in particular. "There is no question of Coward's profoundly cynical view of life and, in particular, his take on domestic relationships. His talent for trivializing everything, especially the snobbish world of the rich, only makes his characters all the more poignant. He illuminates this viewpoint through the paradox of Elyot and Amanda's love-hate relationship. Here we have two people who find it difficult to be in the same room together, yet cannot bear to be apart..."

I tuned her out. Instead, I spent the afternoon imagining what it was going to be like to smack lips with Cynthia Collins—my witty and flippant Amanda. Perhaps this job wasn't going to be such a bore, after all.

Amanda's dull new husband Victor was played by Lane Sewell, a man who hardly needed to act the part of a tedious bore. He was as stiff as a plank, and wore us all down, throughout the morning, inquiring of Diane Frankin what Victor's "motivation" was for this line or that. "Shouldn't I be more upset?" he asked, as we read through the scene in the Paris flat. "I mean, I've just found my wife shacked up with another man. Surely this Victor fellow would be on the very edge of violence. At least, that's how *I* would feel, if she were my wife."

"Well," said Diane Frankin, with the utmost patience, "perhaps if this were an Irish play, Victor might have clobbered Elyot with a handy cudgel and then gone off to the pub for a pint, but since it is a British play, the traditional mix of irony and *stiff upper lip* prevails. I think, Lane, that the success and longevity of *Private Lives* is in itself evidence that Noel Coward knew what he was doing. Victor's dullness works, within the context of the quartet, *because* he is dull. If he were anything other than dull, the dynamics would be all wrong and the play would fail."

Poor Lane couldn't keep up. He required simple "yes" or "no" answers. Anything more just confused him. "So I shouldn't drop a lamp on his head, then?"

"No, Lane."

He chewed his bottom lip. "Just a thought. Never mind."

She couldn't leave him pouting like a child. "Don't feel bad, Lane. I welcome all your questions. It's a necessary part of the process for actors, if they want to discover the true depth of their character. So, don't hesitate to ask."

I could detect the flood of questions rushing to Lane's dull tongue, so I interjected. "I have a question," I said, in the nick of time.

"Yes, Billy?"

"When is lunch?" We all had a laugh.

Completing our ironic quartet as my (Elyot's) sibilant new bride Sibyl was Juliet Saire. She was barely twenty, and this was her first significant job since graduating from the acting program at George Brown College. She had the goods that promised to one day make her an exceptional actress, but she would never be a leading lady. She was not unattractive (after all, Elyot would never endure *plainness* in a wife), but her overbearing sincerity annihilated any sex appeal she might have had. She would never successfully play anything other than the naïve sister, or the good-hearted best friend, or, as in this case, the silly wife. If she had been one of Joe Maiken's clients, he would have kept running and left her to bleed to death alone in the alley; he would have taken his fee from her in cash.

"I'm really sorry about your show, Billy," she whispered to me, when I first sat down beside her.

I nodded, to acknowledge her sorrow over my loss, but I didn't want to talk about it anymore. I was tired of the subject. I was moving on. Besides, I was too caught up in my grief over being abandoned by Selena to care about some tacky television show.

At the end of the day, we all tromped out into the frigid prairie air in search of a drink. Getting pissed together after rehearsal was as much a part of the actor's process as asking inane questions during rehearsal. It was a necessary bonding that pulled a cast together (in most cases). Several worthy establishments came into view as we exited the theatre. There was no shortage of bars in Winnipeg. Largely because five sets of nostrils had instantly stuck shut upon breathing the crystalline air, we ran for the nearest one, directly across the street.

The place was crowded for a Monday evening. We found a table for two near the back and managed to scrounge up three more chairs to crowd around it. I made sure to sit next to Diane Frankin. I wasn't in much of a mood to bond with my fellow cast members, and I knew that if I asked the director a single meaningless question about the play, she would happily drone on at length in answer, permitting me to tune out, except to nod periodically. All I was really interested in was killing as many brain cells as I could with alcohol. Oh, beloved *oblivion!*

Unfortunately, Lane Sewell deliberately took the spot on the other side of Diane. He still had a list of question that I hadn't permitted him to ask earlier. Now that he had her undivided attention, he let loose. That left me with Juliet Saire nestled to my left—whose close proximity inspired in me nothing resembling desire—and Cynthia Collins, who sat across from me in gorgeous indifference. The waitress couldn't bring the bourbon fast enough.

"I don't want to do television, I want to do movies," Juliet said to me, buoyantly. "It must be such a wonderful experience."

"Listen, kid," I said. "Don't dismiss the biggest market available to you. Television has been pretty good to me. And making movies is rarely as glamorous as it seems. In fact, it can be pretty gruelling. For *Alpha Force III*, I had to stand out in the rain for a week, wearing fifty pounds of military gear on my back."

"Oh, you poor thing." She put her hand on my arm. She was the sort of girl who couldn't keep her hands off others.

"Of course," I went on, "it has its advantages, too, but in the end, it's all work."

"Believe it or not, I almost became a hairdresser. I even enrolled in one of those beautician training schools. My mother put a lot of pressure on me to become a hairdresser. But really I think she just wanted me to be anything other than an actress."

I nodded in sympathy. "My mother still calls me on the telephone to remind me that it's not too late to become an accountant."

Juliet laughed.

I put my hand on her leg—a perfectly innocent manoeuvre that might have left room for misinterpretation. "If you set out for a career in the arts, whether it's acting or writing or painting, or anything else, you need to brace yourself for a lifetime of rejection. And the first people to serve up that rejection will be your closest family." I was getting pretty drunk. "They'll tell you they have your best interests at heart, but they're really just mortified by the very real possibility that you will fail. Of course, given the long odds of succeeding, they may be justified, but they don't understand that we need their support, above all else, if we're going to persevere."

My mother can't bear to tell her friends what I do for a living because she will be forced to admit that my hit television show has just been cancelled. She believes my failure to keep *Maiken Trouble* on the air is a reflection of her shortcomings as a mother. And my father cannot fathom the notion that acting is work. He calls it "goofing off." Whenever I return home, his first words to me are, "When are you going to stop goofing off and get a job, Billy?" I once told him how much money I made, and he couldn't disguise his shame. "How can your conscience allow you to take good money just for goofing off?" My sister says nothing, but the look in her eyes tells me everything.

"Even my old friends joke about my success, ask how I dare condescend to speak to the little people. They suggest they won't all fit in the same room with my vast ego. What they don't know is that the more they talk like that, the smaller they become—which leaves more room for my magnificent ego—and the less inclined I am to be in the same room with them. Their little jokes only demonstrate how small they really are, and the world they live in." I couldn't go on until a fresh drink arrived.

Juliet gave my arm a squeeze. "Once I convinced my mother that I wasn't going to change my mind about becoming an actress, she became very supportive. I can't complain about that. In fact, I worry sometimes that having grown up in a stable, loving home might work against me as an actress. I mean, so many of the great ones came from terrible childhoods, and it makes me wonder if that doesn't have something to do with their genius, as if a hard childhood can benefit an actor's performance. What do you think, Billy?"

My attention had wandered. The waitress had arrived with the drinks, and I was watching Cynthia Collins swig with gusto from her martini glass. "How about you, Cynthia?" I asked. It irked me that she didn't seem interested in the rest of us. I wanted to draw her in. "Did you have a tortured childhood?"

She looked up over the rim of her glass. "No, I had a wonderful childhood. But then, both my parents were artists." There went Juliet's theory. Cynthia Collins was a very good actress. "My torture didn't begin until adulthood," she added. She began to nibble her olive.

We looked at her expectantly. We couldn't allow her to leave us hanging like that.

"Marriage," was all she said.

I knew she was married to Russell Kirkwood. Rusty. A two-bit actor. He did commercials, now and again. He couldn't really act, but the camera didn't mind his face. If he was eating breakfast cereal or faking a migraine, he was passable. The last time I had seen him on stage, he amputated the life from *Titus Andronicus* with Shakespearian brutality, and left us all wondering how he had got himself the part in the first place. He did not command the stage, as one should in that role—or *any* role, for that matter. He spoke the text without the slightest comprehension. And he looked ridiculous wielding a sword.

I also knew that Rusty had a titanic ego that surely would have struck my old friends with awe. Because he didn't work much as an actor, he taught. He took semesters at the various local colleges, and offered his services as a private acting coach. His technique as a coach was not bad, but he could not put into practice what he preached.

"Trouble in the nest?" I said, grateful I wasn't the only one trying to kill the effects of love with booze.

She rolled her eyes, waved an impatient arm at the waitress. "What possesses actors to marry each other?" she asked. "It can't possibly work, yet we can't seem to resist the temptation." She eyed her nearly-empty glass with grave disappointment. The waitress was overworked.

"I suppose the reason depends on the actor," I said, in the manner of the profoundly drunk. "If they are both bad actors, they console each other. If they are both good actors, they congratulate each other. If a bad actor marries a good one, it's in the hope that he might gain something by osmosis. Frankly, there is no excuse for the good actor who marries a bad one. That's just plain stupidity."

"Cheers to that," she said, raising her glass to us. She gulped the dregs. "You know what he's doing right now, my husband?" she asked.

We shook our heads.

"Sulking. He's at home sulking. I almost had to turn this job down because he didn't get the part of Elyot. God! Can you imagine how awful he would have been? He puts constant pressure on me to help him get work, which is another way of saying he expects me to *beg* people to give him work. It's wrong. It's just wrong. I shouldn't have to ask people to give him roles out of pity. He's asking me to blackmail producers, to tell them that if they want me, they have to take him. When he lost Elyot to you, he flew into a rage. He called *my* agent and told him to turn the job down. *My* job! Thank God my agent had the wits to check with me, first."

"I know how you feel," I said, trying to regain control of the room—which was spinning out of control. "My girlfriend asked me to get her a part in *Alpha Force III*, and when I couldn't do it, she left me." Cynthia and Juliet both shook their heads sympathetically.

"My boyfriend," said Juliet, "loves that I'm an actress. He's a junior loans officer at the Royal Bank."

Cynthia and I chimed in unison: "Good for you." And we meant it.

My next solid memory is of waking up next to Juliet Saire. So much for the junior loans officer.

"Morning, Billy," she chirped, as one of my eyes opened. Evidently, she was a morning person. "We've got to be at the theatre in twenty minutes, darling. Do you want to shower first, or shall we go in together?"

"What are you doing in my room?" I asked.

"This is my room. You couldn't remember your room number."

"Graagh!" I rolled over, pulled a pillow over my head. But I knew it wouldn't go away: the nagging feeling that I had just done something regrettable.

Our second day was another table session, and, throughout, Juliet Saire rarely left my side. Her effervescence rang like a gong in my throbbing skull. My predicament seemed to cheer Cynthia Collins.

"You didn't waste any time," she whispered to me during a break, after Juliet had run off to get me a coffee and aspirin.

I groaned at her. "I don't suppose you could have interceded on my behalf."

"Ha! And spoil your fun? To be honest, I don't know who to feel more sorry for. She's just a foolish girl. You're the asshole who's taking advantage."

"I'm not an asshole!"

"And she's not as foolish as she seems?"

I wasn't in a mood to argue, so I let it go. "Anyway, I suppose now I'm going to have to play along for the next month. The kid doesn't strike me as the sort who jilts with grace."

Cynthia looked amused. "No, I imagine she'll make all of our lives miserable if you throw her over. But for God's sake, don't get her pregnant, not unless you fancy the idea of having Sunday dinner at her parents' house every week."

"Right," I said, dejected. "Thanks for the advice."

At the end of the second day, I saw Cynthia leave on Lane Sewell's arm, headed back toward the hotel. Well, given that she married Rusty Kirkwood, her taste in men was already suspect.

"Let's stay in, tonight," I said to Juliet. "Let's order room service and have a quiet evening, just the two of us."

"Sure, Billy. Whatever you want." She gripped my arm tightly as we walked. We both sounded as if we had colds; our nostrils were stuck shut. It was already dark at six o'clock. It was a calm night, all the sounds of the city muffled by the thick, dry snow that covered it. Apart from Juliet's shrill voice, it was almost peaceful.

We returned to Juliet's room, and while she drew a bath, I poured myself a tall drink from the mini-bar. I found the dry heat in the room oppressive, so I lit a cigarette and stepped onto the balcony. I breathed in a bit of Winnipeg peacefulness, and my nostrils immediately closed up, but that was still better than the cloying air in the room. I passed my eyes over the city below. Except for the traffic in and out of the countless taverns, the city seemed to go to sleep after six. Not like Toronto, which bustled twenty-four hours a day. I thought about going back in to get my coat—the cold air was creeping up on me—but I didn't want to disturb the calm I had achieved. Another minute, and I just might make it through the night.

A man's voice suddenly called out nearby. "Shall I pour you a gin, darling?"

It had come from the room next door. I thought I recognized the voice.

"Yes, Lane," said a familiar woman's voice, very near to me. "And don't be chintzy with the gin."

I squinted through the blackness and could discern the glowing red ember of a cigarette illuminating the railing of the balcony next door.

"There's nothing quite like Winnipeg in January," I said, to the ember.

I heard a short breath. "The muffled retches of a thousand drunken clods vomiting into the snow banks makes me think of the gently rolling Mediterranean surf," said Cynthia Collins.

"Frankly, I wouldn't trade all this for the south of France, not if you threw in two bottles of nicely chilled Bollinger."

There was a pause in our exchange, and then Cynthia said, "Are we still in rehearsal, or are you actually attempting to converse with me?"

I shrugged. "That's hard to say. I've lost my script."

Cynthia laughed. My eyes were adjusting to the darkness, so I could almost make out her shape. "I see you've got another intimate evening planned with your new bride, Billy."

I dropped my spent cigarette over the balcony. "We seem to be of a like mind," I said, smoothly.

"And how are things between you and Juliet? Still gloriously wonderful?"

"Tickety-boo," I said. "But I imagine life with a ghastly bore like Lane Sewell must have lost its sheen by now. How are you bearing up?"

"There's something to be said for a man with manners and good sense, Billy. You are hardly qualified to comment on that subject. And anyway, I can only imagine the scorching headache you must have after spending an evening with your little mouse squeaking in your ear."

I sighed. "Let's not fight. Tonight should be a night for romance. We should be happy for one another, that we've finally found true happiness. Let's not spoil it by quarrelling."

"I have no desire to quarrel. I'm ecstatic over your newfound joy. I assure you, nothing will delight me quite like hearing your moans of pleasure seeping through the paper-thin walls."

"There you are, darling," said Lane, stepping onto the balcony. "You'll catch your death standing out here. I've brought your drink. Were you speaking to someone? I thought I heard voices."

"Just the thin walls in this cheap dive," I heard Cynthia say, as I slid the door shut on the balcony.

Juliet was hanging up the telephone when I came in the room. "I've changed my mind," I said to her. "I think we should go out tonight."

Her pink face wrinkled with disappointment. "But we can't go out now. I've just ordered us a scrumptious dinner. I've ordered us champagne, from *France!*"

I looked at Juliet, radiant in the glow of youth, unmarred by the welts of life. She dropped her towel. Her body glistened from her bath. Even standing before me, naked, ready to give me everything she had, she could not stir me. It was like spying on my little sister. "I need cigarettes. I shan't be long, darling." I stepped quickly out of the steamy room, leaving Juliet to dress for dinner.

As I rode the elevator down, I wondered how I could possibly extricate myself from this situation. Honesty didn't seem like a practical alternative. Juliet was the hysterical type. One way or the other, a tantrum was coming, but there had to be a way to get out of this without making the entire company miserable for weeks. I knew I could not possibly endure another month of this.

Advice to men: When you are faced with the unenviable task of dumping a woman, do not, under any misguided sense of consolation, tell her you think of her as a sister. To do so is the most vile insult you could possibly inflict. You will be on safer ground telling her that she is too tall or too fat or too large-breasted for your current taste. Better yet, tell her there is another woman—she will believe that! To women, being a sister is to be unappealing and unwanted in every aspect. And think about this: what brother is not forever at war with his sister?

When the elevator doors swished open to the lobby, I stepped out and nearly collided with Cynthia Collins.

"That was fast," she said, looking wry, and a little drunk. "I thought you'd at least get through dinner before you gave her the heave-ho. Nasty business to conduct with an empty stomach."

"I just came down for cigarettes," I said. "What's your excuse?"

"Corkscrew." She held it up as proof.

"There must be one in Lane's room."

She shoved the utensil back in the pocket of her jacket. "Don't tell Lane that." And she laughed. "Well, now that I've got a corkscrew, all I need is a cork."

I shot her my winning smile. "I think I know where to find one of those." I pressed the elevator button. "We'll have to go to your room," I said. "I can't, for the life of me, remember where mine is."

Although Cynthia Collins was in her mid-thirties, she possessed the sort of allure that Juliet would never achieve. Even her inebriated rancour could not thwart her natural sex appeal. She was wasted on Russell Kirkwood.

"What the devil possessed you to marry a loser like Rusty?" I asked, using the corkscrew to open a miniature bottle of Pino Noir. The wine was for Cynthia. I was sticking to the hard stuff.

Cynthia sat on the end of the bed with her legs crossed seductively. She had a dancer's legs, chiselled from marble. She sighed. "I first saw him in *The Last Bridge*. I thought he gave a brilliant performance." She saw my eyebrows shoot up. "It was a fluke. I know that now. I had a friend in the show and she introduced us. I had just divorced Ed, so I was a little vulnerable, and I was in the midst of a rare dry spell. I hadn't worked in months. Rusty was getting the jobs back then, and I refused to believe that his consistently bad performances afterwards were his fault. I blamed the directors, or the lack of rehearsal time. I wanted to believe he really was the actor I had first seen in *The Last Bridge*. I needed to believe it, because the alternative was just too unpleasant to consider. It wasn't until he decimated *Titus* that I knew I had been duped. But it was too late. By then, my career was back on track and his was on the skids, and we were married."

"An honest mistake," I said, to commiserate. "It could happen to anyone."

She took her jacket off and tossed it on the bed. "What about you, Billy? What happened with your model?"

I shrugged. "My last name."

"She doesn't have to take your last name. I kept my maiden name when I married Rusty."

"No. That wasn't it. She couldn't cope with the fact that I *had* a last name. Anyway, she was just using me to advance her own career. We weren't that serious," I lied. One of us was serious. "She went out to buy cigarettes, and didn't come back."

We both laughed.

"So now you're trying out the technique on poor little Juliet?"

"It's worth a shot," I said.

"You know," said Cynthia, "you really are an asshole." And she laughed again.

I don't remember how the fight started. It began sometime after we had made love, and it had something to do—I think—with the fact that the key to the mini-bar went missing. Cynthia accused me of locking it inside the refrigerator. I remember she called me a bigger oaf than Rusty. I called her an old hag and an adulteress—or something along those lines. I think that was when she slugged me in the eye. Naturally, I didn't hit her back. I wasn't that sort of man. All I could do was defend myself as best I could and hope she would pass out before she really hurt me. When she wound up to throw a glass ashtray, I was still sober enough to duck. Unfortunately, she was so drunk, the glass cube went wide and glanced painfully off my ducking forehead.

I was barricaded behind a *faux*-Chippendale chair, rubbing the swelling goose egg on my forehead, when the manager barged in. Cynthia dropped the Gideon Bible she was about to fling at me.

"I imagine," she slurred in the direction of the manager, "this looks worse than it is."

I emerged from my hiding place, still trying to keep some distance between Cynthia and me. "Actually, it's about right."

When Juliet Saire and Lane Sewell stepped in together behind the manager, my heart sank. At least I was wearing underwear, which was more than I could say for Cynthia Collins.

"Oh, my God!" Juliet squealed. "What's going on in here?" She couldn't take her eyes off Cynthia's incredible body.

The manager stepped forward. "There has been a complaint about the noise," he said. He was the sort of thin-necked weasel who wanted to be in charge of a room, but didn't have the character to pull it off. When he recognized me—Joe Maiken, that is—he lost his nerve completely.

"I should have known it was you," said Lane, crossly. He was looking around for a lamp to drop on my head, but Cynthia had already taken care of that. "We could hear the commotion from our rooms upstairs. It sounded like a bloody riot. We thought someone was being killed."

"We lost the key to the mini-bar," I said.

"*You* lost the damned key!" Cynthia shouted. I feared she was about to pick up the Bible again. Instead, she began to sob. She sat down heavily on the edge of the bed and buried her face in her hands. "Everyone get out of my room," she moaned. "Please, just get out."

Lane took Juliet by the elbow. "Come on, darling. Let's go, before I lose my temper."

"Stay in character, Lane," I called, as he led Juliet out of the room. "Think dull thoughts!"

"Well," said the manager, in more obsequious tones, "now that everything's straightened out, good night, and enjoy the rest of your stay at the Ramada." He winked at me and shuffled out the door.

Cynthia would not lift her head, would not respond to my tentative attempt to touch her quivering shoulders. "Go," she moaned, "Please go."

I plucked up the rest of my clothes and hustled into the hallway. I caught up with the manager as the elevator arrived. "I don't suppose you could tell me where my room is?" I asked.

It had taken only two days to transform the entire cast of *Private Lives* from a tight-knit group of professionals into a clutch of sullen children. Even Juliet refused to speak to Lane after that evening. Apparently, Lane had later refused her advances, claiming he thought of her only as a sister. She had a fit. Poor Lane could have used some good advice on how to dump a woman.

When the show finally went up, the fat-assed farm girls came in droves to see Joe Maiken. He didn't disappoint.

Each night, I stood outside the theatre doors and signed autographs for my loyal fans, in spite of the ice crystals that made my nostrils stick together. Many of the girls cried when I told them the show had been cancelled. News travelled slowly in that part of the world. I consoled them by telling them that, if they hurried, they could catch me down at the Cineplex, in *Alpha Force III*. Disregarding Herb's sensible advice, I had read all the reviews. I couldn't have trashed the flick more eloquently myself. I counted down the days to my exit from Winnipeg. And I drank.

Chapter 8

Five minutes after inhaling a Los Angeles winter, I was pining for the crystalline Winnipeg air. My nostrils wanted desperately to clamp shut, but the humidity and the smog caused them to flare in agony.

A garrulous teenage boy with shaggy blonde hair and leather sandals met me at the airport. He told me his name was Myron, but that everyone called him Skid. He didn't say why. He was a production assistant with Miracle Films, the company producing *Painting the Cherry*. He said he had always dreamed of becoming a world champion surfer, but a slight problem with balance had scuppered that ambition. He blamed it on an inner ear weakness, but I suspected it was a fundamental shortage of brain cells.

"Some day, man, I'm gonna be a third AD," he said, careening along the Ventura Freeway at high speed in a company panel van.

"Aim high, kid," I said, encouragingly. "Do you have a cat?" I was thinking of crazy Marcia and poor dead Floyd.

"Naw, man. Too many Chinks in my neighbourhood."

"I'm sure you'll make a fine third AD."

"I drove Jay Leno, once," said Skid, swerving into the slow lane in order to pass a Highway Patrol cruiser. The transport truck that he cut off blared its air horn. Skid was unstoppable. "He just sat there and didn't say much. He wasn't funny at all, man. I've been disillusioned ever since."

"No kidding."

Skid was eyeing me as he attempted to drive. "Hey, man, haven't I seen you in something?"

I shot him my winning smile. "Joe Maiken," I said, smoothly. "*Maiken Trouble*."

He shook his head. "Naw, never saw that one. Must have been something else." He kept staring at me, making me uncomfortable—the way he drove, he needed to focus on the traffic. "*Alpha Force III*," he said, suddenly. "Man, that was a *great* movie! You were in that, right?"

I nodded.

"I saw it twice. It was better than the first two," said Skid.

"It ain't Shakespeare," I said.

"Who?"

When I stepped into Donald Duke's office, I blinked, rubbed the smog from my eyes. I blinked again. I squinted across the vast chamber at the speck sitting behind the massive mahogany desk. Donald Duke was a small man to begin with. At his desk, he looked like a munchkin. "They let you use Louis Mayer's office when he's out of town?"

He stood up to greet me, and it didn't make him seem any bigger. "Have a seat, Billy," he said, shaking my hand. "Would you like a drink?"

"Bourbon, neat. Make it a double."

As I reclined in a cushy leather armchair, he went to the fully-stocked bar to pour my drink. "How was your flight? Smooth sailing, I trust." He brought my drink and sat across from me in what appeared to be an authentic Queen Anne chair.

I surveyed the plush office. "You seem to have recovered nicely." I sipped the bourbon. The sides of my tongue thanked me by tingling.

He moved his shoulders, as if his spectacular recovery was only to be expected. "Jobs come and jobs go. That's the nature of the business. Nobody knows that better than you, I'm sure. But they're only jobs, and when they go, it's nothing personal."

Easy for him to say. It's personal when you are the star of a hit show that suddenly gets cancelled after five great years. It's *my* face that's up on that screen. It's *my* performance that gets reviewed by the critics. When was the last time a critic slammed a producer for botching a film? When was the last time a producer made the cover of People Magazine? Who gets the blame when a film flops at the box office? The producer? I knew that if I were to ask Skid the Surfer who produced *Alpha Force III*, he would give me a vacant stare and probably sideswipe a Toyota.

"You're absolutely right, Donald. I've spent the past year exploring exciting new options. I've rediscovered my roots in the theatre, for one."

"Good for you."

Now that we had dispensed with pleasantries, it was time to get down to business. "So," I said, "*Painting the Cherry*. A great title, by the way." Such an opulent setting inspired sycophancy, to the utmost. "Who's directing? I asked Herb to find out, but he told me no one seemed to know, for sure."

"We were fortunate enough to get Martin Scorsese locked in for the job," he said.

A thrill ran up my spine.

"But we ran into a bit of a snag with that."

"A snag?"

"Eddie Lawson."

"The love interest?"

"Precisely." Donald folded his fingers into a steeple—never a good sign. "He threatened to pull out of the project unless we let him direct."

"Eddie Lawson?"

"Yes."

"The love interest?"

The steeple collapsed into Donald Duke's lap. "His last two movies have each grossed over fifty-million. He had us over a barrel. We let Marty go."

"Has Eddie Lawson ever directed anything?"

"He's assured us he can do it. He has certainly been directed by some of the best. We have confidence he can handle the job."

"So, what you're saying is that he hasn't directed before."

"Correct, Billy."

"And the only way he will act in this movie is if he can direct it, too."

"Also correct."

"And we will all just cross our fingers and hope that he doesn't totally screw up the film."

"That's not precisely how I would have worded it, but, essentially, yes."

"What about Rollie?" I asked. "Can't you get him to do it?"

He put his hands up in a gesture of surrender. "If it were up to me, I'd have kept Marty. I'm a firm believer in directors. I think every film should have one. But in this case, we had no choice."

"What does Jeanette Winters think about this?"

"She gave back her points and took more money instead."

"Smart kid."

The two stars had made their respective reputations doing the sort of coming-of-age drivel that I never watched. I hadn't seen any of their films. Eddie Lawson I knew only by name. I couldn't have picked him out of a police line-up. Jeanette Winters had been a model, until last year, when she took the next logical step in her career.

"Can either of them act?"

Donald Duke looked thoughtful. "I find there's a subtle distinction between an actor and a movie star. The two don't necessarily go hand in hand. The trick for us, as producers, is to draw the crowds with the movie stars, and keep them from falling asleep in the theatres by surrounding the movie stars with actors. It's one of the more complicated aspects of my job."

Skid was waiting for me out front. "Did they let you use the hot tub, man?"

"No. What hot tub?"

"I heard they got a hot tub in there," he said, skidding around a corner at high speed. "Only a few people know about it. It's for the big shots and the movie stars. I heard they got live fish swimming in it. And naked girls."

"I didn't see any hot tub." The way Skid looked at me, I could tell I had diminished in his estimation.

"Did you check the lines?"

"Lines?"

"Yeah, man. The panty lines. I heard the girls there aren't allowed to wear underwear. It's a rule, or something."

"Well," I said, "I guess my mind was on other things. I didn't notice."

"You a fag, man? Most actors are, you know."

"Hardly. You've been reading People Magazine, haven't you?"

"It's the Bible, in this town."

"Come to think of it, I may have noticed the lines on Donald Duke's secretary. She was over sixty, so I thought it was a bit inappropriate for her not to be wearing underwear." I didn't need this little twerp spreading rumours about me.

"This is California, man. Over sixty just makes her gorgeous *and* rich."

"Maybe I can introduce you."

Skid's eyes widened. He tailgated a low-rider crammed with Latinos wearing blue bandanas, then careened around it with the horn blaring. "You'd do that for me?" he asked, over the wail of the horn.

"Sure, sure," I said. Live and learn.

Our van screeched to a stop in front of the Holiday Inn. "Are Eddie Lawson and Jeanette Winters staying here?"

"Naw. Lawson reserved the top floor of the Four Seasons, until he found out Winters checked into the top floor of the Highland, which is two stories higher, so he moved over to the Palaise Royal. Last I heard, Winters is negotiating with Mel Gibson to rent his penthouse at Winston Towers. I think Lawson will have to rent the Goodyear blimp if he wants to get any higher."

"Sounds pretty childish, if you ask me," I said.

"Welcome to Los Angeles, man." He dropped my luggage on the sidewalk and sped out of the hotel driveway, prompting a chorus of protesting horns.

When I got to my room, I unlocked the mini-bar, but somehow it seemed inadequate. I closed it up again and went down to the hotel bar. I brought the script for *Painting the Cherry,* in case I felt the urge to learn my lines. It was three in the afternoon, so the lounge was populated with only a smattering of tourists who were working up the courage to venture into the city. I took a window seat that gave me an unobstructed view of cement. What the hell, I wasn't there for the view.

Three tall bourbons later, I was having a bit of trouble concentrating on the script. I began to wonder about the hot tub that I hadn't seen at the Miracle Films offices. Was Donald Duke holding out on me? Did his ancient secretary peel off her frock and scrub the backs of movie stars? Should I be grateful to have been spared that experience? Before I could make any decisions, I was brought out of my rumination by a woman's voice.

"Hi, Maiken. Nice to see you."

I must have been crazy, expecting to see Selena standing over me. Wishful thinking is the last bastion of unrequited love. I looked up at the owner of the voice and was genuinely surprised to see that it wasn't my one great love. This girl was forty, at least. The blonde curls shot off her scalp like springs from an old mattress. She was thinner than most models I knew, and her tight clothing emphasized her thinness. She had small breasts with prominent nipples—and no bra to hold them back.

"My name is Billy," I said, without a trace of reproach. "Billy Fox."

"Nice to meet you, Billy Fox. I'm Glenda."

I spied her suspiciously. "Glenda *what?*" I wasn't taking any chances.

"Walker." She aimed her nipples at me and let me have it, right between the eyes. "Are you going to invite me to join you?"

I waved a hand toward the empty chair. "Are you an actress, Glenda Walker?" I found surprising pleasure in giving credit to her full name. Good-bye, Selena.

A crack of laughter peeled through the lounge, jittering the nerves of the anxious tourists. "Do I look familiar to you?"

I squinted at her. With three double bourbons coursing through me, I tended to squint at everything. "I don't know your face, but your name means everything to me,"

She laughed again, causing the windowpanes to shudder. "I don't know what that means, but I like it."

I waved at the waitress. She must have been an actress, she was useless. She glared at Glenda.

"I'll have what he's having," said Glenda.

The waitress shuffled away at low speed.

"If you're not an actress, what do you do, Glenda?"

"I party." She didn't laugh, so I knew she meant it.

"That pays the rent?"

"You bet your sweet ass it does." She leaned toward me. "Do you like to party, Billy?"

"I was having a pretty good bash, before you showed up."

"I hope I didn't spoil your fun."

"On the contrary—"

"I know a place where the service is a lot better than this," she said.

Moments later, I was settled in a convertible Mercedes, headed for North Hollywood.

"You know," Glenda was saying, "the passenger seat of this Mercedes was designed specifically for gorgeous men."

I enjoyed the wind fluttering my longish bangs. "How many pairs of shoes do you own, Glenda?"

She gave me a sideways glance. "You know better than to ask that." In a softer tone, she said, "What are you doing in Los Angeles?"

"*Painting the Cherry*."

"Hmm. Eddie Lawson's gig. Good for you."

"He bumped Scorsese out of the director's chair."

"I know. Most of us think he was doing Marty a favour."

"You know Martin Scorsese?" Glenda impressed me.

"Marty and I go way back, and I can tell you he's not losing any sleep over this. He only agreed to do it in the first place as a favour." As we rolled gently along, the houses were getting farther apart, and the driveways were getting longer.

"Where are we going?" I asked, catching brief glimpses of columned porticos through the tall hedges and rod-iron gates.

"My place."

"I thought we were going to a party."

"Precisely," she said, as we pulled into one of the long driveways. "Jay Leno lives across the street."

"I hear he's not funny."

"Actually, he's a riot."

We came to a stop in front of a Spanish-style bungalow. Lush shrubs coloured the façade a deep green, while a stand of palm trees lining the drive protected us from the brutal California sun. Inside the front door, we took three steps down, which added two feet to the height of the interior rooms. The air conditioning sent a chill through me as I followed Glenda through room after room, tidy and expensively furnished. There didn't seem to be anyone else in the house.

"I thought there was a party going on."

"Patience, darling."

The bungalow seemed to go on forever, not as quaint as it had appeared from the outside. At last we reached the back patio, where a kidney-shaped pool shimmered.

"You have lovely hair," I said. She pushed me down onto a chaise lounge and fucked me, next to the pool.

Her terrific nipples hovered over me for the rest of the afternoon, and between lovemaking, she kept up with me, drink for drink. As the sun was setting, I awoke and noticed the others. I don't know when they arrived, but more than one chaise lounge was squeaking to the irresistible rhythm of Donna Summer, and the pool was occupied by a half dozen naked women, their rippling limbs illuminated by underwater lights.

"Who are those people?" I asked, pulling myself up into a seated position.

"Just a few friends," said Glenda. She glistened in the soft light of dusk.

"The party's finally starting, then."

She slapped my thigh. "You sure know how to make a girl feel unappreciated, Billy."

"I didn't mean it that way."

She leaned over and kissed me. "The best party is a party of two."

I had to agree. After she brought me another drink, I asked: "I still don't understand how you make a living at this."

She shrugged. "It's not very complicated, really. I bring men here and party with them, and they give me things. That's about it."

"You mean money?"

"Sure, sometimes. Or cars, or works of art. One of my friends sent over his contractor to redo my kitchen. That was really sweet."

"So you're a prostitute, then." It should have occurred to me earlier. "I'm supposed to pay you for this."

She smiled and shook her head. "I'm not a prostitute. You don't have to pay me, and you don't have to give me anything. It's just that some men do. They do it because they want to, because they really enjoyed partying with me." She leaned back against me and we watched the girls frolic in the pool. "You have to understand, Billy, I don't have any professional skills. I can't type, I don't have a degree in anything, I'm not a trained nurse, although I've taken CPR training—you know, because of the pool. It's come in handy, once or twice, too. I only really do one thing well, and that's party. The men I party with appreciate that skill, and they want to give me something for it. They're mostly successful men, like you, who know that nothing in life is ever really free. But in my case they're wrong. I am totally free, Billy. No charge. I'm no high-priced call girl. I'm no Hollywood Madame. If it makes these men feel better to give me presents, I would be selfish to declined them. And I would be even more selfish if I charged money for doing what I do."

"It must be an L.A. thing," I said. "The girls in Toronto expect you to buy them dinner before they'll party with you, and then they expect you to marry them, afterward. The only other choice is to pay twenty bucks to have some tramp transmit a vile disease in the back seat of your car. My Corvette doesn't have a back seat, so that pretty much eliminates option two."

Glenda's laughter tore through the evening sky. "I've had my share of marriage proposals, come to think of it."

"You've never been tempted to take one seriously?"

"I'm perfectly aware of the effect I have on men. I'll bet the thought of marriage passed through your mind, as I was lying on top of you. Am I right?" She was. "But the feeling always passes. In the light of a new day, you'll look back at this and congratulate yourself for not going through with it. While the party is going on, you want it to last forever, but no man could ever be happily married to a party girl. Not for long, anyway."

"Don't you long for a solid relationship with one man?"

"It's a career choice. Anyway, darling, in a few short years, I won't be able to cover the hag beneath all this with makeup and fashion. I suppose I'll have to start acting my age. Maybe I'll get myself a real boyfriend. In the meantime, the party rages on." She leapt off the chaise and dove into the pool.

I was dreaming. In the dream, I was being rolled down a hill by my old girlfriend and nemesis Tracy Ford. I was rolling out of control, and every time I tried to get up, she slapped my face and pushed me, sending me spinning farther down the hill...

"Wake up! Wake up, man!"

I groaned and rolled over.

"Wake up!"

I fell off the chaise lounge. A foot struck me in the kidney. That pretty much woke me up. I wanted my eyes to stick shut, but they were lubricated by the damp seaside air. They slid open, taking in the harsh morning glare and the ruffled mug of Skid. "Where am I?"

"You're late, man. Let's go!" He nudged me again with his sandal.

I managed to gain my feet, but they were confused, each attempting to go in a different direction. I staggered a bit. "Are we experiencing an earthquake?" I asked. Everyone knew that California was scheduled to sink into the Pacific Ocean at any moment. "The ground seems to be heaving." I looked at the pool. The surface was a flawless mirror.

"Come on, man," said Skid. He took my arm and pulled me through the bungalow, toward the exit.

"Where's Glenda? I have to say good-bye." I spotted a wine bottle on the mantle and grabbed it on my way past. It was three-quarters full. I put it to my lips, and nearly lost a tooth as I tripped on the steps up to the front door. Skid didn't look back. He had a firm grip on my wrist. He pulled me along as if I were a misbehaving child.

The van was parked in place of the Mercedes. Glenda was out, no doubt looking for a new friend to party with. I was pushed fairly roughly into the passenger compartment, and then Skid jumped into the driver's seat. When he saw the bottle in my hand, he snatched it away and tossed it out the window, littering Glenda's professionally landscaped lawn. Anyway, it was almost empty, and I was beginning to feel better.

Skid was doing over forty as he veered out of Glenda's driveway. He managed to swerve at the last minute, avoiding the golf cart that was puttering along the right hand curb. I stuck my head out the window to make sure the old geezer in the golf cart was safe, and I could have sworn it was Jay Leno who was shaking his fist at me. I waved.

"I think that was Jay Leno you just about killed, back there," I said to Skid.

"Whatever." Skid was uncharacteristically quiet.

After a time, I asked, "How did you know where to find me?"

"I asked at the hotel bar. The waitress said you left with Glenda."

"You know Glenda?"

"Everyone knows Glenda, man."

It took over an hour to get to the set. We spent most of that time idling on freeways, inhaling exhaust along with twenty thousand other sweating motorists. At last, a security guard waved us through the gates of the Miracle Films studio lot. The van stopped in front of a massive cinderblock warehouse. Sound Stage 13B. People of all shapes and sizes milled about. Some held scripts in their hands and I suddenly remembered that I had abandoned mine in the lounge, back at the Holiday Inn. "I forgot my script," I said to Skid.

"Whatever, man."

I misjudged the step down from the van and fell ungracefully to the pavement.

"Jesus," said a voice in the background. "Nine o'clock in the morning and the guy's already drunk."

I wasn't drunk. Not very. The gruelling stint on the California freeway system had worn away the effects of the bottle of wine I'd had for breakfast. I looked up into the sky and saw the face of a boy even younger-looking than Skid. Evidently, Miracle Films employed the entire U.S. Olympic surfing team during the off-season. I stuck my hand out, so the new kid could help me up.

Once again upright, I brushed the pebbles off myself and looked around. "Who's in charge around here?" I asked.

"That would be me," said the surfer.

I gave him a charming smile of indulgence. "No, no. I asked who's *in charge*. I think his name is Eddie Lawford."

"Lawson," said the surfer. "Eddie Lawson. That would be me."

"Sorry, kid. Didn't recognize you. Must be the morning light." I had never seen even a photograph of Eddie Lawson. "You look bigger on screen."

"I am bigger on screen," said Eddie. "And don't call me *kid*. I'm Mister Lawson."

"Sure, okay," I said. I spotted Donald Duke standing at the studio door with a clutch of shrunken old men in blue suits.

"Why are you late?" asked Eddie.

I refocused on him. He was a beautiful boy. Almost as beautiful as I had once been. But Eddie Lawson spoiled his natural good looks by sneering. "I was in Winnipeg," I said. That was as good an excuse as any.

He let it drop. "We're starting with page thirty-three. Your first meeting with Nelson Fairchild." He snapped his finger and a lackey instantly appeared at his side. "Get him to makeup. He's got ten minutes before we roll." He strode away, leaving me with the lackey.

"I suppose you're a surfer, too," I said.

"Yeah, man. I suppose you're a drunken fag," said the lackey, leading the way to makeup.

"One out of two, man," I said.

PAINTING THE CHERRY
SC. 42A

FADE IN:

INT. OFFICE. DAY.

Inside the plush penthouse office of NELSON Fairchild. The room is opulent to the extreme, with rich mahogany wainscoting and deep leather armchairs. A massive desk is featured. The desk is tidy. NELSON Fairchild is a detail-oriented man, who likes everything to be in its proper place.

(the intercom on the desk beeps.)

          A WOMAN'S VOICE
  Mister Fairchild, Mister Ketchum
  is here.

          NELSON
  Send him in.

JOE Ketchum enters the office. He is impressed, as he should be. If NELSON Fairchild looks like a million bucks, JOE Ketchum looks like two dollars and change. He is wearing the only suit he owns, which he has owned since his high school graduation, twenty years earlier. He is shabby, but confident in his skills as a private investigator.

          NELSON
  Sit down, Mister Ketchum.

                            JOE
(looking around.)
          Nice digs.

                          NELSON
          We can skip the pleasantries,
          Mister Ketchum. I have a job
          for you, and I need to know
          that you can do it fast, and do
          it right.

                            JOE
(nodding.)
          Those are the very words I live
          by, Mister Fairchild.

                          NELSON
          I want to add one more thing to
          the list. Discreet.

                            JOE
          That one goes without saying.

                          NELSON
          In this case, it's worth
          saying, Mister Ketchum. This is
          a sensitive matter that
          requires the greatest delicacy.
          It involves my daughter, you
          see, and there is nothing in
          this world more important to me
          than Daisy.

...and on it went. I barely needed my script. I was able to remember at least half my lines, and the rest I filled in with clichés, or a wry grin that became Joe Ketchum's trademark throughout the film. No one seemed to notice I was making up large parts of my dialogue as I went along.

Later that afternoon I discovered how I was able to get away with changing or inventing so much of my dialogue. We had finished shooting my scenes for the day, so I had been released. After scraping off the makeup and returning the cheap suit to wardrobe, I had returned to the studio to find out from the production assistant when my next call time was. They were still shooting in Nelson Fairchild's office—a two-walled set with no ceiling, and with a sky and cityscape painted on the wall outside the window. Magic!

Nelson was conspiring with his corporate minions to conduct a shady business deal. I stood in the background and watched with only superficial interest as the scene unfolded (no actor is really interested in any scene he's not in). Eddie Lawson, sneering star and novice director, sat in his folding chair behind the camera. He appeared to be so deeply intent on following along with the dialogue that his eyes never left the pages of his script. He paid not the slightest attention to what his actors were doing, or how they were framed in the camera. Nelson Fairchild could have been dressed in a clown suit, and Eddie Lawson would not have noticed. When I took a step closer, I could see that Eddie's script was open to a different page altogether. He was learning his own lines, as he was supposedly directing. After Nelson Fairchild stopped speaking, I saw the cinematographer's foot gently nudge Eddie's ankle.

"Cut!" shouted Eddie, at last looking up. "Print that one. That was great, guys. Just great."

A buzzer sounded and people started moving about, getting ready for the next scene. The cinematographer leaned down to Eddie and whispered in his ear.

"Wait!" shouted Eddie. "Let's try it again. One more time." The cinematographer had pointed out that Nelson had flubbed his line, halfway through the scene. Another take was required.

Eddie's method of directing involved giving his actors the freedom to act in any way they felt was appropriate or natural, to use, in other words, their "instincts"—a method that, in the hands of someone with talent and vision, could be regarded as brilliant, but which in Eddie Lawson's case was nothing short of monumental incompetence. As long as we hit our marks for the camera (which the cinematographer insisted upon), Eddie didn't care what happened. He gave me not a single suggestion about how he wanted me to play Joe Ketchum. He gave no notes to any of the actors. If not for his talented cinematographer, he wouldn't have got a single coherent scene in the can.

After a while, I wandered over to the craft table to get a piece of fruit. But when I got there, I discovered the gaggle of producers had just finished clearing every scrap there was. I spotted them—Donald Duke among them—lounging on the sofas against the back wall, where they could sit comfortably and bad-mouth the actors.

"Can I getcha something?" asked the craft services lackey. He was a massive hulk of manhood, who must have once wrestled professionally. But his wide grin was open and genuine. "Sorry. Not much left, today."

I surveyed the remaining crumbs on the table. "I don't suppose you've got a bottle of half-decent bourbon?" I asked, joking.

"You're Billy Fox, aren't you?" he asked.

"Yep."

"I'm Marvin." He offered a giant paw to shake. "Too bad about your show. It was the only good thing on, Thursday nights."

Cripes! Will no one let me forget? "Yeah, too bad. It's also too bad you don't have a bottle of Knob Creek stashed away back there."

Marvin's eyes made furtive sideways motions, and he jerked his head sharply to the right. He was about as subtle as a runaway freight train.

I followed him behind the double fridge, where he knelt down and unlocked an old steamer trunk, covered in travel stickers. It must have once been a prop. And I was suddenly looking down into a treasure chest for anyone with a penchant for mind-altering substances. One side was an orderly jumble of baggies and pill bottles, the other side a well-stocked bar.

Marvin began lifting the bottles up by the necks, so he could read the labels. "What was it you asked for, Knob Creek?"

"Any bourbon will do," I said. The sides of my tongue were tingling wildly.

"No, no. I think I got the KC. I had one left over from Burt Reynolds's last movie."

As Marvin was clinking the wares in his magic trunk, in search of my relief, I heard quick footsteps approaching.

"There you are, Marvin!"

I turned, and was face to face with Jeanette Winters. She was Selena's age. She was nearly as beautiful as Selena, but she lacked an element of grace that Selena possessed. Her movements were jerky and unnatural, like a robot with a faulty servo. Her face wore a hard expression that fought against the well-moulded features. I could see that she might have had a certain appeal in a still shot, but in motion she was awkward.

"Hi," she said, quickly, when she noticed I was ahead of her in line. But her eyes did not linger on me for more than a second, they went straight to the open trunk. "Come on, Marvin. I need my diet pills. Hurry. I have to get to wardrobe." She couldn't stand still.

Without looking up, Marvin handed a bottle of pills over his shoulder. Jeanette Winters snatched them greedily and clipped away without another word.

"Nice to meet you," I called, to her retreating backside.

"Don't waste your time," said Marvin. "You'd have a deeper conversation with a banana—Aha!" He stood up and presented the KC like an award. "Let me get you a thermos."

"I don't need a thermos."

Marvin compressed his lips and looked down on me with mild-mannered brutality. "You can't walk around with the bottle, Billy. This may be California, but even here you can't do that." He opened a short green cabinet next to the trunk, in which were rows of thermoses, in various styles and sizes, lining the shelves. He grabbed a large silver one and filled it with the bourbon, and then he took a marker from his shirt pocket and penned my name on a piece of tape that he stuck on the side. "Don't want someone else picking up your thermos by mistake," he said, handing it to me.

"Thanks, Marvin," I said.

"Fifty dollars is all the thanks I need."

Was I going to argue? Not a chance. I paid up. As I roamed the set, I noticed that I was not the only one carrying a thermos with a nametag. Marvin had a pretty good business going on the side.

At first, I was disappointed to discover I did not have a single scene in *Painting the Cherry* with Jeanette Winters. Despite her drugged-up edginess, she was something to behold. I always liked to have a pretty girl around, something to give relief to the eyes. But after two weeks on the set, I changed my mind about the flick's young starlet. I began avoiding her. I tried not to be in the studio when she was shooting her scenes. If I did nip into the sound stage, it was to pay a quick visit to Marvin at the craft services table, to get my thermos refilled. That silver canister was my constant companion throughout the shoot. As I retreated to the daylight with my drink, Jeanette Winters's latest tantrum would cause me to wince, and quicken my pace. She was impossible.

"Why am I not in close-up?" I heard her shout. "Why do *you* get the close-up?" She was shouting at Eddie, the director.

Another time, I overheard this:

"This dress makes me look fat! That *cunt* in wardrobe is trying to ruin my career!"

She walked off the set for half a day, until the wardrobe girl was replaced.

"I'm not saying that line, Eddie! I wouldn't say that. This is shit! This was obviously written by a man! I'm not saying this shit!"

Or, in the middle of a scene, she might suddenly burst into tears.

"I can't do it," she would wail, burying her face in Eddie's shoulder. "I'm just not good enough."

I had to agree. She couldn't act. She was capable of flying into a convincing rage, or falling into the deepest despair, until the camera started rolling. Then she became just another model who felt that acting was the next logical step in her career. She was dreadful. And she was sufficiently messed up by Marvin's "diet pills" that there was no hope of ever getting a performance out of her. Her best work was wasted, off camera, as she shouted or cried into Eddie Lawson's face.

Any dreams I might have had of striking up a friendship with her vanished quickly. She was too young for me—a thought that depressed me, made me feel old for the first time in my life, caused me to drink more.

As an actor, Eddie Lawson was no better than his co-star. He spoke as if his mouth was recovering from a shot of Novocain. I could see the wheels spinning, as he tried to remember his lines, usually without success. He finally gave up and had cue cards placed strategically around the set. But his eyeballs moved as he looked over Jeanette's shoulder to read the cards. And he couldn't read any better than he could memorize.

"It's all about the money," wailed Jeanette's character. "That's all you care about."

"I don't care about you, darling, fortunately," Eddie read.

"What?"

He tried again. "I don't care about you, fortunately, darling."

"Is this a joke?"

"What I mean to say is, I don't care about your fortune, darling. That's what I've been trying to tell you." He finally got it out.

"I can't work like this!" shouted Jeanette Winters. She stomped off the set.

Eddie fired the cue card boy, just to let off some steam.

Later, he said to me, "You know, Billy, I really like the whole drunken angle you've given to Joe Ketchum. Keep it up."

Drunken angle, I wondered? What drunken angle? When I thought about it for a moment, I realized I was drunk during nearly all of my scenes. Of course I was giving a drunken angle to my character. Of course. During the final week of shooting, Donald Duke also had something to say about my drunken acting. "You're better than this, Billy. Sober up and prove to me that you are the actor I think you are." The next day, Marvin was replaced.

What do you suppose the odds were of *Painting the Cherry* being a hit? Consider this: the script was a scene by scene, word by word, rehash of every romantic comedy ever churned out by the Hollywood machinery, the outcome was as predictable as the L.A. smog, the title was stupid, and Jeanette Winters *did* look fat in that dress.

Now consider: it starred two of the cutest, hottest movie stars in Hollywood, there was an impressive supporting cast of real actors (among which I include myself), there were opulent settings in vast mansions and swanky restaurants, a two-hundred-thousand-dollar Rolls Royce got demolished during the climax of the movie, and there was a great deal of kissing.

It was a runaway hit, obliterating the rest of the trash released in the summer of 1981. It just goes to show that the public is not prepared to think too much. Let that be a lesson for Dave Small and his cerebral cronies.

I got paid and sent home to my empty loft. On my last day in Los Angeles, Donald Duke said to me: "I won't hire you again, until you sober up." (That was nearly twenty years ago. I have been sober now for five years. I have still not heard from Donald Duke. I called his office once, a few years back, to let him know I was back in business, so to speak, but he did not return my call. Such is life.)

Chapter 9

Beep..."Hi, sweetheart. Listen, didn't you tell us you were in that *Heritage Creek* show, the one that's been on television for a few weeks? I'm sure you said you had a part in that show. Well, we've watched three episodes, so far, and we haven't seen you once. Maybe you can let us know which episode you'll be in, and then we'll be sure to watch it. I'm sorry to say this about something you're involved with, honey, but the show is really unbearable to watch. If your poor father has to sit through another hour of wholesome men in cover-alls, he just might lose his mind. He missed the beginning of the hockey game last week, and he was fit to be tied. Anyway, we still haven't heard from you about coming home. We all want to meet that girl of yours. And speaking of girls, I ran into Gail Jerome at the Co-op, the other day. She's still as pretty as ever. I'll never understand why you two didn't get married. Of course, it's too late now. She married Todd Fleckman, the dentist. You remember Todd, darling. He was in your class, I think. They have a lovely home in Bonavista, right on the lake. They seem to be doing quite well for themselves. Well, let us know when you'll be coming."

Beep..."Jesus Murphy, Billy! What happened out there? I just got a lashing over the phone from Donald Duke. He said you were drunk for the entire shoot. Sylvia Parker called last month to say more-or-less the same thing about the Winnipeg job. What's going on, Billy? Don't blow it now, not when things are starting to fly. We can't afford to have you get that kind of reputation in the business. I want you to come by the office tomorrow. I might have a job for you, but first I need you to give me your personal assurance that the booze isn't going to be a problem. I need you to do that for me, Billy."

Beep..."Hi, Mister Fox. This is Kelly Boyce. We met after your performance of *Waiting for the Smoke to Clear*. I hope you remember me, but I won't be offended if you don't. I'm sure you meet lots of girls. Anyway, I'm calling just to tell you that I missed my period last month. I know I told you that I wasn't one of those crazy girls who stalk famous people, and I meant it. I'm not crazy. But I think I might be pregnant, and I just needed to tell you about it. If I am, it's your baby. Like I said, I don't expect you to do anything about it. I'm not asking for money, or anything like that, but I thought it would be the decent thing to do, to tell you. It wouldn't be fair to keep it from you that you're going to have a child out there somewhere. I'll understand if you just ignore this message. You're such an important person, you must have lots of things to deal with, but if you wanted to call, you know, to talk about it with me, I wouldn't mind if you called me. My number is five-five-five, three-O-seven-seven."

I called my mother to tell her I couldn't come home at the moment, because I had just enrolled in Dental College, and was too busy with homework. I figured that would clam her up for a while. I called Herb Farley to tell him that I would almost certainly be too drunk to come to his office, the next day. I called Kelly Boyce.

The first step to recovering from alcoholism is to admit that you have a problem. In 1981, after Selena walked out on me, after bringing a "drunken angle" to Joe Ketchum in *Painting the Cherry,* after impregnating my number one fan, I was a long way from that first step.

A man answered the telephone. Mr. Boyce, I presumed. "Can I ask whose calling?"

"Joe," I said. "Joe Ketchum."

There was a long pause at the other end, and I momentarily wondered if he'd hung up on me.

"Hello?" I said.

"Just a minute." I could hear muffled voices.

"Hello?" asked a vaguely familiar voice.

"This is Billy Fox," I said.

Little Kelly Boyce burst into tears.

I came round in the Corvette to pick her up. She lived with her parents in a tidy working-class neighbourhood in the west end. I rolled to a stop in front of a quaint red-brick post-war bungalow. When I spotted the pristine '67 Galaxy 500 in the driveway, I knew that I could not go to the door. It was Mr. Boyce's car. I knew that he had owned it since 1967, had paid cash for it, way back then, and had fastidiously maintained it for fourteen years with such zealous care, it probably still *smelled* new. I knew the type. I had encountered fathers like him when I was younger, and dating girls who still lived at home with their parents. I always got along best with the fathers who drove rusted out beaters, held together with coat hangers and duct tape. The ones who polished the spokes in their hubcaps with a toothbrush every Saturday morning were invariably impossible to please. My own father was one of those men.

I beeped the horn. Three weeks later, Kelly and I were married.

Advice to men: Always try to maintain at least one good friend, at all times. He will be there for you to intervene when you are about to do something rash. He will get you drunk and talk the sense back into you. He will throw you into the backseat of his car and drive you to Las Vegas, if that's what it will take to put your life into perspective. He will call the girl who is the cause of your rash behaviour and tell her that you have the clap, and suggest that she sees a doctor. (That usually does the trick.)

When Kelly Boyce jumped into the passenger seat of my Corvette, I had no friends left. Even my old friend, the writer, was mad at me after I drunkenly accused him of stinking like shit. There was no one left to save me.

"If we're going to get married," Kelly said to me, later, "I want to do it before I'm showing. I don't want people to think that we did it because I got pregnant."

"We *are* doing it because you got pregnant," I said.

Advice to men: ...well, the stupidity of that last comment speaks for itself.

Before the big event, I took Kelly to Yorkville and introduced her to my hairdresser. Kelly confessed that her mother had always cut her hair. That much was evident. Once Alex was through with her, she was almost a new woman. All she needed now was a completely new wardrobe, so we went shopping. Four hours and a thousand dollars later, she could have been one of Selena's friends. She was stunning.

"Billy, if I break an ankle on these high heels, it'll be on your conscience," she said, wobbling along Cumberland with a fist full of shopping bags. At least she wasn't calling me Mister Fox anymore. And I was growing accustomed to that adoring, unblinking gaze of hers. "I know you've been avoiding it, Billy, but you're going to have to meet my parents, sooner or later."

"Later is preferable, darling." When I looked down on her, I saw that she was quietly crying. "What's the matter?"

She sniffed. "That's the first time you've called me 'darling.'"

It's the little things in life. "You know, seeing you in that new dress makes me want to tear it off and ravish you, right here on the sidewalk."

Her eyes widened, and the tears really spilled out. She dropped her shopping bags and flung her arms around my neck, and kissed me so deeply, I gave serious consideration to carrying out the threat, throwing her down on the Yorkville cobblestones and giving her a special moment.

"Billy," she whispered in my ear, "you can do anything you want to me. *Anything.* If you want to tie me up, or spank me, or have your way with me in a public place, you can. If you want me to wear naughty underwear, I will. I've always dreamed of wearing naughty underwear, just for you."

"I think your dream is about to come true."

We spent two hours in La vie en Rose. Kelly held every skimpy and see-through item in the shop up to herself. "Do you like this one? Does this one make you want to ravish me? Do you prefer pink or black? Do you like the two-piece instead of the one-piece?" She was devastated that she was not permitted to try them on in the store—for obvious hygienic reasons.

In the Corvette, Kelly began peeling off her dress. She couldn't wait until we got home. She was struggling in the cramped space of the passenger seat with a sheer black nightie that left nothing to the imagination. After we stopped at a red light, a nearby horn honked. I looked over at the car in the next lane, and a fat bastard in a rusted Lada blew a kiss at me. When I saw Kelly wave to him in my peripheral vision, I gave him the finger and revved my powerful motor. Will that stupid fat bastard never learn?

And Kelly wasn't kidding when she said I could do anything to her. Back in the love loft, after I had tied her securely to the bedposts and spanked her a few times (at her insistence), she said, "If you want to invite some of your friends over, so they can have their way with me, you can, Billy."

"I don't have any friends," I said. She almost seemed disappointed. I began to wonder about her predilections.

"They don't have to be *good* friends. Anyway, it's just a thought. I just want to please you. Whatever you want."

Two days later, she bought me a gift. "Where did you get this?" I asked, holding up the vintage telephone repairman's jacket. The name "Bud" was stitched on the breast.

"In one of those used clothing stores on Queen Street. Do you like it?"

I looked at it warily. "I suppose so. I'm not really sure what to do with it. Are you suggesting a career change for me?"

She laughed. "No, darling. I just thought that if you put it on, you could come to the door sometime, you know, pretending to be the telephone repairman. I would pretend to be the pretty young wife, all alone at home during the day, while my husband is at work. Naturally, I would have forgotten you were coming, so I would answer the door in my negligee. Then, as you were fixing my phone, you would be so overcome by my beauty, you would have to ravish me. I would struggle, but you're such a big strong man, I would be powerless to resist you. You would make me to do all sorts of dirty things with you."

"Are you sure you were a virgin, when we met?" I had to ask.

"Billy! How could you even ask that?"

When we filled out the marriage certificate, I discovered she was twenty-five. "Jesus. I've never heard of a twenty-five-year-old virgin."

"I was saving myself for you, Billy. You're the only one for me."

"Me and Bud," I said.

She smiled. "I think the telephone is on the fritz, Billy. Maybe you should call the repairman."

She *was* crazy. And I was a drunk. We were a pair.

"It's not too late to change your mind," I said. "You don't really know what you're getting into, by marrying me."

"Oh, Billy! This is a dream come true for me. You're only saying that because you don't want to marry *me*."

"Of course I do," I lied. "It's just that, well, things aren't going so well for me, right now. I have a lot of stress. And I'm older than you. I just think you should consider this carefully. I don't want you to regret it, down the road."

"As long as I'm with you, I won't regret anything. You're my reason for living."

I wished I could have felt the same way. I really did. The truth was, I wasn't sure why I agreed to marry her. I wanted to believe it was because it was the right thing to do, since she was pregnant, but that didn't seem to fit with my character. There had to be more to it than that. It may have had partly to do with her knockout good looks—which were enhanced dramatically after our day in Yorkville. It occurs to me now it might have been due to her blind and unflagging devotion to me. With fewer and fewer people stopping me in the street to call me Joe, it's no wonder I was attracted to a single acolyte who would have slit her wrists for me, if I had asked her to. She gave herself to me completely, in every way. How could I fail to be attracted to someone like that? She wanted me to do everything to her, and I did. During the years we were married (ten, in all), she never had a harsh word for me, never criticized my drinking, or my philandering, never threw my fading glory back in my face. But she was prone to cry. That was her weapon of choice. For any reason, or no reason at all, she would flood the love loft with tears, until I was up to my neck in unwarranted despair. I would thrash about until I could persuade her that I loved her still. Or, I would put her over my knee and give her a spanking. That never failed to reassure her.

When I booked the wedding with a Justice of the Peace, Kelly cried, once again.

"I've always dreamed of a white wedding."

"You can wear whatever colour you want."

"In a big church, with two hundred of my closest friends watching me go down the aisle with Billy Fox. My mother will be devastated."

The Boyces were not invited—another cause for tears. "We're only allowed to bring two witnesses," I said. Another lie. "And I've already arranged for Dave Small and his girlfriend Donna to stand in. It's too late to change it, now."

Two weeks after Kelly Boyce became Missus Billy Fox, she got her period.

"Didn't you go to a doctor, to find out if you were *really* pregnant?"

"I was so sure." she sobbed. "I never miss my period."

"Cripes. This is a real shock."

"Aren't you happy with me, Billy?" Her eyes were turning to glass.

"No, no. It's not that," I said. But that was it, exactly. "It's just that—" I didn't have the right lie at the tip of my tongue. I needed a script. And a drink.

Kelly hugged me. "Don't worry, my love. We'll just have to keep trying. I'll get pregnant for you." But she was missing the point. Furthermore, it was a promise she couldn't keep. She would never have my baby. Not from lack of trying (although, I confess, my heart was never in the task, and I was not as disappointed as I may have seemed to my wife).

I had the decency to wait until Herb swallowed his coffee before I broke the news to him.

"Whoa! Billy, are you off your rocker?" His arm twitched and knocked over his coffee mug, sweeping brown, sticky java across piles of file folders.

"I hope those are someone else's contracts," I said, indicating the soaked folders.

"What did you say her name was?"

"Kelly."

"Kelly what?"

"Kelly *Fox*. Jesus, Herb. What did you think her name would be?"

Herb dabbed at the damp mess with a tiny napkin. "I was hoping you would say 'Just Kelly.'"

I crossed my arms. "Believe it or not, most people have a last name."

"I'm perfectly aware of that, but jeepers, did you have to marry one of them? What were you thinking? Why didn't you warn me? I might have saved you."

"Saved me from what?" I was indignant. He was my agent, not my father. (Frankly, I knew my father would approve of the marriage, which made me all the more uneasy.)

Herb gave me his fatherly look. He sighed. "How much have you drunk today, Billy?"

"Do you have a job for me, or did you just call me in to nag me?"

Herb found a box of Kleenex in his desk drawer. He plucked all the tissues out of the box and spread them around his desk. "*Heritage Creek*."

I nearly slid out of my chair. "You're killing me."

"It's a one-day guest spot."

"I'm not auditioning for those bastards again."

"No audition. Les Dodd gave you a recommendation and the producers agreed."

The room began to spin. I hadn't been drinking much, but it spun anyway. "Tell me the truth, Herb. I kicked the bucket, and nobody told me."

"What are you talking about? It's a double-scale job on a popular show."

"The day Les Dodd gets me a job is the day I've died and gone to hell."

"Word is that Les is getting a Gemini nomination this year. He's pretty good. I'm trying to get him onto my roster, but he has every other agent in town running after him. Have you even seen the show?"

"Ha! You're having a hypoglycemic reaction."

"Do you want the job or not?"

"Yeah, sure." What the hell. I've done enough favours for the waitering community in this town. It's about time I got something in return. "I've always wondered what I looked like in cover-alls."

"That's the spirit, Billy. And be sure to say hi to the little lady for me."

```
HERITAGE CREEK
EPISODE #13 -- THE HOMECOMING.

FADE IN:

INT. JUD'S GENERAL STORE. DAY.

A busy day in JUD's store. Women in white
bonnets are picking over bolts of cloth, men
are browsing the selection of shovels and
pickaxes. Young children hover near the front
counter, where the candy jars entice them.
There is a genial buzz to the store, everyone
happily going about their business. Until
NATHAN Cooke walks in. All the men in the store
stop browsing and look nervously in his
```

direction. The women hide their faces behind their bonnets. Even the children stop squealing for candy. JUD looks angrily at NATHAN Cooke. They have a history. NATHAN walks up to JUD at the counter.

     NATHAN
 Bin a long time, Jud.

     JUD
 (looking disgusted)
 Not long enough, if you
 ask me, Nathan.

     NATHAN
 (smiling...)
 Now, is that any way to
 speak to an
 old friend?

     JUD
 We may have been
 friends once, but those
 days are long past,
 Nathan. You're not
 welcome round these
 parts, I reckon.

     NATHAN
 Last I heard, this was
 still a free country. I
 haven't broken the law.
 You make it sound like
 I'm some sorta KILLER,
 Jud.

     JUD
 I know exactly what you
 are, and I don't like
 it. I don't like it,

> one bit. No sir. This
> here's a nice little
> town. People round here
> just want to live in
> peace. We don't need
> men like you bringing
> your kind of trouble
> in.

               NATHAN
> That's not very
> neighbourly, Jud. I'm
> an honest, hardworking
> fella, just like you. I
> don't want no trouble.

                 JUD
> What is it you want,
> then?

               NATHAN

Looking around the store, ignoring the nervous customers.

> Just a few supplies.
> I'm movin into the old
> Chelsea place, out past
> the river bend. Gonna
> plant me some corn,
> keep some goats. I'm
> not here to bother no
> one.

                 JUD
>   (squints warily)
> Those are just words,
> Nathan. And I heard 'em
> before. But I'm a fair
> man. I'll take you at

>   your word, for now. But
>   I don't trust you. Not
>   after what you did, all
>   them years ago. I
>   cain't forget the past
>   so easily.
>
>   NATHAN
>   Fair enough, Jud. Just
>   a chance is all I'm
>   askin' for.
>
>   JUD
>   Every man deserves a
>   chance.
>
>   MAN IN HAT
>   (angrily, to NATHAN)
>   Why don't you just go
>   back where you come
>   from? We don't need
>   your kind in our town!

That was me: Man In Hat. It's a living.

Les Dodd was doing his best to make me feel like a bit player.

"Say, Billy," said Les, "if you want to use my trailer, you know, to have a little rest or make a phone call, you're welcome to it. It's the big one at the end of the row. You can't miss it. My name is on the door."

I shot him my winning smile. "That's great, Les. Thanks a lot." The mealy-mouthed prick. He knew I didn't have a trailer of my own. I was herded into the back of a U-Hall, to dress with the rest of the plebs. O, how the tables turn on us all! And Les had to rub my nose in it.

At least I had my silver thermos to comfort me on the set. I'd brought home Marvin's little trick from Los Angeles. There was one close call, early in the morning, when the key grip picked up my thermos by mistake (actually, I suspect him of attempted thievery). I flung myself at him before he could unscrew the lid and get a whiff of cheap whiskey. He pretended to apologize for mistaking my thermos for his, and I learned an important lesson: don't forget to stick your name prominently on your thermos.

Even though they shot my scene first and I was effectively finished by ten-thirty in the morning, I was asked to remain for the day, in case there was a last minute call. I didn't mind spending the day. I found Jackie Knowlton loitering outside the makeup trailer, looking stunning.

"Oh! Hi, Billy—" She took two steps back. I couldn't blame her, really, given the history of my hands suddenly finding their way onto her breasts. But this time her breasts were safe. One of my hands was safely stowed in a pocket, and the other was clutching possessively at the handle of my thermos.

"You look well, Jackie," I said, smoothly. I took in our surroundings as if I owned the set, as if it were *my* series. I suddenly regretted not having called her back quickly enough, after she had left that eager message on my machine, last year. Although I hardly wanted to admit it to myself, I could see by the look in her eyes that she would rather be somewhere else—or, more accurately, she would rather *I* was somewhere else. I must have smelled like a distillery. And even then my face was showing the early signs of alcoholism. Those faint lines that were tracing around my eyes and mouth were deepening with every refill of my silver thermos. When I looked at my face in a mirror, I thought I was seeing the belated elements of manhood asserting themselves, but it was a delusion. I was becoming a wreck.

"You look good, too," she said, sinking into a folding chair. She was good with the lies.

Any seasoned drunk will tell you that acting sober is relatively easy if you remember a few simple rules, the most important of which is that standing still is a sure giveaway. I wasn't even consciously aware I was trying to act sober, it was second nature to me. But I soon realized my constant pacing was unnerving Jackie Knowlton, so I stopped pacing and put my free hand on the back of her chair, to keep myself steady.

"I hear *Private Lives* was quite the success in Winnipeg," Jackie said, leaning away from me.

Her chair began to wobble, so I let go and began pacing again. "I thought it went pretty well. Of course, if only *you* had been my Amanda—" I let that one hang for her.

"Cynthia Collins is a fine actress," she said.

"Sure, sure. But she wasn't the easiest person to work with, if you want the truth of it. We had our moments."

"So I've heard."

"Hmm. Is there talk going around?"

"Cynthia is an old and dear friend of mine."

I was seized by a hot flash as I recalled those fantastic dancer's legs and that vicious temper. I suddenly needed to get out of the sun. My thermos felt like a dead weight at the end of my arm, but when I attempted to set it down on a small table, next to Jackie's chair, I missed by a foot, and it fell to the ground. I heard the faint tinkle of breaking glass. I straightened up, pretended that I meant to drop it, and then promptly forgot about it.

"Juliet Saire had a nervous breakdown, after the show came down," she went on.

That surprised me. Juliet hadn't been in the business long enough to qualify for a nervous breakdown. "That doesn't surprise me, one bit," I said. "She was having a tough time of it with Lane Sewell. They had some sort of thing going. You know how it is with small casts."

"Oh, yes," said Jackie, smoothly. "I know how it is."

"So, how is Cynthia? I really should give her a call."

"She's divorcing Rusty."

I blew out some air. "Well, that's a bit of good news, anyway. How's Rusty taking it?"

"He thinks she's leaving him because she's jealous of him."

That made sense. Before I could tear into a speech about what a loser Rusty Kirkwood was, Les Dodd came up to us. He was still wearing his cover-alls. (I had wasted no time changing back into my street duds, once my scene was finished.)

"Hi, you two," said Les. He leaned down and gave Jackie Knowlton a lingering kiss on the mouth. I must have looked alarmed, or disgusted, or some combination of the two, because Les was quick to explain. "We're living together," he said. "I suppose you didn't know that."

"I've been out of town," I said. I'd been back for months, but I hadn't spent much time at the Epicure Café—which is the hub of industry gossip.

"Say, Billy," said Les, "I just heard the most bizarre rumour. Someone told me that *you* just got married. I knew it had to be a joke, of course."

"It happens to be true," I said. I couldn't expect People Magazine to report on everything that goes on in my life. I tried to focus on two gaping mouths. "I was married a few weeks ago."

The two mouths began to work, like fish gulping plankton. "Well…um, congratulations, Billy," said Les, finally. "What's her name?"

"Kelly."

"Kelly what?"

"Kelly Fox," I said. "Missus Kelly Fox."

Chapter 10

I couldn't stall any longer.

"It won't be so bad, Billy, you'll see. They're very nice."

A month after legally bonding with Kelly Boyce, I was compelled to meet her parents—a situation I had been energetically avoiding since I had spotted that vintage Ford in the Boyce driveway.

I probably should have jumped right in with both feet on that first day, strode up to the front door and collected the young damsel like a man—like a big shot movie star. I should have confronted Mr. Boyce with the supreme confidence of a (relatively) young man of position and substance. I turned out to be a coward. After so many weeks, the issue had become a massive boulder, rolling downhill, gaining dangerous speed with every turn. The longer I waited, the more devastating the impact would be. It was time to get it over with.

"I don't know what you're afraid of," said Kelly, in the car.

"Assault and battery, for one," I said. But that just made her laugh.

"No one is going to assault you. My parents are very big fans. They can't wait to meet you."

"Fans?"

"Sure. I never would have known who you were if they hadn't watched your show faithfully every week. *Maiken Trouble* was their favourite show. After it was cancelled, they vowed never to watch NBC again. My father even wrote a letter to the president of the network to say so."

Jesus. A whole damned family with squirrels in the attic.

When we pulled up to the house, the Galaxy 500 was gone. "Your father's out," I said. I didn't know what to make of that, but I was relieved.

"What makes you say that?" asked Kelly.

"His car is gone. The Galaxy."

"That's my uncle's car. My father doesn't drive. Neither of my parents has a driver's license."

I was speechless. I had never heard of anyone who didn't drive, unless they were crippled, or only nine years old. Everyone I knew drove, even if they didn't own a car. "Are they cripples?" If they were, I wanted to be prepared.

Kelly squeaked with laughter. "Of course not. They just don't want to pollute the air. And they don't want to support the oil conglomerates. They get around fine on their bicycles."

"Bicycles—"

"You know, those things with only two wheels and no motor? You make them go with your feet. You must have seen them around." She was teasing me.

They were waiting for us on the front step.

"Here they are, at last," said Mr. Boyce. He spread his arms in a welcoming gesture. He wore blue jeans and Birkenstocks. His remaining hair was graying, pulled back in a short ponytail. He squinted through round, rimless glasses. Mrs. Boyce stood behind him, a bundle of homespun clothing and straw hair that was held in place with an elaborate system of clips and ties.

My God, they were hippies!

As we came up the walk, Kelly leaned into me and whispered, "Whatever you do, don't let Daddy talk to you about politics. And don't mention John Lennon. They're still in mourning."

And then we were one big happy, hugging, hand-shaking family.

"Welcome, welcome," said Mr. Boyce. He pumped my hand, limply. "So wonderful to finally meet you, Mister Fox."

"Billy," I said. "Call me Billy."

"Sure, okay. I'm Dan, and this is Dawn." He pulled Mrs. Boyce away from her daughter and thrust her at me. As we embraced, I noted that she smelled like a haystack. I backed out of the hug and looked more closely at her.

Advice to men: When you are selecting the woman you will spend the rest of your life with, it is wise to give close scrutiny to the girl's mother. She will, more often than not, be a fairly accurate representation of what your potential life-mate will look and act like, in just a few short decades. The mother is a crystal ball, permitting you to see into the future. Take note: if you have neglected to check out the mother *before* you have committed yourself to the girl, close scrutiny is not recommended.

I was surprised to note that they didn't have a lava lamp. There were no black lights or beaded curtains. The living room was what I expected in that neighbourhood: plain, uninspired, tasteless in a middle-class sort of way. They had a dog, of course.

"Down, Dean! Down!" shouted Dawn.

Dean was an enthusiastic black Labrador with a thick tail that he swung like a truncheon at everything at coffee table height. As Dean was stencilling my shirt and slacks with muddy paw prints, his tail swished a crystal candy dish onto the floor.

"Dean! Stop that!" shouted Dawn, relentlessly.

I pushed him off me, and there went the coasters that had been stacked neatly on a side table.

"Good boy," said Dan, patting Dean heartily on his oily back, as if he had obeyed. Dean circled the room, setting the fireplace tools to chime, flinging the latest issue of National Geographic onto the carpet, and jamming his dripping nose into Kelly's crotch (it may have been an accident, but even a smart dog can play dumb and get away with it).

"You'll get used to him," Dan said to me.

Why would I want to?

Kelly and her mother went to the kitchen to fetch us drinks. I needed one fairly urgently. The several I'd had earlier, to fortify myself for the visit, were wearing off. Dean followed the women, smart dog. Dan and I sat down.

"We were all pretty upset when your show was cancelled, Billy."

Here we go. "I can assure you," I said, "no one was more upset than me."

Dan nodded. "Clearly, the network wasn't aware of how important the show was."

Well, it was important to me, to my reputation and to my bank account. Otherwise, I couldn't imagine what might be important about it. "What do you mean, Dean?"

"Dan."

Damn.

Dan settled back. "You see, on the surface, *Maiken Trouble* seems like any other run-of-the-mill television drama. The plots are predictable, the characters are cliché and the language they speak is simple enough to be understood by the common man. But after watching a few episodes, it dawned on Dawn and me that there was a deeper meaning to the show. It wasn't just an hour of mindless fluff. I mean, sure, we all couldn't wait until the end, to see if you were going to get the girl, and we certainly knew that you were going to get your man. Those things are obvious. But the way I see it, the show was really a metaphor."

"A metaphor," I repeated. I nodded, crossed my legs, wondered what was taking so long with the drinks. "Interesting."

Dan was on a roll. "*Maiken Trouble* addresses a conflict we've been struggling with for generations: gender identity."

What?

"Ever since Susan B. Anthony raised the flag of women's rights, we've been confused about our roles—both men and women. Suddenly, men are trying to be *sensitive,* while women are trying to be ruthless. It's an impossible mission. Now, Billy, I'm the first to admit that a man *should* try be sensitive to a woman's needs, but I also believe that there are gender-specific roles that humans are meant to fulfil, and there are valid and practical reasons for us all to embrace and encourage those roles. I'm not here to say that the clocks should be rolled back, that women should be oppressed, or treated as chattel. I don't condone violence against women. Let them vote, and let them be educated. But let's face it: as men, it goes against our nature to be kind and understanding. Those qualities have always been the woman's domain. And it's just as unreasonable to expect women to meld into the cut-throat world of business or politics without feeling confused or disillusioned. After all, women have a conscience, whereas men have merely *guilt*. It's an important distinction, one that brings balance to Nature."

At last, the Boyce women arrived with the drinks. They passed the glasses around quietly, careful not to distract Dan from his speech.

"The business of living in a civilized world can be complicated and difficult. But it becomes much easier to cope when you know where you fit in. We spend so much time wondering how we are supposed to act, as modern men and women, we let the important things fall through the cracks. Should you hold a door open for a woman, Billy? If you do, you might be insulting a woman who wants to prove to the world that she can open the door herself. If you don't, you might be insulting a woman who would have appreciated the help. Either way, you lose. You have wasted all that mental energy wondering what to do, instead of pondering the more important issues in life. And the women lose because they are being insulted. A hundred years ago, the question never would have entered your mind. You would have held the door open, and the woman would have been grateful."

Dawn was nodding and nodding. Clearly, she had heard this all before. Kelly sat beside me, listening with riveted interest—her mother's daughter.

"Just imagine an army where all the grunts decided that they wanted to be Generals. What if infantrymen suddenly decided that they didn't want to be infantrymen any longer, that they wanted to be paratroopers, instead? What if radiomen wanted to be medics? It would be bedlam. Civilization, like the army, works best when we all have carefully laid out roles. There needs to be the proper balance of leaders and followers if it's going to function successfully.

"All this is to say that *Maiken Trouble* was important because it portrayed gender as it should be, as many of us, consciously or not, want it to be in real life. It may have seemed like just another detective show, but it was really a fantasy, reminding us all of what we have lost over the years. In other words, it was a show where men were men and women were women, in the most traditional sense."

"How interesting that you picked up on that," I said, as if the metaphor had been my idea.

"Daddy's a social worker," Kelly said, proudly.

"Really?" I looked at him. "That explains your keen insight." I was as full of shit as Dan.

"Mother's a social worker, too," Kelly said.

I nearly lost a mouthful of bourbon. "Oh? You work?" After the speech I just got from Dan, I wondered that Dawn was wearing shoes.

Dawn smiled pleasantly. "Dan and I met in the Peace Corp. We were stationed in Rhodesia. When we saw how awful things were over in Africa, we just had to do something. At first, we were going to stay there, to help any way we could, but Dan realized that it would be more appropriate if we came home, to help our own people. Take care of your own family, first. That was our motto. That's how we became social workers."

"Isn't that romantic?" Kelly swooned, dropped her head on my shoulder.

"Terrific," I said.

Dean was circling again. His tail suddenly swept away two wine glasses. My own glass was safely at my lips.

"Dean!" shouted Dawn. "Stop that, Dean!"

Dan patted the dog as he shuffled by. "You rascal," he said, scratching the dog's ears. What did Dan care? It clearly wasn't *his* job to clean up Dean's messes.

Beep... "Hi, Mom. You can tell Dad I will be in this Thursday's episode of Heritage Creek. It's the opening scene, so don't be late switching on. I'm pretty sure there's no hockey game that night. By the way, I got married last month. Her name is Kelly. Just thought you'd like to know."

Later that day, there was a horrible screeching noise emanating from my answering machine. At first, I thought the machine had finally packed it in, but then I realized it was just a message from my mother. Apparently, mothers don't like to be kept out of the loop, when weddings are being planned. Live and learn. To mollify her, I mailed her an official wedding photo, taken by Dave Small (our official photographer), of the happy couple standing in front of old City Hall. In the photograph, the tops of our heads are cut off, but at least the shot is more or less in focus. Only a few of the other snaps turned out at all. My beloved Selena was not the only one who needed glasses.

I arrived at Herb's office ten minutes late.

"You have to wait, Billy," said Mrs. Semple. She was a stern and efficient secretary, who had been protecting Herb from the outside world for more than twenty years. If she had a first name, no one knew what it was. Even Herb called her Mrs. Semple. During the twelve years that I had been with the agency, she had never asked me to wait.

"Wait?"

"Have a seat, Billy," she said, organizing the important documents on her desk. "He needs a minute."

"Since when does Herb need a minute? Is he a goddamned movie star, all of a sudden?"

Mrs. Semple gave me a look that drew all the blood to my lower limbs. She knew how to handle thugs. "Sit down, Billy."

A minute later, Les Dodd walked out of Herb's office. He spotted me sulking in the corner. "Hey, Billy! What a coincidence. Herb and I were just talking about you."

"I'll bet," I said, shaking his hand, anyway.

"I just signed on," he said. "I had a lot of offers, but I chose Herb because he represents you. I figure if he can do for me half of what he's done for you, I'll be in great shape."

I'm certain I saw Mrs. Semple roll her eyes.

"Sure, Les, sure."

"Listen, I have to run. They're remodelling my trailer today and I have to make sure they don't botch the colour."

"Right." If I'd only had a pen, I'd have stabbed him in the throat. "Give my regards to Jackie."

"We broke up," he said, casually. "She was only using me to advance her career." He strode away, like a smug bastard.

I stalked into Herb's office.

"Go ahead and sit down, Billy," said Herb.

"I've *been* sitting," I said, sitting.

"What?"

I jerked a thumb over my shoulder. "Out there. Missus Semple made me *sit*."

"Don't be a baby. Missus Semple makes everybody sit."

"Not me," I said. "She's never made me sit before. Today, she made me sit. She said you needed a minute."

"Well, she did the right thing. I did need a minute. Didn't you see Les Dodd leave my office?"

"Sure. He managed to insult me several times before he left. I suppose it's your turn, just to make my day complete."

"You're not my only client."

"I've single-handedly financed your children's college education."

Herb nodded. "That's more or less true."

"And this is the thanks I get. Missus Semple makes me sit."

"I needed the minute, Billy."

"So I heard."

"Anyway, I thought I had something for you, but it fell through."

That wasn't what I needed to hear. "I'm just about broke, Herb. The insurance on the Corvette is due, and I can't afford to pay it."

"I don't want to sound like a broken record, but I keep hearing about your drinking. It's a problem that you need to get a handle on. You're on the shit list."

"I quit drinking, last week," I lied. I supposed I could give it a shot, but I didn't see why I should put myself out just to make up for Herb's shortcomings as an agent.

"Good, good. That's a start. In the meantime, you should think about taking on some smaller jobs. I know you don't want to hear that, but you need to demonstrate to the Donald Dukes out there that you've still got it."

"Get me anything that pays." I had to keep my car on the road.

"That's the spirit, Billy. By the way, how's married life treating you?"

"Super."

Herb's mouth was smiling, but the rest of his face was a frown. I knew he wanted me to say we were at each other's throats, that lawyers would soon be involved. Bully for him. To be honest, I was beginning to enjoy married life. I couldn't figure out what everyone else was complaining about. Anyone with imagination and a telephone repairman's jacket can make it work. I never knew what I was going to come home to. Sometimes, when I walked through the door, Kelly would scream, and make a run for it. I always caught her easily, quickly subdued her, although she would squirm and struggle until I had forced myself upon her. Once, she nearly clobbered me with a frying pan, trying to get away. Another time, she had somehow bound her own arms and legs so expertly, I had trouble getting her out of it. "Did you like that, Billy?" she asked, every time, when it was all over. One day, I lashed her to a support beam and forced her to eat an entire loaf of Wonder Bread. "Let's have a party, tonight," she'd said, after swallowing the last crust. "I want to meet your friends." One of these days, I thought, I'll take her up on it.

"I'm here for the recording session," I said to the receptionist.

"Which one? We have seven studios."

"The commercial."

"All of our sessions today are commercials. You'll have to be more specific."

The foyer wobbled drunkenly. "I don't know. It could be a beer commercial."

The receptionist ran several blurry fingers along her schedule. "That narrows it down to four. Do you know who the agency is?"

"Uh…Something & Something."

She huffed. "That doesn't narrow it down at all. Have a seat."

First Mrs. Semple, now this one. It was some sort of conspiracy. "No thanks. I'll stand," I said, collapsing into a chair. I shut my eyes in a futile effort to stop the room from spinning.

"Are you Fox?" shouted a voice behind me.

When I opened my eyes, I was struck with wonder and awe. There was definitely something wrong with the cosmos. The man who had called me was somehow standing on the ceiling, which, as far as I knew, was impossible. "How are you doing that?" I asked.

He ignored my question. "You're over an hour late. Let's go!"

I tried to get up, and realized that he only appeared to be upside down because my head was tipped over the back of the chair. I lost my orientation as I tried to fall up, and fell down instead. Next thing, an arm was gripping me, lifting me roughly to my feet.

"You drunken asshole," shouted the man. I believed him, completely.

"I'm not drunk," I slurred.

Two hands grabbed me by the collar and shook me.

"Hey! Stop that! Do you have any idea who I am?"

Two bloodshot eyes stared into my face. "You're a drunken asshole. Now, I'll tell you who I am. I'm the guy who is signing your paycheque for this session. I'm the guy who's going to deduct the cost of this studio from your paycheque for the hour you wasted. I'm the guy who's going to get a performance out of you, in spite of your condition. I'm the guy who's going to make sure the agency doesn't know you're a drunken asshole because, if they find out, it will make *me* look like an asshole. Got it?"

I shut one eye, to reduce the number of paycheque signers by half. That seemed to help. "I missed the part after 'You're a drunken asshole.'"

The hands let go of my lapels. "Is that a grape juice stain? What the fuck are you wearing?"

I looked down. "Pajamas."

"Pajamas—"

"You say *pa-ja-mas*, I say *py-jah-mas*—" I did a little soft shoe, a manoeuvre that might have been mistakenly interpreted as an attempt to fall down. "You say *tomay-to*, I say—"

The hands pushed me toward a corridor. "Don't speak to anyone. Do everything I say and just nod. If you embarrass me, I'll see to it that you never do another commercial again, with anyone."

"Commercials are for losers," I mumbled. I was pretty sure his shoe struck my buttocks.

I was put on a stool in front of the microphone. I couldn't see the window to the control room; the paycheque signer had moved a portable baffle between me and the two-inch glass—for acoustical reasons, he said.

"We're ready to take a stab at it, Billy," said the intercom, finally. "Are you ready? Just nod. We can see the top of your head."

I nodded.

"Okay, Billy. We're rolling. Anytime..."

I unleashed my glorious voice upon them. Drunk or not, the plumbing still worked. I got my paycheque, minus the hour of studio time, of course, and I never did another commercial voice-over.

"Have you ever thought about getting a job?"

Kelly stroked my forehead and kissed my cheek. "Of course not, Billy. I wouldn't do that to you."

"Right."

"It wouldn't be fair to our children," she said.

"What children?"

The tears poured out.

Advice to men: Avoid causing unnecessary tears. When the man of the house is upset, he is a ridiculous cry-baby who can be ignored. When the woman of the house is upset, it is customary for everyone else in the house to be upset, too. Her tears cannot be ignored, nor can they be called ridiculous (see earlier Advice re: ridiculous). There can be no peace until the woman is pacified.

I sold the Bang & Olufsen. I inquired at a pawn shop, but the greasy lout behind the glass told me that he never paid more than two hundred for anything.

"If you bring a fucking Rolls Royce in here, two bills is the best I could do," he said. "I have to draw the line somewhere."

"I paid forty-five hundred for it, two years ago. It's in perfect condition. It's worth at least half that. But I'll settle for two grand."

"Take a zero off, and you've got a deal."

I looked at him more closely. There was something familiar about him. "Do you drive a rusty Lada?"

"Yeah, why?"

"Fat bastard!" I stomped out. I advertised the stereo in the paper, and sold it for seven hundred dollars. Just enough to keep the Corvette on the road for another year.

Since I had no work, and I was already sunk into a suicidal depression, I took Kelly to Calgary to meet my family. I had stalled the trip, claiming temporary impoverishment, and my mother rendered my argument moot by sending two airline tickets.

"We're here for you, honey," she said, over the telephone. "If you need money to get your life back on track, all you have to do is ask. To be perfectly honest, your father and I have been expecting this for some time. You gave it your best shot, but we're all glad you've finally come to your senses. I knew that the responsibilities of having a family would make you see the light. I know it's a shock, but everyone goes through it. Just wait until your first child is born, Billy. Your life will never be the same again."

Fortunately, I let the answering machine pick up that call. There's no telling what I might have said to my mother. When Kelly heard the bit about our first-born child, she burst into tears and fled to the bathroom. She was desperate to get pregnant.

"If I can't have your baby," she wailed, "what use am I? What have I got to give you, other than children?" Lately, after making love, she would leap out of bed (or wherever) and stand on her head, leaning her heels against the loft walls. The first time I witnessed her doing this, I thought she wanted me to do something new to her, but she shooed me away. "I'm letting gravity help your little babies find the mark," she said. One time, she remained in that position until she passed out.

"Whatever makes you happy, darling."

"I'm doing it to make *you* happy."

Her mother's daughter.

Five minutes of a Calgary December was enough to set my stomach to churn. It was the one place I hated to go more than anywhere else. A desaturated sprawl of "earth tone" bungalows and pickup trucks. A poky downtown core that aspired to cosmopolitan *chic* the way the Japanese aspired to western-style pop music credibility—both hopelessly provincial. A patchwork of homogenized suburban conformity that bred dullness like mould and hewed the rest like a cancerous tumour. A hive of accountants and insurance adjusters and civil engineers. A city of failed expectations—for me, anyway.

As we disembarked, I said to Kelly, "Let me to apologize in advance for my family."

She had learned to ignore my cynical remarks. Strolling toward the arrival gate, my wife attracted many curious and leering glances. She carried a coat over her arm, which allowed the international population in the terminal to take in the full effect of her new dress. We couldn't really afford to shop, but she wanted so desperately to impress my family, I relented, putting another charge on my over-burdened credit card. The dress was red and short and just loose enough to swish intoxicatingly when she walked. There were no discernible lines beneath the garment, as if she worked for Miracle Films as a hot tub maiden. ("Just in case you want to have me," she said, before we boarded.) She could have passed for a model. The only thing she lacked was a love of the lens. In all her photographs, she looked a little frightened.

My parents were waiting for us. "Hello, honey," my mother said, almost hugging me. She was not an affectionate woman, keeping the physical contact to a minimum—which suited me. "Welcome home."

Right. My home was over two thousand miles away, appreciating with each passing year, as the trend setters began to discover what a loft was.

"You must be Kelly," she said, offering up a similarly vague embrace to my wife.

But Kelly came from a family of huggers. She was never going to be satisfied with my mother's vagueness. She pulled my mother in and kissed both her cheeks. "It's so wonderful to finally meet you, Missus Fox," she gushed. "I only wish we had some special news to give you, but we're trying very hard to start a family. I promise. We can't wait to have a baby!"

Jesus! She was pouring it on pretty thick.

My father lurked in the background. He looked the same as always: blank. He had acquired the blank look years earlier, in order to mask his disenchantment with having a son who was determined to "goof off" for a living. He shook my hand. "Hello, Billy." He was built like a man who had spent his entire life at manual labour, but he was not tall. I had looked down on him since my seventeenth birthday. Still, I always found his obvious strength intimidating.

Whenever I looked at my parents, I couldn't help wondering where I got my looks. Even after removing the deleterious effects of the railroad from my father, he was never anything more than a dog-faced brute. And I had seen enough photographs of my mother as a young woman to know that her most redeeming feature was a set of ears that didn't stick out like jug handles (in contrast to the rest of her family). As for my sister, Jane, there was no mistaking who she got her looks from: she was a dog-faced brute, too.

(It had been a long-standing fantasy of mine to one day discover I was adopted, that I had beautiful and loving biological parents out there somewhere, who followed my successful career in show business with silent pride. But a few years back, I learned the hard way that I was indeed my father's son. I had inherited the congenital heart defect that put him in an early grave, before his sixtieth birthday, and nearly sent me along after him. I persist to live. I am not eager to meet his blank gaze at the Pearly Gates. "I'm not finished goofing off, yet, old man.")

Kelly gave my father a typical Boyce-style greeting. The poor man couldn't tear his eyes away from her red dress, and its lack of lines. He probably hadn't been hugged in thirty years.

We fell into the spacious and pristine vinyl seats of William Fox Sr.'s 1963 Pontiac. Nearly two decades later, it still smelled as new as it looked. A slight depression in the driver's seat was the only indication that the car hadn't been driven off the lot yesterday.

As a teenager who clearly required guidance in my development towards becoming a useful citizen, I had been enlisted by my father to spend a part of my Saturday mornings helping him clean the Pontiac. But I had stubbornly refused to use a toothbrush on the spokes in the hubcaps. It just didn't seem right to me. Our relationship went downhill from there. I was irresponsible. I was lazy. I didn't appreciate the value of things. Worst of all, I was aimless. The fact that I knew, by age fourteen, that I was going to be an actor did not persuade my father that I had direction. Ambition was related to serious things, such as a welding apprenticeship, or a Class D driver's license. Acting was not serious, in Senior's view (yes, we all called him Senior—even my mother).

I sat up front, with Senior. "There's no snow," I said. A blanket of snow would have spared me the full impact of the offensive "earth tone" theme that pervaded the city. Everything was a shade of brown that caused my jaw to clench.

"Wait fifteen minutes," said Senior. That was the closest thing to a joke he ever told.

"Jane couldn't come," said my mother, from the backseat. "She's just started her new job at Eaton's."

"She's really making something of herself, that girl," Senior chimed in.

"Junior Assistant Buyer."

"She and Cliff are finishing their basement. They're putting in a pool table and a dart board. Cliff's putting in a wet bar."

"They drive a van, now."

"They're taking the kids to Disneyland in March."

How times change! Jane and I spent the better part of a decade begging my father to take us to Disneyland. "What makes you think I'm prepared to spend a week putting you two ingrates on rides and stuffing your faces with ice cream, when I could spare myself the aggravation and just throw all that money out the window?" He never took us anywhere that didn't require us to sleep on the ground. His favourite trick was to send us to summer camp, so that he and my mother would be excused from that particular discomfort.

"How nice for them," I said, distantly.

"You bet it is."

The start of a long week.

Jane and family arrived for dinner. I was always surprised to remember what a bore Cliff was. He worked as a cameraman at the local television station, and therefore felt he and I—both being in show business—had something in common.

"We had Eddie Lawson in the studio, last week," said Cliff, handing me a drink. (Kelly was in the kitchen with my mother and sister, no doubt being told what a loser she had just married.) "He was promoting his new movie, some piece of shit that I'll probably rent when it comes out on video, just because it has Jeanette Winters in it."

"Right."

Cliff's goal in life was to have met more famous people than me. It was a competition he pursued with vigour, and one I couldn't be bothered to engage in. If it made him feel better about his small life in the backwoods, let him have his little victories. "I don't suppose you ever met him, eh?"

I shrugged.

"He's fucking Jeanette Winters," he said. "He told me himself."

That was untrue on both counts. First of all, Eddie Lawson would never confide in a peon like Cliff. I also have a foggy recollection of witnessing Eddie in a grope with a well-rippled clapper boy behind a stack of apple boxes on the set of *Painting the Cherry*. Maybe it was true, what they say about all actors these days. In any case, I wasn't going to let my goofball brother-in-law draw me into this ridiculous discussion. He evidently had no idea I was in the movie, and I was not inclined to enlighten him, for the simple reason that such a disclosure would just prolong our conversation. I let him go on and on until he ran out of steam.

I was saved from Cliff when one of my anonymous nephews was spotted in the living room attempting to swing Senior's nine iron. He managed to dent the stereo cabinet and knock over a teak magazine rack before the club was wrestled from him. There were two more nephews lurking, and they were all out of control. My sister and her husband did not believe in discipline. They had read a book, after the first boy was born, that suggested love, rather than a good spanking, would guarantee a well-adjusted child. The book had to have been a joke, but they took it seriously. As a result, their three sons were growing into magnificent vandals, running amuck with impunity, utterly lacking in regard for authority or property. And because of all that bad behaviour, they were hugged and kissed relentlessly. If only Senior had read that book, thirty years ago. Some kids get all the luck.

My father filled the empty spot Cliff left. "We watched that show of yours," he said, trying to sound casual. We had never known how to talk to each other. There was nothing easy between us. "The Heritage thing."

"Uh huh."

He made a sucking noise with his teeth. "You could have been nicer to that fella."

"What?"

"That fella in the cover-alls. You were pretty disrespectful. I don't want to tell you how to run your life, but you're never going to get anywhere talking to people like that. I may only be a railroad man, but I know how to treat somebody with respect. It's no wonder you can't get yourself a real job, talking to people like that."

"It's called acting, Dad. I was acting."

"Give it a fancy name, Billy. It still adds up to disrespect, in the end."

"Yes sir," I said. Why bother? It wasn't worth the effort.

He sucked his teeth some more. He couldn't look at me. "How's the dentistry thing going?"

"The what?"

"Your mother said you were in dental college. I suppose you've been kicked out of that, by now."

I nodded. "Yeah. They kicked me out. I didn't have the stomach for it, anyway."

He nodded. "No doubt."

I had to give him credit, he was at least trying to communicate. He wanted to find something about me to be proud of, and I wanted him to have it, but I knew it would never happen, so long as I was an actor—a "goof off." (If Senior were alive today, I know what he'd say to me: "Son, it's taken you half a century, but you've finally found respectability. Being a waiter is nothing to be ashamed of, son. Take it from an old railroad man. No job is menial. I'm proud of you." He might even look me in the eye.)

Something in another room shattered. Childish shrieks resounded. I heard Cliff's heavy feet pounding down a hallway. My father shuffled away to inspect the latest catastrophe.

Jane emerged from the kitchen with Kelly in tow. They carried trays of crackers and carrot sticks and dip. I watched my sister as she arranged the trays on the coffee table. She resembled my father too much for me to like her. She thought she was fashionable, but the way I see it, if you put a three-piece suit on a monkey, you have a monkey in a three-piece suit. Every time I saw her, she was a little fatter than the time before. She worked too hard at her hair. A cresting wave of bangs rolled out toward me ominously. She must have spent an hour staring into the mirror, gluing the wave in place, ignoring the rest. From any angle other than directly frontal, the neglect was apparent. She never checked her own profile, had no idea what was going on behind those bangs. She made me think of the back lot at the Miracle Films studios, where the well-dressed façade of a house is propped up from behind by a mesh of raw timber.

"I tried to tell that girl of yours what a loser you were," she said, coming at me with those bangs. "But she claims not to notice."

Kelly proved it by pressing into me and kissing me deeply. As her tongue was working my mouth, I was keenly aware that, in all likelihood, no one had ever kissed Jane like that. Cliff had probably stopped kissing my sister years ago. Who could blame him? Who wants to kiss a blow-dried dog?

I didn't look up any of my old friends in Calgary. I couldn't face them. And I was uncomfortable introducing Kelly to them, given her predilections. I allowed a steady wash of bourbon to carry me through the week. I permitted my family's derogative commentary to roll over me. By the week's end, I decided that I didn't need my family any more than I needed my old friends. I was through with them all. I never wanted to set foot in Calgary again. I meant it, this time.

Chapter 11

Tired and dejected after a long week with my family, I was glad to be home. We rolled up to the love loft after midnight, only to find the front door open. To be precise: the door had been *kicked* open. I discovered it's no use having a metal door if it is hinged on a rotting wooden door frame. Live and learn.

I was suddenly glad I had already sold the Bang & Olufsen. There was not much else of value. The thief left the television, which was too heavy to carry off. The rock-hard pinstriped loveseat that Selena had left behind had been slashed into rags, and the matching valances had been pulled off the walls. This burglar had some taste, I confess. I had meant to do the same, myself. Once the mess was sorted out, I discovered that the only item missing was my telephone repairman jacket, the one with the name "Bud" sewn onto the breast pocket. Kelly was devastated.

"I told you to get out of that crummy neighbourhood, Billy." That was Herb, offering his usual sage advice. "What if the thief comes back when your wife is alone at home?"

I wondered about that for a moment. I couldn't be sure Kelly would mind.

Herb sipped his coffee and winced.

"Why do you put all that sugar in your coffee? I get all puckered up, just watching you drink that shit."

"I'm trying to quit the stuff. My stomach's bad. I figure if I put enough sugar in it, it'll put me off it for good."

"You've been spiking your coffee with a dozen sugar cubes for years."

"Yep. I think it's starting to work. I'm down to six cups a day."

"You're killing me, Herb. What have you got for me? I'm running on fumes. I need a paycheque."

His shoulders dropped. "Not much on the table, Billy. These are lean times. There's not much coming in for anybody, right now."

"I'm not anybody."

"These slow periods never last long. I hear Woody Allen's casting his new movie. He has a pretty tight group he likes to work with, but he's got a couple of spots open. I'll drop your name in the hat and we'll see what happens. In the meantime, you should think about the summer."

"What about the summer?"

"There's a lot of regional stuff going on."

"Regional stuff?"

"You know, stuff in the regions. Out of town stuff."

"You're talking about summer stock, aren't you?"

"Yes. Yes, I am."

I sighed. I tried to swallow, but my mouth was as dry as Wasaga Beach. I looked at Herb. He looked well fed. This year, Les Dodd would pay for his office renovation. "So, this is what it has come to. Billy Fox does summer stock."

"You're not the first actor to hit a dry spell. Look at Brando. Look at Tony Curtis."

"Bernard Schwartz," I said, distantly.

"Who?" He shrugged. "Whatever. What I'm trying to say is that it happens more often than we think. Writers get blocked, artists lose their inspiration, actors have slumps. They bounce back."

"Not always."

"Sometimes."

"Where does that leave me?"

"The Huron Country Playhouse in Grand Bend, this July. They're doing *The Mousetrap*, and they need a Detective Sergeant Trotter."

"Jesus. Another bloody detective. I might as well be Gilligan."

"I can put out feelers. See if they want you."

"Why wouldn't they want me?"

Herb just looked at me. "We're done, here, Billy. Leave it with me. I'll send a package to Mister Allen, and call Huron."

I had a little trouble on the way home.

After leaving Herb's office, I was admittedly in a foul mood. The growl of the Corvette's V8 always made me feel better. When I spotted a rusty Lada two blocks ahead, I might have accelerated beyond the limits of speed permitted by law. It's just possible I swerved into the oncoming lane in order to get around several slow-moving motorists, but I zealously deny that I clipped the rear bumper of a parked van, and I am willing to testify before God (or anyone in authority) that the cyclist simply wasn't paying attention, and ran himself up the curb (and, out of embarrassment, he had to blame someone else).

The first indication I had that anything was wrong was when I spotted the flashing lights in the rearview mirror. I slowed down and pulled to the right, to let the cop pass, but the cruiser angled in behind me and stopped. I recapped the thermos and slid it under the passenger seat, as a precaution. Not that I was worried. The uniforms and patrol cars did not intimidate me. Joe Maiken had had many friends on the police force. Of course, he didn't put much stock in their abilities. In fact, he counted on their incompetence. It meant more work for him. In Joe Maiken's experience, the cops always showed up at the end, after it was all over, after he had already done the work. All the cops did was haul the thug off to jail and take the credit. Not that Joe cared about credit, he wasn't in this business for the glory—he was in it for the women.

I watched in the side mirror as the cruiser door opened and a pair of legs emerged: female legs. What luck! I unfastened one more button on my shirt and fluffed my hair. I checked my teeth in the mirror, switched the radio to the jazz station, and gave the V8 a sultry little rev.

"Please shut off the engine, sir," said the coppette, filling the space outside my window with wonderful hips.

"Yes ma'am," I said. I turned the key back one notch, allowing the jazz to continue, setting the mood for our exchange.

"Please shut off the radio, sir," she said, probably a country music fan. That didn't bode well.

I turned to face the coppette, giving her the full impact of my winning smile. She didn't appear to be impressed, which I took as a personal blow. My winning smile had never failed before. This coppette was inscrutable.

She was not gorgeous, but she was attractive, and she looked strong. Her hips moved slightly, next to my face. She gave no indication she recognized me, but I knew that cops were trained at the police academy to maintain that steely gaze under the most extreme conditions. This gal was a real pro. She must have been at the top of her class. "What can I do for you, ma'am?" It was exciting to call her "ma'am."

"Have you been drinking, sir?"

"Drinking?"

"Alcohol."

"You know," I said, trying to bring the conversation around to a more personal level, "I suspect we both share a common interest."

The steely gaze was chiselled in granite. "What's that, sir?"

"Speed. I'll bet your cruiser is an even match for this Corvette, at least on a straightaway. I'll bet you get a rush out of hitting the gas pedal, hearing the roar of all that horsepower."

"Speed kills, sir," said the coppette. "Especially when alcohol is involved. Step out of the car, please." The hips moved away.

This was my opportunity to really impress. I unfolded myself from the driver's seat, all six feet of me, and looked up at her. She was an Amazon! I thought I would burst with lust.

"You were travelling at a high rate of speed, sir." She was all business.

"It's hard to tell, in a Corvette."

"You crossed into the oncoming lane, twice."

It's hard to tell, when you are drunk, and speeding. I wisely chose not to say that out loud. "I was trying to catch up to a fat bastard in a rusty Lada. Did you see him? He's been terrorizing women at stoplights for some time. Some sort of pervert. I almost had him when you stopped me. I have reason to believe he's a pawnbroker."

"That's very interesting, sir," she said, showing no interest at all. "Are you aware that you nearly struck a cyclist?"

"Well," I said, smoothly, "I think 'nearly' is the operative word."

"Are you aware that you struck a parked vehicle, three blocks back?"

Suddenly, I was indignant. "I most certainly did not!" I slurred.

"A red van, sir. I witnessed the collision."

"I think I would know if I was involved in a collision, ma'am." Calling the coppette "ma'am" was losing its thrill.

"Come with me," she said, leading me to the passenger side of my car. "How do you explain the dent in the front quarter panel, with streaks of red paint, sir?"

The sight of the dent caused my heart to flutter. My beloved car was brutalized. "I—"

"Sir, now would be a good time for you to show me your license and registration."

Still reeling from the shock of seeing my crumpled fender, I complied.

She looked at it for a long time, and then looked at me. "I suppose you're trying to tell me that your name is Krisha Bottomly, and that you are a seventeen-year-old girl, *sir*."

Rats. "I don't know how that got in there."

"Your daughter, perhaps?"

Cripes! How old do I look? "She's my assistant." I wasn't about to confess to porking a minor. This coppette was a straight lace. "Look, don't get any funny ideas. I never touched her. I'm a married man. That girl did *not* sleep with me in Algonquin Park, and she certainly wasn't living with me during the month my girlfriend was in New York."

"I thought you said you were married, sir."

"I am. I mean, I wasn't back then, when Krisha was living with me."

"I see."

I handed her my real driver's license, took back Krisha's.

"William Fox, Junior," said the coppette.

"Billy," I said, smoothly. "Billy Fox. Believe it, or not, that's my real name."

"Why wouldn't I believe it? Do you have other names?"

"No. It's just that I'm an actor. Maybe you recognize me." I gave her the suave grin of a private eye who has just satisfied another gorgeous client.

"I don't watch television. It rots the brain."

I nodded. "I've always said that, myself. Anyway, I do mostly feature films, and theatre, of course."

"Hmm. Is this an old picture?"

Advice to men: It is rarely a good idea to raise your voice and call police officers names. The rule of thumb, during any exchange with law enforcement, is this: no matter how wrong, rude, stupid or unfeeling the officer is, she is always right. If you happen to forget, be aware that, unlike in the United States, in Canada you are not constitutionally entitled to a telephone call. But, if you ask nicely, they will often permit you that privilege.

After I was arrested, I began to have superstitious thoughts for the first time. Were the gods toying with me? Was Fate having a little fun at my expense? I tried to recall if I had broken a mirror lately, or stepped on a black cat, or whatever.

At seven o'clock the next morning, they threw me, and twenty or thirty other hapless and detoxicated victims of Fate, out of the drunk tank and into the quiet streets of January. We gripped our own shoulders and drifted away, in twenty or thirty different directions, in search of a four-leaf clover.

On my way out, I had inquired about my car, and was told I should contact Traffic Services, in order to find out which impound lot it had been towed to. I asked if I could use the telephone, but I must have not asked nicely enough. The ruddy-faced brute behind the glass told me to "fuck off."

"Yes, sir," I said.

By the time I let myself in, the loft was quiet. It was early. My plan was to get into bed without waking up Kelly, and hope that she wouldn't notice I had been gone all night. I kicked off my shoes and padded softly toward the bathroom (back in the drunk tank, I had refused to urinate in front of twenty or thirty malodorous derelicts), when I suddenly saw a blur in a nightie flash before my eyes. I thought I caught a glimpse of a stainless steel colander arcing toward my skull, right before my lights went out.

I woke up in a hospital bed.

When I groaned, Kelly was suddenly on top of me. "Oh, darling!" she cried. Her voice sounded raw, as if she had been crying for a long time. "I'm sorry, darling. I didn't mean to hit you."

"Was that a colander you swung at my head?"

"You always duck. Why didn't you *duck?*"

After a long, sleepless night in the pokey, my reflexes had been a bit slow. "How long have I been here? My back is aching." So was my head, but at least I knew why.

"Two days."

I began to panic. "Cripes, you'd better pack your stuff and get out, before Selena comes back. She'll be here any day, and if she catches you in the loft, there's no telling what she might do."

By now, Kelly was really bawling. "Oh, Billy!" was the only intelligible thing she said before she fled.

I admit I was a little confused. A solid klune on the head will do that to you. I had been dreaming of Selena for two days. Technically, I may have been conscious, but my addled brain was still shrouded in the mist of those dreams. If Kelly had stayed a little longer, I might have called her Krisha—or Marcia, for that matter. I didn't know what was what. And by the time the fog lifted and I understood what I'd said, my wife was long gone, presumably back at the love loft, packing.

I slid out of bed to find a telephone. As soon as I got upright, my legs began to wobble, and a wave of nausea flooded me. I vomited on the floor, and then collapsed in it. Except for the vomit, it felt good to lie on the floor. It felt better to be horizontal again, and the coolness of the floor tiles helped with the nausea.

"What on Earth…" A set of thick ankles and white shoes appeared before my eyes. "What are you doing out of bed, Mister Fox? For heaven's sake." Unseen hands pulled at me.

I wasn't much help. "Just leave me here," I said, weakly.

"You're lying in a mess. I can't leave you on the floor."

"I'm not so thrilled with the puke, myself, but the floor is nice."

"If you needed something, you should have rung the buzzer." The ankles were strong. I felt myself going up. "You'll feel better, once you're back in bed."

"I need a telephone," I said, involuntarily falling back onto the warm mattress. "There's been a mistake. I think my wife is leaving me."

The ankles were gone, and a plump, stern face had taken their place. "I don't know the circumstances, Mister Fox, but I imagine you deserved it," she said. "Men usually do."

"What are you talking about?"

She took my wrist to check my pulse. "I've been married for thirty-one years, and there have been times when I wanted to crack my husband on the head. I'm sure your wife had her own reasons."

"Sure," I said, not quite appreciating this stranger's honesty. "She wanted me to ravish her."

The plump head nodded briskly. "That's what you all think."

"No, really—"

"I have to ask you some questions, now, Mister Fox," she said, cutting me off. "We need to determine how serious your concussion is." She consulted a clipboard. "What year is it?"

"Nineteen-eighty-something." At the best of times, I'd be hard pressed to know what year it was.

"Who is the Prime Minister?"

I had never followed politics. "Er…someone named Fitzpatrick, I think."

"Subtract seven from one hundred, then keep subtracting seven until you reach zero."

"Not a chance." This was some kind of cruel joke. There was only one way to end this: I closed my eyes, feigning sleep. I threw in some phoney snoring, just to convince her that question period was over.

"Hmph!" She tapped the clipboard with her pen. "I never liked your show," she muttered, as she was leaving.

"I heard that!"

Beep…"Darling, don't go. I didn't know what I was saying. My brain was scrambled. I was confused. I need you to stay. I need you. I'm coming home this afternoon. Please be there. I love you."

After I hung up, I realized I meant all that. It made me wonder if I could have been so sincere with Selena. I often regarded Kelly as a somewhat pale imitation of Selena. There was a crucial element missing in Kelly that prevented her from rising above the ranks of the ordinary—an element that Selena had to spare. Yet, despite that crucial shortcoming, it seemed I truly loved her. I was afraid of what I would feel if she really did leave me. When Selena took her flit, I felt betrayed, angry, all the usual stuff. But mostly it was my ego that was hurt. If Kelly abandoned me, I knew my heart would break. Go figure?

I checked myself out of the hospital without asking a doctor's permission. I found my clothes in the closet and simply walked out the front door. No one stopped me. When I arrived home, all trace of Kelly was gone. Once again, the loft looked empty. All the furnishings remained, but Kelly's essence was missing. She had taken her wardrobe, including an extensive array of lingerie, and a few framed photographs of her family. She had left a window open, so even her smell was quickly evaporating.

There was no bourbon left in the cupboard, so I cracked a bottle of red wine. I used a glass, just to convince myself I wasn't a lush. When I woke the next afternoon, I went out to the street, only to remember that my car was still at the impound lot. I made a phone call, hailed a taxi, stopped on the way to pick up Dave Small (since my driver's license had been revoked for three months), and had an argument with the bully at the impound office—which had closed for the day, five minutes earlier.

"What took you so long getting here? This isn't a goddamned parking lot."

"I was in the hospital. I couldn't get here any sooner."

"Not my problem. There's an extra charge for every day the car's here."

"Then let's get this over with. I'll take the car away."

"We're closed."

"But you're still here. How long can this take?"

"You should have been here two days ago."

"I was in a coma!"

"Not my problem. Come back at eight o'clock tomorrow morning."

"I need my car now. I'll pay you for the extra day. Just let me take the car now. Please," I said. I had learned my lesson, dealing with authority.

Another two hundred dollars on my credit card, but I had my car. My beautiful, dented car. I permitted Dave to drive off the lot, and then I switched places with him, dropped him at the Epicure, and then I drove to the Boyce residence, obeying all the speed limits. I had no idea it took so long to get around, driving at the speed limit. How does anybody get anywhere? Even the V8 whined.

Kelly agreed to see me, provided her family could be present. Dean began the meeting by sweeping my teacup onto the carpet with his tail, and then burying his nose in Kelly's crotch in mock shame. Just as well. I wasn't planning to drink the tea.

"Good boy," said Dan.

Dawn glared at me in silent protest, as she cleaned up the mess. I watched mutely as Dean's enthusiastic tail swished near her head. It was only a matter of time. When it finally struck, a shower of clips and straw rained to the carpet, disrupting one side of Dawn's complicated hairdo. "Stop that, Dean!" she shouted. She pushed a small fist into the dog's haunch and shoved his backside away.

His tail began to club Dan's knee. "Ow!" said Dan, laughing.

"What do you want?" asked Kelly. She sat across from me, with her arms folded across her chest. She was wearing one of her old dresses, a homemade frock that made her look like an extra from *Heritage Creek*. All she needed was a bonnet to complete the illusion.

"I want you to come home," I said. My own directness surprised me.

"That isn't what you wanted yesterday."

"I was delirious, darling. I just came out of a coma, for Christ's sake."

"You weren't in a coma."

"I had a serious head injury." I resisted the temptation to remind her that *she* had caused the injury. "I didn't know what I was saying. I was all doped up on painkillers."

"You weren't on painkillers. I wouldn't let them give you drugs."

No wonder I was delirious. "I had a dream—"

"I had a dream, once, too," she said, tearing up. "My dream was to marry Billy Fox. I thought my dream had come true. And then he threw me out."

"I didn't throw you out."

"Do you want me to remind you of what you said?"

"I know what I said, but I didn't mean it. I was confused. I had a concussion, you know. I didn't even know what year it was. I couldn't tell the nurse who the Prime Minister was."

"You never know what year it is, and you have never followed politics."

Dan clucked his tongue at that revelation. "As long as the Liberal Party carries a weak foreign policy, they will never—"

"How can I ever trust you again, Billy? From now on, I'll live every day in fear that if I do one little thing wrong, you'll just throw me away like a piece of garbage. I can't live like that."

"Speaking of garbage," said Dan, "did you know that recycling—"

"I want to feel secure in my marriage. How can I have your children when I can't be sure we won't suddenly be thrown into the streets?"

172

"You're absolutely right, darling," I said. "It won't happen again. I promise."

"I had a dream once," said Dan, dreamily. "Remember that dream, Dawn? The one with the monkey?"

Dawn nodded, tried to push her collapsing hair back up. By the look on her face, she didn't remember the dream quite as fondly as Dan did.

"I'm sorry," I said, to Kelly.

"Don't be sorry, Billy," said Dan. "That's the nature of relationships. Sometimes they're going great, sometimes they're not so great. That's what makes human beings so interesting. You never know what's going to happen next. But this is good. You two are talking it through. Keep the lines of communication open, that's the important thing. If you can do that, you'll be as happy as Dawn and me, some day. Am I right, honey?"

"Right as rain," said Dawn, unconvincingly. She passed a menacing glance at Dean, who was snoring wetly in Kelly's lap.

"Now, what I was about to say about recycling..."

Kelly came home.

Les Dodd got the part in Woody Allen's movie. They wrote him out of *Heritage Creek* at the end of the first season so that he could pursue his movie career. He (Jud) went out to the old Chelsea place, past the river bend, to finally have it out with Nathan Cooke, and got a slug in the chest for his trouble. After murdering Jud, Nathan Cooke fell to Fate's brand of justice when he was trampled in a buffalo stampede.

Beep..."Look, Billy. I know it's you who's been calling and leaving those hateful messages on my machine, and I think it's really childish. I thought we were friends, but I guess you only want friends who aren't as successful or important as you. Get off the booze and go see a shrink, Billy. That's my advice as a friend and a colleague. Get help. And stop phoning me. Next time, I'll call the police."

Beep..."Les, this is Billy Fox. You must have your cover-alls cinched too tight. I'm sure I have better things to do with my time than call you. It was probably just some poor waiter you offended. Who knows? Anyway, you can rest assured I will never dial this telephone number again."

Because I was hand-picked from the acting program at York University and dropped effortlessly into a string of films, before making a splash on television that rocketed me to fame, I was spared the drudgery of spending the early years of my career doing summer stock. Don't get me wrong. I like Neil Simon, I like Agatha Christie, but their work rarely gets due justice in the summer playhouses. On the other hand, there are worse places than Grand Bend to spend the summer. Except for the droves of squealing, jostling tourists that clutter up the narrow streets with their campers and their station wagons, it is a peaceful enclave in a lovely lakeside setting.

Walter Campbell was directing *The Mousetrap*. I knew the name. He had risen to prominence in the early Seventies for his daring interpretations of Shakespeare, at the Stratford Festival. He had shocked and bewildered audiences and critics by injecting song and dance numbers into his famous production of *Othello*. He was considered a genius, until he ran out of new ideas. His rather small bag of tricks had been used up before he was thirty. I hadn't heard his name spoken in years.

"You can run to a bottle of gin," he whispered to me, during our first day of rehearsal, "but you can't hide in it."

Gin was not my drink.

He singled me out of the cast as a confederate, perhaps because I was the only one with any real acting credentials. Everyone else in the company was a bore. Everyone else in the company considered this job their big break. Only Walter and I had *descended* to the pitiable depths of summer stock. We shared a common shame in being there that separated us from the rest.

Walter was bored from the first day. He gave no grand speeches about his take on the play, or the playwright. "Learn your lines and hit your marks," he shouted, from his fifth row seat. "Wake me when it's over." One afternoon, I thought he had really gone to sleep, but partway through the second act he shouted, "Stop!"

I wasn't in the scene. I was slouched in the front row.

"Giles Ralston," he said. "Step forward." He didn't bother to learn his actor's names. He referred to everyone by their character's name. Except for me.

Giles (a thick-limbed kid with no ears named Chester) stepped forward. "Yes, sir?"

"What sort of accent should you be speaking with?"

"British, sir."

"I'd settle for mid-Atlantic."

"I beg your pardon?"

"Can you sound like Barbara Stanwyck in *Ball of Fire*?"

"Um—"

Walter waved a lazy hand. "Forget it kid. Listen, maybe you can just tell me why you sound like Gandhi."

"My family is Welsh, sir. I can't seem to help it. Whenever I try to do British, it comes out Welsh."

"It comes out Paki. You sound like a fucking New York cabbie."

"I'll try harder, sir."

"Splendid. Carry on."

Near the end of the third act, he stopped us again. "Missus Boyle!"

"Hello?"

"What are you doing after your line?"

"I'm standing here, next to the sofa."

"Take a step back!"

She took a step back.

"Take two more steps back!"

She complied.

"One more!"

"I'll be in the wings," said Mrs. Boyle.

"Right you are! Carry on."

At four o'clock, he called it a day. "You're all boring me. I'm leaving, now."

"We still have two more hours of rehearsal," said the pretty girl playing Miss Casewell.

"Learn your lines!" he shouted, and then left.

I followed him out. I knew my lines. I was enjoying my third drink at the nearest bar when I spotted Walter at a table in a dark corner. I didn't join him. He seemed to be enjoying his solitude as much as I was. We nodded to each other and hunkered down to the task at hand. Later, a weight lifter approached me.

"You Billy Fox?" He looked like an over-inflated water toy. "My girlfriend says you're Billy Fox. We have a bet." He jerked a muscular thumb toward a table across the room. I looked at the sculpted blond girl sitting there. She blew me a kiss.

"I get that all the time," I said. "Everyone says I look just like him."

"I knew it," said the hulk. He stalked back to his table, to gloat. I heard them arguing, but kept my eyes down.

Advice to men: Body builders are always right. No amount of alcohol can change the fact.

I did not bond with the other cast members of *The Mousetrap*. I made no passes at the women. They all seemed of a generation that I no longer belonged to. We had nothing in common, except for the deepest longing to be recognized by perfect strangers, to be adored by the public, to live the good life that comes with fame and fortune. Twice, I was mistaken for Lorenzo Larson as I strolled the beach amidst the tourists. I smiled and signed their autograph books anyway. It was the least I could do for good old Lorrie (who was, I heard, busy shooting *Alpha Force IV*, now that his ankle had healed).

Kelly came to Grand Bend for the opening. I got her a front row seat, and played the show exclusively to her. She was swept away by my performance. The reviewer for the Grand Bend Chronicler perceptively noted the "drunken angle" I brought to my character, Detective Sgt. Trotter.

"See you in hell," Walter Campbell said to me, during the opening night party. (Although I have been to hell and back, I have not seen Walter Campbell since that night.)

Kelly stayed with me for the duration of the run. I was glad for the company. By then, she no longer needed to lean against the wall. She could stand on her head, perfectly balanced, without any support. She was getting nose bleeds, but she was determined.

"If you can think of a better way to get pregnant," she said to me, "I'd like to hear it."

"Knock yourself out, darling."

I was in constant contact with Herb. I didn't want him to forget about me, now that he had Les Dodd's magnificent career to nurture.

"I've got something cooking, Billy. I don't want to talk about it over the phone. You need to keep your mind on what you're doing, out there in Grand Bend. When you get back, we can get into it in detail."

"This is all pretty mysterious, Herb. I don't know what to make of that."

"It's a little different. That's all I'll say, for now. Don't worry."

With the money I got from the Grand Bend show (I am too ashamed to call it summer stock again), I got the dent in the Corvette hammered out and repainted. My car was whole again. As long as I had my Corvette, I could have moments when I could believe that I was still on top, still Joe Maiken, still an actor worthy of the biggest trailer, still in a position to help my struggling confrères. An illusion, maybe, but one I needed to hang on to, for my own sanity.

At Herb's office, Mrs. Semple made me sit, again.

"Who does he have in there, this time? Robert DeNiro?"

"He's on the phone, Billy. Sit down."

"Probably pitching Dave Small for the lead in Scorcese's new film."

"Sit!"

I sat. Ten minutes, this time. Ten minutes!

"Sorry, Billy. Unavoidable conference call. Took longer than I expected." The office had been remodelled again. Art deco. It was tasteful, but not Herb's style. All that brushed steel reflected the wrong colours into his complexion, made him look sickly.

I dropped into a poorly padded—but trendy—chair. "So, this is what Les Dodd's bustling career gets you."

"Don't be cynical. You know as well as I do how this business works. It's cyclical. You were hot last year, Les is hot this year. Who knows who'll be hot next year? It could be you again, if you keep a cool head and stay sober."

"You make it sound like I have a drinking problem, Herb."

He let that one pass. He sipped his coffee, which left white froth on his moustache.

"What the hell is that?" I asked.

"Cappuccino." He licked his moustache.

My stomach rolled. "You're killing me."

He looked at me, studied my face. I wondered what he saw.

"Okay. What's the big secret? What is it you couldn't tell me on the phone?"

Herb held up a videocassette.

"What's that?"

"A videotape," said Herb.

"I know a goddamned VHS when I see one."

"Actually, it's Betamax. Better than VHS. VHS is on its way out."

"Spare me the sales pitch. I can get that at Bay-Bloor Radio."

Herb shook his head. "They're pushing the VHS. They're digging their own grave, if you ask me."

"Are you going to tell me what's on the tape, or shall we discuss signal-to-noise ratios for a while?"

"I'm just trying to help, Billy. My brother-in-law is the local distributor of Betamax, and he tells me VHS is on its way out."

"So you've said."

"I don't want to see you invest in obsolete technology. I'm just warning you, in case you were thinking of buying a machine."

"I'm not thinking of buying anything. I'm broke, Herb. I'm *selling* stuff. That's why I'm here, so you can get me a job that will pay me money. Then I can think about buying something, like food, perhaps, or electricity. All my lamps are more useful to me when they have electricity to power them. Electricity makes them more than just pretty objects, lying about the loft."

"I think you're being cynical again."

"Yes, Herb. Yes, I am."

"Okay, okay. Let me plug this in." He got up from his desk and went to his brand new Betamax machine. After a lot of clicks and whirrs, a picture appeared on the television set.

Some chirpy music began to play, and the picture faded up to some crudely rendered pencil animation in primary colours: a dancing stick-man with a pirate's hat. The title of the show drew itself on the screen, as if in crayon: *Captain Binky's Ship of Fun*. A sock puppet with floppy ears and a black nose popped up from bottom screen.

"Ahoy, kids!" said the sock. "It's smooth sailing ahead, now that Captain Binky is at the helm. Come on aboard! There's plenty of room for everybody. There's nothing fishy about Captain Binky's ship. We'll have a whale of a time. We're ready to set sail on *Captain Binky's Ship of Fun!*"

I rushed over to the Betamax and shut it off before my head exploded. I turned and looked at Herb, smug in his new chair, behind his new desk.

"Well?" he said. "What do you think?"

"About what?"

"The job is yours. All you have to do is say yes."

I must have fainted. I don't remember anything after that. It's a completely blank spot in my memory banks. I suspect Herb of taking advantage of my unconscious state by moving my writing hand across the bottom of a contract, committing me to the first season of Captain Binky.

Chapter 12

Captain Binky's Ship of Fun was produced by CJRK television. The half-hour children's show was just a small part of the station's ongoing efforts to keep its broadcast license by developing original Canadian programming. Since the American shows got the ratings and made the money for the station, few people cared about these locally produced "fillers." They were done fast and they were done cheap. And the children's shows, in particular, were scraped together from the very bottom of the budget barrel. The only show that went up cheaper than Binky was the T.O.Day Show, an interminable sixty minutes of soporific interviews with homespun authors and gardening experts.

When I entered the foyer of CJRK for the first time, I was walloped by the overworked—and seemingly angry—air-conditioning unit. An arctic wind came at me from all directions, tousling my hair and causing me to grip my arms in pain. No expense could be spared, evidently, to make the lobby welcoming to visitors. A splotchy and threadbare sofa sat against the wall, decomposing next to a fake palm tree whose plastic fronds were dropping away with suicidal bravado. Above the sofa hung the four massive extruded station call letters, threatening a concussion, at the very least, for anyone who dared sit below.

The reception desk was designed to be leaned on by tall men. I thought nobody was there, until I came up to the desk and leaned on it. From that vantage, I looked down and spotted the receptionist below, hunkered over a switchboard that blinked like a Christmas tree. From within the reception pit, there was no way for her to see anyone come or go. As I stood above, waiting for her to acknowledge my looming presence, busy people passed through the lobby, shouting greetings at the unseen receptionist, to which she would raise her hand and wiggle her fingers. She was wearing a parka. I could see her breath as she spoke into the telephone.

"Yes, ma'am. I'll put you through to the complaints department, right away." I saw her finger jab the red disconnect button. She pressed one of the blinking lights. "CJRK, how can I help you?" There was a brief pause. "No, sir. We won't evacuate the building again. We'll just have to take a chance, and hope that your bomb is a dud." She hung up on him. She selected another line. "CJRK, how can I help you?" A faraway voice squeaked out of the earpiece. "No, ma'am, I did not hang up on you. Your complaints are very important to us. Let me put you through to the complaints department." She jabbed the disconnect button and finally noticed me. "Yes?"

"I'm Billy Fox," I said, shooting her my winning smile.

"How nice for you. What can I do for you?"

"I'm here for the Captain Binky show."

Her eyes narrowed. "A bit old, aren't you?"

"No, no. *I'm* Captain Binky. I'm Billy Fox."

"That way, Captain," she said, pointing to a corridor to her left. She selected another blinking light. "CJRK, how can I help you?" She listened a moment. "Sir, I don't like all those commercials, either, but they pay the bills." Pause. "Yes, they are louder. We charge our sponsors extra for that service. Thank you for calling CJRK."

The corridor led to a vast open space with a low drop-ceiling and banks of flickering, unflattering fluorescent lights. The Production Room was a jumble of desks, cork boards and filing cabinets. A few areas were partially enclosed by low cubicle walls, giving the appearance of privacy to the lucky occupants. I stopped at the first occupied desk. The man sitting there was completely bald, and compensated by sporting a wilderness-man beard that hung like a wild shrub around his chin. He was talking on the telephone. He frightened me, so I moved on.

A thin, sickly girl sat at the next desk, nervously thumbing through a computer printout four inches thick. "Oh, my God," she mumbled, over and over. She looked up at me like cornered prey. "I've lost Ed Allen," she said.

"I'm sorry to hear that." I wondered who Ed Allen was.

"He was supposed to be on at six-thirty. My finger must have slipped when I punched him in. Now I can't find him. I'm going to be fired for this."

"I wish there was something I could do," I said. "But before you go, perhaps you could tell me where I should be."

"Oh, God! You're lost. I suppose *that* will be my fault, too."

"Actually, I think it's the receptionist's fault." This poor girl needed some reassuring.

"Nothing is ever her fault, believe me."

"Nevertheless—"

"Oh, my God!" she shouted, suddenly. "You're Joe Maiken!" She stood up, took a step back.

"That was a long time ago," I said. It seemed like a long time, another life.

"You can help me find Ed Allen."

"Er, I'm not really in that line of work, anymore."

Her shoulders sagged. "Really?"

"I'm more of a sailor, these days. Got my own ship. In fact, that's why I'm—"

"Couldn't you just help me? I'm going to be fired if I don't find Ed."

"Sure, sure," I said. I knew how to deal with nutcases. "The first person I need to speak to is whoever is in charge of *Captain Binky's Ship of Fun*."

"Captain Binky? Do you think he has Ed?"

"Well, I don't know if he *has* Ed, but he may know something about his disappearance. I ought to start there, see what I can find out. In the meantime, you can continue leafing through your paperwork."

She nodded.

"And don't say anything about this investigation to the others. Let's keep this our little secret."

"Okay, Joe. Whatever you say."

"So, which way to Captain Binky?"

"I think that's one of Bobo's shows," she said.

"Bobo's shows?"

"Bobo." She didn't laugh, so I assumed she was serious.

"Is Bobo a clown, by any chance?"

"Oh, no. He's right over there." She pointed to the wilderness man.

Rats. I went back to Bobo's desk. As I stood there waiting, he regarded me through square yellow lenses. The world was a sepia tone to Bobo. He must have pined for the days of old, as I did. He put down the receiver.

"You Fox?"

"Billy," I said. "Billy Fox."

He adjusted the lenses on his nose. "You don't look like a sailor."

"You don't look like a producer," I said. I may have hit rock bottom, but I wasn't going to take abuse from Grisly Adams.

"Good one," he said, without smiling. "Sit down, Fox."

"Call me Billy." I sat. Behind me, I could still hear the sickly girl moaning over Ed's disappearance.

Bobo heard it, too. "What's with her?"

"She lost Ed."

"Again?"

"So," I said, hoping to leave the mystery of Ed behind, "tell me how this will work. I've never done a studio-based show before."

"Pretty simple. You and Goober come up with the ideas for the shows, and I do the rest."

"Goober?"

"Goober. The dog. Didn't you see the tape?"

"The Betamax."

"Go with VHS. Betamax is on the way out."

"That's not what I've heard."

"It's your money, kid."

"Anyway, you were telling me about the sock."

"The what?"

"Goober."

"The dog."

"The dog and I come up with the ideas?"

"Right."

"What sort of ideas are we talking about? I mean, usually someone gives me a script and I read the lines. I'm not sure I'm comfortable writing the script, myself."

"You don't have to write anything down. You can make it up as you go. I don't really care. We'll have four cameras in the studio, lots of coverage for whatever you decide to do. Work with Goober. He's full of ideas."

"The dog." None of this seemed real to me. I wondered if I was going to wake up, find myself in my old trailer on the *Maiken Trouble* set. Maybe this was all a bad dream. I didn't hold out much hope that that was true, though.

"Monday mornings you and Goober go over your ideas for the shows. Monday afternoons we have a meeting to discuss your ideas. We tape on Tuesdays and Thursdays, three shows each day. Fridays we edit and package. The show airs at seven o'clock every morning, except Sundays."

"Right after Ed."

"Right."

"And I just sort of make things up?"

"Just remember you're Captain of the Ship of Fun. You're a man of the sea. Think of all the fun you could have with your own ship. Places you could go. Strange sea creatures you'd meet. Talk to the seagulls about what it's like to fly."

"The seagulls can talk?"

"Sure. Anybody can do anything. It's a bloody kid's show, Fox. Use your imagination. Kids love it when animals talk."

"And socks."

"What's all this *sock* business? Don't go getting weird on me, kid."

"When do I get to meet Goober?"

"I know who you are."

"Billy Fox."

"I know."

"And you're Goober."

"No. I'm Neville Fallingstock."

"Bobo said you were Goober."

"My dog is Goober."

"The sock."

"My dog."

"Right."

Neville Fallingstock was in his forties, thinning hair, weather-beaten face, short for a man, but trim. He looked as if he worked out. He looked like the sort of man who used power tools on the weekends. He probably knew how to mix his own cement and dig post holes.

"What's your background, Neville? Carpentry?" If I was going to work with him, I thought we should get to know each other.

"Fuck off!"

"Fuck off? What sort of answer is that?"

"Listen, Fox. I had my own HBO series. I did six seasons at the Stratford Festival. I toured Europe in *Waiting for Godot*. How dare you call me a fucking carpenter?"

"So, you're an actor?"

"Of course I'm an actor!"

"I had my own series, too. *Maiken Trouble.* Maybe you saw it?"

"Mindless crap."

"It was a metaphor."

"It was crap."

"It made the top twenty for five seasons."

"Congratulations. My show never made it into the top fifty."

"It must have been good."

"It was smart, funny."

"*Funny,* people will watch, but they don't want smart."

"You got that right."

"What are you doing here?"

"Same thing as you. Paying the bills. Once you turn thirty-five, the camera stops loving you."

"I'm only thirty-two," I said.

"You must be a drinker, then."

"I think I need a new agent."

"You need to get off the bottle."

"I'd rather just get a new agent."

"Naturally, you would."

I looked him over more carefully. He couldn't have been a leading man at Stratford. Probably just another disgruntled spear-carrier, jealous of the taller, better-looking actors who got the "kissing" roles. Knock off twenty years and put him in a loincloth and he might have been a halfway decent Puck, but he would never be Oberon.

"Is that your real name: Neville Fallingstock?"

In a Universe where time collapses and galaxies spiral inexorably toward the anti-existence of black holes, in a cycle of Natural Order that fosters new life, only to sweep it away in a firestorm, in a world where David Hasselhoff reins King...what, I ask, is the probability that *Captain Binky's Ship of Fun* will succeed?

How can a man call the odds in a world where a two-bit waiter flies to New York to star in a Woody Allen movie, and an adolescent pretty-boy gets the Oscar nod for directing *Painting the Cherry?* Never mind the laws of probability. Keep your sines and your cosines and your tangents safely stowed in your pocket calculator, sir. They will not help you unravel the secrets of success. Instead, find the nearest carnival and throw a few darts at some poorly inflated balloon, toss some plastic rings at bottle tops, go fishing with magnets. Prick your ears and listen for the *clickety-clickety-click* of the Wheel of Fortune, for that is where the future lies. Pick a number, any number…

Captain Binky's Ship of Fun. Episode #1.

(In the CJRK studios, on the set of Captain Binky, we have a saying: "Scripts are for wussies!" Where there is no script, there can be no proper script formatting.)

Music fades. Dissolve to camera 2.

"Ahoy, Captain Binky!" Goober (the dog?) is ecstatic. His ears *floop!* with excitement.
"Ahoy, Goober! Ahoy, kids!" Captain Binky waves his sabre in the air, slicing off the yellow feather that pokes jauntily from his pirate hat. The feather falls away, off screen. Eighty-two children shriek with laughter from the studio risers. They have just witnessed the most hilarious event in the history of the universe.
"Good thing I'm not a parrot," says Goober. "I'd be a gonner."
"Holy Harpoon, Goober. That was my favourite yellow feather. My snostrich feather!"
"Ostrich! Ostrich!" shouts the audience.
"Wait, kids," says Goober. "Captain Binky's right. It's not an ostrich feather, it's a *snostrich* feather."
"That's right, kids. Goober and I sailed for forty days and about fifty-seven nights, to the faraway land of the Grublickey-doodoos—"
Shouting, shouting, from the peanut gallery. "You can't…There can't be forty and fifty-seven…Too impossible…" And so on. A smart mob. Yet…
"Wait a minute!" shouts Captain Binky. "Hold on for just one whale of a second!" He regains control of the mob. "Now," he resets

his hat, which is lopsided without the feather on it, "have you ever been to the land of Grublickey-doodoo?"

"No! No! No!"

"There you have it," says Captain Binky, waving his sword arm in victory. Goober ducks the blade, sparing himself decapitation.

The crowd goes wild.

Captain Binky looks nonplussed. Goober ruffles his ears and gives the Captain a stern look.

"In the land of Grublickey-doodoo," the Captain resumes, "magical things are bound to happen. Not only do the snostrich birds fly backwards…" He waits for the laughter to wane. "…but the nights do not automatically follow the days. While I was there, there were thirteen nights in a row, without a single day. And after that, there were twenty-two days without a single night in between. And I can tell you, it's not easy catching a bit of shut-eye with three suns beating down on your head and the figligabutts nibbling your eyelashes."

The studio audience falls about itself with mirth. Kids love anything with the word "butt" in it.

Captain Binky twirls the ends of his mustachio. "Hey, I'd take you there myself, but you've got school tomorrow. We'd never be back in time."

Groans of disappointment resound.

"I have an idea," says Goober, *flooping*. "Let's go somewhere else. Somewhere closer, but just as magical."

"Jumpin Swordfish, Goober! Good plan! We've got this ship, right here. The Ship of Fun. We can go anywhere we want. Climb aboard, kids. Let's take a little journey!"

Cheers!

"Wait a minute, wait!" shouts Captain Binky. He pats himself down, feeling his pockets. "Where did I leave the keys to the ship? Goober, did I give you the keys to the ship?"

"Haven't seen them, Cappy."

Captain Binky slaps his forehead. "Zoinks! I've left them in the ignition."

"Again?"

Laughter.

Music up. Dissolve to bumper animation. Commercial break #1.

I admit: I was disappointed that Goober got more fan mail than I did. Neville Fallingstock was a crafty fellow. He somehow made me the patsy. I was being manipulated by a sock with a black button for a nose, and there was something unfair about that. Still, it was steady work, and I was once again being recognized on the street—this time by a squealing throng of pint-sized acolytes shouting: "Binky! Binky!" As a bonus, some of the moms were lookers.

But I discovered the kids weren't all fans.

"Are you Captain Binky?"

I was in the mall, getting a new passport. I turned and looked down on a boy, about ten, with a scour pad haircut and a sunburnt face. "Ahoy, mate," I said.

Advice to actors: never alienate the fans, even if you have recently been dealing with a government agency. The fans do not care that you have been standing in a line-up for over an hour, only to be told by a downtrodden and slack-faced civil servant that you have to fill out the *long* form, not the *short,* and it must be completed *before* you arrive at the counter, not *after.* The fans do not permit you the luxury of having a bad day, nor do they like it when you step out of character. They expect you to be *on* at all times, and to give them your time and your full attention, even in the mall. And know this: the younger they are, the more honest they will be.

"You're a *mo,*" said the scour pad.

"I beg your pardon?"

"A mo. A *homo.*"

I couldn't believe my ears. "I most certainly am not a homo."

"My brother says you are."

"Maybe your brother is the mo."

"Where's your moustache?"

"I shave it off, on the weekends."

"You look stupid without it."

"Does your mother know what a bad boy you are?"

"My mother thinks you're stupid."

"Does her head look like a scouring pad, too?"

"My sister likes you, but she's only five. I think the sock is smarter than you."

"I suppose you think Santa Claus is a *mo*," I said. I had a brief fantasy in which I tipped the scour pad upside down and scrubbed the floor with it.

"At least Santa Claus is real. You're nothing but a stupid phoney."

"Actually, Santa Claus is the biggest phoney. Your parents made him up so that you'd try harder to be good."

"That's not true!"

"Sure it is. Have you ever *seen* Santa Claus?"

"I sat on his lap, right here in this mall. I even got a picture taken."

"That wasn't really Santa. That was just some old guy with a pillow stuffed up his shirt."

"You're a dirty liar and a homo!"

"Next time, pull his beard. Ten bucks says it comes off."

The scour pad ran off, in search of his mother.

"Say hi to your little sister for me!" I called after him. Little bastard.

There were small victories, as well.

On Tuesdays and Thursdays, after locking in three more shows, I lingered in the dressing room—actually, a carpenter's shop that rarely got used because it was too small, and because it was a terrible mess that no one wanted to clean up. I needed a nice, slow bourbon to wind down with after six hours of screaming kindergarteners.

"You're never going to get on top of your game again until you get off the bottle." That was Neville Fallingstock, putting in his two cents.

"What's your excuse?" Even though we liked each other, we never really became friends during the five years of Captain Binky's run, and rarely had a civil word for each other.

"I'm too old and too short and too ugly. Nothing I can do about that. You, on the other hand—"

"Put a sock in it, Goober."

He huffed and left me alone.

Outside, in the parking lot, there was always a small group of my most ardent fans waiting to get a pat on the head and an autograph from the captain. A forest of impatient mothers loitered amidst a shrubbery of blonde ringlets. I had learned early on that I should emerge from the studio in costume. Five-year-olds apparently can't fathom the transformation from Captain Binky to mere mortal. They didn't want Billy Fox. They didn't want some thirty-something actor with faded chinos and whiskey on his breath. They wanted Captain Binky. They wanted the pirate hat, the black mustachio, the sabre.

"Where's Goober?"

"He sleeps in a sock drawer, backstage."

"Where do you park the Ship of Fun?" They all looked around, expecting to see it moored in the CJRK lot with the Mazdas and Volkswagens.

"It's anchored nearby, in Knob Creek. I have to drive my Corvette to the shore, and then row a boat the rest of the way. I'd take you with me, but there are too many gronkadiles, this time of year. It's dangerous for little kids."

The last remaining mother leaned into me. "You have no idea what your show means to me," she said, blowing the familiar fumes of whiskey into my face.

"You're not exactly the target audience."

"If it weren't for you, these two would be jumping on my head at seven o'clock, instead of seven thirty." She waved a ringed hand at the twin girls who were tugging at her hip and poking each other. "That extra half-hour is a real gift."

"Glad to help." I looked more closely at the mother. She was once a beautiful girl. She still had a figure. If she hadn't been beaten down by life—and twins—she would have been a head-turner. Instead, her beauty was shrouded in a mist of disillusionment and domestic chaos. Her blue eyes darted, endlessly in search of the mischief her daughters were making. If it weren't for the mist, I might have hit on her.

"Got somewhere to go?" she asked.

"What?"

"Got time for a drink?"

"Sure." I didn't have anywhere to be. Except home. Dinner. With Kelly, my wife.

"We're not far. You can follow me."

I sat in my car, patiently waiting the fifteen minutes it took to get two wiggly five-year-olds buckled in. I doffed the hat and peeled off the mustachio. Captain Binky punches out for another day. As I waited, I realized I didn't even know the mom's name. I remembered the thermos under the passenger seat, and was grateful. Once in a while, life throws you a random kindness.

At last, the rusty Volvo station wagon farted out blue smoke. One side of the rear bumper was swinging in the cradle of a coat hanger. As I followed it out of the parking lot, I stayed well back, in case it dislodged. We wound slowly through a new subdivision: fresh turf, gas barbeques, red tricycles, not a tree in sight. What a life! The subdivision soon led to what had once likely been a quaint village, a two-day buggy ride from the city, a century ago, now just another seedy district for the poor saps who couldn't afford fresh turf and gas barbeques.

The Volvo stopped in front of a two-storey clapboard house that should have been permitted to fall down decades earlier, but was held together against the will of Nature. There was no driveway. There was a yard that resisted the outbreak of grass. There was a muddy array of Fisher Price stock strewn about the property. On a brighter note, there were many ancient maple and oak trees lining the street. Score one for the poor people.

For some reason, it is just as hard to get a pair five-year-olds out of a car, as it is to get them in. After some struggling, and a few choice maternal expletives, Mom gave up the fight. She left the twins to fend for themselves.

"Come on," she said, waving me in.

I followed her in, and just had time to register the pervasive smell of wet newspaper when she turned and kissed me.

"You could have kept the moustache," she said, after we separated.

"Shall I get it?" I had stuck it to the dashboard.

"Do you mind?" Most women, I have found, prefer their men to be clean-shaven. The few who favour facial hair tend to be fanatical about it.

As I skipped back to the Corvette, I noted that the twins were still in the backseat of the Volvo, poking each other with glee. After being thumbed onto the dusty dashboard, the mustachio was losing its stick. It was mostly sweat that prevented it from dropping off my lip.

Mom smiled when she saw me.

"Ahoy!" I said.

"This way, Captain. The Ship of Fun is upstairs." She led the way.

"Where have you been?" After the incident with the colander, Kelly was less inclined to ambush me when I arrived home. She was wearing a housecoat and slippers.

"I had a late meeting with Neville, to go over some ideas," I said. "Sorry."

"He was here two hours ago."

A heat wave rolled over me. My forehead began to vibrate. "Here?"

"He dropped this off." She handed me a pamphlet: *Is There An Alcoholic In Your Life? The Twelve Step Program can help.*

"What does this mean?"

"He thinks you have a problem."

"I don't have a problem. Do I have a problem?"

Kelly put her arms around my shoulders. "He's just concerned. That's all."

"The only problem I have is my agent. My problem is that Herb can't seem to get me the good jobs, anymore. That's my problem."

"He seems nice."

"Herb?"

"No, Neville. He seems nice."

"Honey," I said, "I think the fact that he spends his days as a sock named Goober is conclusive evidence that nice guys finish last." I folded the pamphlet into a small square.

"If you weren't with Neville, where were you?"

Rats. I thought I had ducked that one. "Actually, I had a very important conference call with Lorenzo Larson. We were discussing a potential project that we might do together. I didn't say anything about it because I didn't want to get your hopes up. I didn't want you to be disappointed in me."

"I could never be disappointed in you, Billy. I love you."

I poured myself a drink, tossed the folded pamphlet into the wastebasket.

Chapter 13

While I brandished my plastic sabre and traded banter with a sock, Kelly took Yoga classes—a natural progression from the headstands.

"Pinderjit says I need to relax my uterus," she explained to me. "I need to refocus my energy."

"Knock yourself out, honey." It never occurred to either of us that her inability to get pregnant might have been my fault. And I never would have believed, at the time, that Yoga would lead, indirectly, to a tragedy.

As I was heading into the fifth season of Captain Binky, my father, Senior Fox, died. His heart packed it in. The doctor declared the cause of death a "myocardial infarction," triggered by a "mitral valve prolapse." In other words, natural causes.

My father was a Fatalist—although he would never admit to being anything other than a "railroad man." He felt it was his lot to work for the CNR for four decades. "If I was meant to be a doctor," he said to me, once, "why aren't I wearing a white smock and driving a Jaguar?" I had asked him why he chose to work for the railroad. I was seventeen, and needed to know that I had options in my life. I knew I wanted to be an actor, and I was afraid I might wake up some day and find myself greasing door hinges at the Ford plant. "Good solid union, down there at Ford," said my father. "You could do worse for yourself, Billy."

I flew to Calgary for the funeral. The pews were lined with craggy-faced men with rasping coughs and missing digits. Railroad men, all. "He was the best lineman on the track," they said to me. The parking lot outside the church was a museum of '67 Pontiacs, all in original condition. While Jane and Cliff railed against God (I had no idea they had recently joined a church), my mother remained dry-eyed and stoical about Senior's death.

"There's only so much sand in the hourglass," she said to me. She was a Fatalist, too.

I didn't know how to feel. Sitting in the austere cavern of Grace Lutheran Church with my family and my father's weather-beaten cronies, I felt duty-bound to spurt out a few tears to satisfy my solemn audience. After all, should not the son weep for his father? But remember: I was an actor. I was capable of turning on the taps at will. I could have cried at Hitler's funeral, if there was box-office at stake. The truth was, I never liked my father much, but I loved him. It was a fairly typical failure to communicate that put us at odds with one another. For many years, I blamed him for not accepting the choices I made in my life. (Nowadays, I see that I was equally culpable. I never gave him due credit for *his* choices. I was unwilling to recognize, until it was too late, that he was happy with his life on the track, living in the "earth tone" suburbs with his pristine automobile and my overbearing mother. He strove for the constancy of a quiet, uncomplicated life as vigorously as I pursued fame and fortune. We were more alike than I would have liked to admit. I want to believe that if he were alive today, we would find it easier to tolerate each other's company. We would sip our drinks—mine a tonic water, thanks to a new abstemious lifestyle—and laugh about our weak hearts.)

Kelly remained faithfully at my side throughout the funeral, complementing my grief with her own sorrow, which was so deep and genuine, she almost compelled my mother to well up.

Back in Senior's living room, as the wake took place in small groups of muted conversation and solemn smiles, I spotted my renegade nephews setting up for nine holes of golf. They were shaggy and morose teenagers now, a trio of conspiring dog-faced vandals. They had operated with immunity for so long, they took completely for granted the destructive fun they were about to have. I had no idea what their names were.

"Hey, you!" I said. I could still conjure Joe Maiken's voice of authority when I needed it.

The tall one gave me a steely look. "Course etiquette, man. Cut the chit-chat. I'm lining up a shot."

The junior thugs could not intimidate me. "Not much of a challenge in a ten-by-sixteen living room," I said. "If you tee off from the front yard, you can try and drive the ball over the neighbour's roof. Just be careful of the windows," I added, knowing how that would motivate them.

They shouldered Senior's clubs and bunked off to the front yard. What the hell. With any luck, the neighbours would call the police and have them hauled off to jail, where they might learn a lesson or two about life.

As for their lenient parents, I avoided unnecessary contact. As the newest members of the Church of Christ, they wore their badges of zealotry with a glazed passion typical of recent converts. Now that God had taken Senior away, they felt betrayed. Cliff snuck up on me. I was watching out the front window as the boys were teeing off.

"It's an outrage," said Cliff.

"Actually, his grip is pretty good, but his left foot is back too far. That's why he's slicing." The tallest boy arced one nicely into a chimney, two doors down.

"Huh? What are you talking about?" Cliff was looking out the window, but (as usual) wasn't seeing what was going on outside.

"Never mind." I looked at Cliff. His face was red and puffy.

"God really screwed up, this time." Clearly, he had something to say about Senior's death, and he needed to say it to me.

"This is God's fault? I thought it was a bad heart."

"Precisely. And whose fault is that?" he said, with vehemence.

I shrugged. "That's life. Some people are born with a hair-lip, some with six toes, some with a bad heart. It's just bad luck."

"There is no bad luck, Billy. Everything happens by God's design."

"Then He must have had a reason for giving Senior a bad heart."

"How can there be a reason for striking a man down in his prime?" Poor Cliff hadn't been a zealot long enough to hold court effectively. He didn't have the rhetoric down.

"Senior was somewhat past his prime."

"It's an outrage." He had run out of argument. "Jane and I are praying for you," he said, finally.

"Knock yourselves out." It couldn't hurt to be prayed for, as long as I didn't have to hear about it.

"By the way, have you seen the boys?" he asked.

I shook my head and shuffled away, wondering if his prayers wouldn't be better spent on his sons? I went to the kitchen to pour myself a drink, and found my mother pulling a ham out of the oven. I permitted her to hug me in her vague way.

"He was very proud of you," she said.

"The 'goof off,'" I said, perhaps more bitterly than I had intended.

"He watched every episode of *Maiken Trouble*. Did you know that?"

I didn't.

"He went to the Odeon three times to see that *Alpha Force* movie. And you know how your father felt about movie theatres."

I knew. He thought it was a crime to pay for a movie, after he had already grudgingly shelled out good money for cable television—ostensibly to get the sports. It figured that I would find this out after he was dead. If my mother had an ounce of compassion, she would have spared me the guilt. There is no comfort in discovering secret truths about someone after he is dead, after it's too late to do anything with the information.

"Have some ham," she said, handing me a plate.

As always, I was glad to be leaving the remains of my family far behind. As always, I vowed never to go back.

Beep..."Billy, I have a film script for you. You're on the short list. Call me when you get back and we can go over the details."

I was late getting to Cirro's. We had technical problems during the taping of Captain Binky. Goober had failed to duck my sabre quickly enough, and Neville suffered two broken fingers. Sid, the floor director, taped up the fingers with gaffer tape and the show eventually went on, but after the accident, Goober was clearly out of sorts. His woolly mouth was stiff and slow, and he didn't *floop* with his usual verve. We had to stop a second time when a spot of blood appeared on Goober's chin. It wasn't our best show.

"There you are," said Herb, as if he hadn't made me wait before. He was looking at me strangely.

"What's the matter, Herb? Too much sugar in your coffee again?"

He tapped his index finger on the space between his lip and nose.

Rats. In my haste, I had dashed away with my mustachio still affixed.

"Hi, Mister Farley. Hi, Captain," said the waiter, before I could remove the rat's tail from my face. Derby Underwood. He used to work at the Epicure Café. He might as well have called himself a writer, for all the acting he had done over the years. Soon enough, he would find out the tips were better back at the café. The rich bastards who ate at Cirro's were all cheapskates.

"Moving up in the world?" I said.

"Some of us," said Derby, making his point. At least I wasn't nicknamed Dirty Underwear.

If I hadn't been so harried, I might have asked him how long it had been since his agent had taken him out for dinner. "Bring me a bourbon. Double." Herb caught my eye, puckered his lips. "Make it a single, Dirty."

Derby stiffened. He surely must have known what people called him behind his back, but I imagine this was the first time since the fourth grade anyone had said it to his face. He stood frozen for a moment as he decided how to respond. He made the sensible choice and went away.

I exchanged a glance with Herb. "If they can't even act like good waiters," I said, "imagine what they do with Shakespeare."

We promptly forgot about the surly waiter and got down to business. "This could be the break we've been waiting for," said Herb, passing me the script. "It's a murder mystery."

I read the title: *Murder in Herring Cove*. "No kidding."

"Based on a true story. You probably remember the case. Ten years ago, a young girl went missing and they pinned a rape and murder rap on some local bumpkin who wasn't smart enough to deny the charge, got a speedy trial and a life sentence. It turned out there was plenty of evidence he *didn't* do it, but of course the authorities didn't want to admit they'd screwed up. They let the guy rot in prison for six years, until some local reporter uncovered the truth. The movie covers the retrial. You would be playing the sole eyewitness who can set the innocent bumpkin free. The only problem is, you're a drunk."

"I am not," I said. Not really.

"Not you, the witness."

"Right."

"Anyway, it's not a big-budget Hollywood extravaganza, but it's a solid production that could relaunch your film career."

"Who else is up for the part?"

Herb suddenly looked shifty. "You know…the usual," he said.

"If I didn't know better, I'd say you were dodging the question."

He sighed. "Les Dodd," he said. "Les is up for it, too."

That figured. "Back from New York, is he? Woody finally noticed he was a two-bit waiter and sent him packing?"

"Between you and me, Billy, he's in Arizona."

"Working on his tan, no doubt."

"He's in a clinic. Seems he's developed a taste for cocaine. He gets out next week, in time for the audition."

"Another sprained ankle. Jesus, Herb, I can't figure these guys who need the drugs, as if fame and fortune isn't enough for them."

"Uh-huh."

"Anyway, Les is no match for me. Let him give it his best shot."

"You could show a little compassion, Billy."

"What do you care? You get your cut, either way."

Herb rustled some papers, to change the subject. "They'll be shooting on location in Nova Scotia, in October. That means there's a conflict with your show. Your contract with Captain Binky runs through the end of December. I've had an initial conversation with your producer—"

"Bobo." I liked to say his name. It made me feel better about being Captain Binky.

"Yes. Bobo. He didn't appear receptive to releasing you early, but I'm going to work on him. I'm confident we can work something out."

"Leave it to me," I said.

After Goober's accident, he was not the same. Not only did he loose a perceptible measure of his former vim, but he seemed skittish, tense. His little button-eyes were forever on the lookout for swooping blades. He hovered at the far edge of the raster, positioned to flee at any sudden movement from my direction. Neville blamed me, of course. He would not have admitted that, at his age, his reflexes might be slowing. My thrusts and parries were well practiced and consistent. I knew my mark and I hit it every time.

"Your pacing was off, today," I said to him, after we stopped tape.

"Thanks to you, I have almost no mobility left in those two fingers."

"I don't think blaming others is the way to solve your problem, Goober."

"For the last time, my name is Neville!"

"Try using your left hand," I suggested.

He took my suggestion, but it was a disaster. He couldn't synchronize his mouth with his left hand. It was like watching a foreign film with dubbed-in dialogue. And because of the limited space behind the railing where he had to crouch, he couldn't twist his arm around far enough. Goober spent thirty minutes looking off-screen, speaking out of synch. Half way through the show, I had to improvise.

"Ahoy, Goober! Looks like you've got a stiff neck today. What gives?"

"That's right, Captain Binky. I *do* have a stiff neck today."

I clucked my tongue. "I told you not to wax the floor of the bird's nest, Goober. It's a long way down to the poop deck."

The kids went wild. The only thing funnier than the word "butt" is the word "poop."

"I sure learned my lesson, Cappy."

"Ho ho!" I had a laugh at his carelessness.

At the end of the day, I sought out Bobo at his desk. He was on the telephone, as usual. I had heard all the rumours about Bobo's wife: that she was depressive (the kind opinion), that she was a raving, needy nutcase (the more accurate opinion). No one had ever seen Mrs. Bobo. Apparently, she didn't venture out. She passed her days sitting by the telephone, waiting for her husband to call. Bobo spent every available moment of his working day muttering comforting words into her ear. As I stood waiting for him to wrap things up with the little lady, I wondered if his tinted glasses had to do with Mrs. Bobo, as if her (reportedly) bluish hue required a shot of yellow to give her the impression of natural skin tone. I reckoned she had money. Why else would he go through all the trouble?

At last, he hung up. "Sit down, Fox." He tipped his chair back and pointed his beard at me.

I wasn't intimidated. The station was overrun with politics and intrigue. Every manager from News to Programming to Mobile Sports was vying for power. They all wanted the General Manager's job, and went about the business of giving the current G.M. an early stroke with ruthless joy. They were all assholes, Bobo included, but he was my boss, so I couldn't ignore his existence, as I did the others. "How are things at the top, Bobo?" The bigger the asshole, the easier he flatters.

"Jenkins is hanging on by his nails," he said, chuckling. Jenkins was the current General Manager.

I laughed right along with him. What did I care? It wasn't my business. Every man for himself. "Listen, I was wondering about my contract."

"I already talked to your agent."

"Yes, well, I just thought that you and I—"

"What do you think this is, fucking amateur theatre? You think you can sign contracts and then just walk away from them when you get a better offer?"

"As a matter of fact, yes." It was a fairly standard practice among actors.

"What about the kids, Fox? Captain Binky is a hero to them. How do I tell them that their hero is really just some slack-assed weasel without any moral fibre?"

"You could tell them I was lost at sea. You could say I was eaten by a gronkadile."

"Very funny." He was not smiling. "You have a responsibility to those kids, and to this station, and I have a contract in my filing cabinet that says so. You can do whatever the hell you want after Christmas. Until then, the Ship of Fun sails daily, at seven o'clock sharp." The next day, I overheard him complaining to his production assistant that someone had slashed his tires and scratched the word ASSHOLE in his hood. Vandals are everywhere.

I decided to do the audition for Herring Cove anyway. I told Herb that I had been negotiating with Bobo, myself, and was confident I would be available for the movie. Over the years, I had learned a thing or two from Bobo about ruthlessness. If I got the role, I'd worry about Bobo.

I put all my energy into preparing for the audition. I was determined to do it off-book, but for the first time in my life, I was having trouble remembering my lines. It had always been the part of the process I found easiest. One or two reads and I'd have it. It was a knack I knew was rare, and I took it for granted. At the time, I attributed my failing memory to the fact that I had spent more than four years working without a script. Captain Binky worked off the cuff, running with a theme that was discussed, in general, beforehand.

I also considered the possibility that my colander-induced concussion had done permanent damage, although I did not voice that theory to Kelly. (Nowadays, I might more accurately blame it—along with the rest of my deterioration—on the booze.) In further preparation for my audition, I drank a bottle of whiskey. I didn't have the confidence I could convincingly *act* the part of a drunk. I needed to be sure.

At the studio where the auditions were being held, there was only one other man waiting in the foyer. He appeared to be drunker than me. He must have been really desperate for the work. The man looked well into his sixties, with a face like a dried up riverbed, soaked in the cheap brandy that I could smell wafting off him. Like the professionals we were, we exchanged friendly nods, and then I sat across from him, so that I could intimidate him with my own impressive drunkenness. He had the years behind him, but I was Billy Fox.

I intended to address him only with my steely gaze, but my mouth apparently had other ideas. "You're here for the drunk?"

His old skin crackled. "He's more of a druggie, actually," said the geezer. The fool.

"That's not the way I see it," I said. Had this old fart even read the script?

He looked ashamed. "I blame myself. I should have done more." He knew he was beaten.

I suddenly found a measure of pity for the old guy, and baited him no more.

Five minutes later, Les Dodd emerged from the office. He looked like hell. He'd lost weight that he couldn't afford to lose, his face was collapsing on itself and his skin had lost its colour. His eyes were open, but he appeared to see nothing, including me. "Come on, Dad," he said. "Let's go."

The old coot sitting across from me launched himself slowly from the chair and followed Les toward the exit. "Nice talking to you," he said, quietly, as he shuffled out.

How is it that fathers manage to give the worst part of themselves to their sons, I wondered? (Les Dodd's inheritance was a knack for mind-altering substances. Mine was a faulty ticker.)

Needless to say, they offered me the part, pending release from my current contract. Now all I had to do was sink the Ship of Fun.

Captain Binky's Ship of Fun. Episode #1024.

Music fades. Dissolve to camera 2.

"Ahoy, Captain Binky!" Goober is ecstatic. His ears *floop!*

"Ahoy, Goober! Ahoy, kids!" Captain Binky waves his sabre in the air, slicing off the yellow feather that is poking jauntily from his pirate hat. The crowd goes wild. The feather thing never seems to get stale. "Ho ho! Kids! Keep it down! Captain Binky has a scorching headache today."

"What's up, Cappy?" asks Goober, full of concern. "Knock your head on the poop deck again?"

Just a tinkle of laughter. Unlike the feather, the word "poop" is losing steam with the kindergarten set. They are a sophisticated bunch.

Captain Binky looks sideways at Goober. "Say, Goober, don't tell me you've forgotten last night?"

Goober somehow manages to look surprised—a tricky thing when you don't have eyebrows. "You mean the gronkadile hunting we did after supper? Hey, kids, you should have seen Captain Binky fight off those gronkadiles!" He *floops* again.

"No, no," says Captain Binky. "*After* that. I'm talking about all those strippers I fought off at Peelers. Whoa! Hey, lady, don't point those things at me! Ba-boom ba-boom!" Something sharp digs into Captain Binky's right calf, but he manages to control the pain, thanks in part to all the bourbon coursing through his bloodstream. "Surely you remember getting your ear caught in that snapping g-string, Goober? Well, maybe you'd had too many Black Russians by then."

"I don't know what you're talking about, Cappy? What's got into you?"

Captain Binky winks at the stunned audience. "Just a raging river of Knob Creek, my little sock-like friend. A barrel of bourbon has got into me. And while I've got you all here, I just want to say—" But the pain in his calf suddenly escalates. "Ow!"

"I think you've just been bitten by a calf-eating wuggum fishy, the most dangerous creature in the sea!" says Goober

The audience laughs tentatively. They aren't sure what to make of this scene. Goober looks around wildly. A calf-eating wuggum fishy could swallow him whole. "You'd better lie down, Cappy. You're delirious from the poisonous fangs."

"Sorry about barfing on you in the parking lot, Goober. It looks like you managed to clean off most of the chunks, though."

The kids roar with laughter. They all appreciate a good barfing story. Captain Binky knows his audience.

Goober is trying to push Captain Binky off-screen. "You better rest, Cappy. You're delirious. You don't even know what you are saying."

Captain Binky will not be moved by a mere sock. "Sure I do, Goober. What I am saying is that a woman's funbags can never be too big. There are so many neat things you can do with—"

Fade to black.

I sat at Bobo's desk and witnessed the destruction of my contract with CJRK television. Anyway, Bobo had just learned he'd got the General Manager's position. Jenkins had had enough. Bobo had other things to worry about, now.

"Say hello to the little lady for me," I said, on my way out. "Bye-bye, Hilda," I called to the receptionist pit as I passed through the arctic foyer for the last time. Hilda's fingers wiggled above the ledge. I made a mental note of the giant C that had fallen off the wall, and was resting on the sofa beneath. There appeared to be a blood stain. Tough luck, sucker. I was out.

I stood in the parking lot and blinked. I felt like a convict released from prison after countless dark years, thrown out into a different world, a new era. Still, I was strangely optimistic because I knew things could never get worse. I was bound for Herring Cove, and all the adventures that awaited me there. The only thing missing from the scene was a powerful musical score, ranks of violins and French horns to bring a tear to the eye. I rubbed my sore calf and sank into the driver's seat of my Corvette. It roared to life and sped me into an October sunset.

Beep..."Hi, Billy. It's Herb. I just talked to Bobo, and he's agreed to release your contract. I told you I could do it. He turned out to be a pretty reasonable guy, after all. Anyway, that's a bit of good news. I already called the Herring Cove people, to let them know you're officially available. We should be all set to go. By the way, have you seen Les Dodd, lately? I haven't heard from him for a couple of weeks. I'm sure it's nothing to worry about, but if you happen to run in to him, tell him to give me a ring. Thanks, Billy."

Chapter 14

Five minutes of a Nova Scotia autumn was enough to make me pine for Winnipeg. The raging westerly gale caused my ears to whistle. A thick-limbed kid with a Moosehead baseball cap met me at the airport in Halifax. He whisked me away in a '73 Monte Carlo held together with rust and barnacles. The kid told me his name was Bob, and that was the only coherent syllable I squeezed out of him during our drive to Dartmouth.

"You live around here, Bob?"

"Eh."

"This is my first time on the east coast," I said.

"Uh, yur," said Bob.

"I was thinking of getting my wife a baby seal-skin coat. I guess I can get a pretty good deal on something like that around here?" I was only trying to get a rise out of Bob. I didn't hold out much hope.

"Huh."

"You ever do any surfing, Bob?"

"Whuf—"

The lobby of the Seaward Inn smelled of chlorine. There was an indoor pool, but a sign informed me it was closed for seasonal maintenance. My next disappointment was the discovery that there was no mini-bar in my room. My trek back to the lobby only depressed me further when I read the notice informing me the hotel lounge had had its liquor license suspended.

A dried-up coot with a sad face manned the front desk. When his eyes came up to meet mine, I had a sudden impulse to burst into tears. "Welcome to the Seaward Inn," said the sad sack. "Do you have a reservation?"

"I've already checked in," I said.

"Are you checking out?"

"No. I just got here. I need you to tell me where the nearest bar is."

"The Harbour Lounge."

"Where's that?" I asked.

"You can't miss it." He pointed toward the locked door across the lobby.

"Let me rephrase my question. Where is the nearest bar that's open?"

"Halifax."

"Halifax?"

He pointed in the general direction of Halifax. "Over yonder."

"Doesn't anybody in Dartmouth drink?"

"I reckon they do."

"Where do they go to do their drinking?"

"Halifax."

"Right." I looked at his gold plastic nametag. Bob. Of course. "Well, Bob," I said. I had been around long enough to know that, if you want better service, learn the names of the little people, no matter how offensive they seem. "How do I get to Halifax?"

"You can get there by car," said Bob.

"I don't have a car."

"That will make it harder."

"Call me a cab."

"I'll have to bring one over from Halifax."

"You don't have a taxi in Dartmouth?"

"Bert doesn't drive to Halifax."

"Bert?"

"The taxi. He's afraid of bridges."

"Bridges?"

"The war," he explained. He looked particularly sad about that.

I didn't want to know any more. "Isn't there another way besides a bridge?"

"Sure, but it's a long way round. Bert gets sleepy if he has to drive too far."

"Maybe Bert needs to rethink his career choices."

Now Bob looked offended, as well as sad. I assumed he was somehow related to Bert. "Do you want me to call Halifax?"

"Sure, Bob." Clearly, further negotiations were pointless.

Forty-five minutes later, a taxi pulled up. I climbed into the back seat.

"You call a taxi?" asked the driver, after I had settled in.

I regarded the back of the driver's head, looking for any markings that might indicate recent brain surgery. At least he spoke English, more or less. "Take me to the nearest bar," I said.

"Okey-dokey." He steered the cab out of the parking lot.

"Isn't the bridge the other way?" I could see the steel crosshatch looming over the rooftops, out the back window.

"Yep," said the driver.

"Where are we going, then?"

"The nearest bar." He veered into a parking lot, half a block away from the Seaward Inn, came to a stop in front of Crabby Joe's Tavern. A giant neon crab with a sailor's cap snapped its claws at us from the roof. "Here we are, fella. Thirty-seven fifty."

"Bob told me the nearest bar was in Halifax."

"Bob's a moron," said the driver.

I dropped a couple of twenties in his lap. "I need a receipt," I said, just before he sped away, back toward the bridge.

There was a bang on the door.

I ignored it, reasoning that if it was important, whoever it was would have had the decency to knock softly, first.

There was a soft knock on the door. Well, what did I expect? Everything in this part of the world was backwards.

I looked down on the grizzled fisherman who stood outside my room. All the men in Nova Scotia looked like damp driftwood. "Who are you?"

"Bob." (I should have guessed.) "The cair is doonstairs, awaitin."

I screwed my pinkies into my ears. "The *what* is *where?*"

"The cair. She's doonstairs."

"I don't suppose you know sign language?"

"She's awaitin," said Bob.

"I'm going to make an assumption, Bob," I said. "You're here to drive me to the set. Am I right?"

"Ayuh."

207

I took that as affirmative. "Give me a minute." I swung the door on him, but the old net flinger jammed his driftwood foot against the doorjamb before it could latch.

He pushed the door open. "The cair's not awaitin fer a minute."

"Okay, okay. Keep your gumboots on, Bob. I'm coming."

Going down the elevator, I tried to engage Bob in conversation. I've never been comfortable with lingering silences. "So, Bob. Where's the other Bob?"

Bob stared at the panel of buttons in the elevator. "Payroll."

"Payroll? Is it payday? He's gone to pick up his cheque?"

"Payroll," said Bob. "He gone meet his payroll officer. Got to check in every week."

"Of course." I was gaining a new appreciation for silence.

The "cair" turned out to be a van, and it was crammed with bit players—such as myself. I squeezed into the only remaining seat, next to an obese woman who was to be the ubiquitous but silent court stenographer in the trial scenes.

Advice to men: A woman's hips are not a topic a man should bring up in conversation, no matter what the context—and particularly if that context has to do with those hips occupying half the man's seat. The subject of a woman's hips can only be safely broached by another woman. Even the most effusive compliment a man might give about a woman's hips will unfailingly be interpreted by the woman as derogatory. Hips are the gateway to trouble.

It was a twenty-five minute drive to Herring Cove that Bob managed to stretch into an hour. He seemed unaware there was a *minimum* speed limit on the highway. As the horns blared and the passing transport trucks caused the van to shimmy, I daydreamed of Selena.

It wasn't that I longed for her, so much as that I longed for that period in my life when I was on top of the world, a time when the name Billy Fox meant something. And Selena was an important part of that former life. I thought I was indestructible, impervious to the whims of Fate. And Selena was a living manifestation of the perfection my life had achieved. I wouldn't have believed it could have ended. Rolling across the bleak moonscape of Nova Scotia, squashed by a flabby hip, too sober for comfort, I had trouble believing it could ever happen again. I could not even conjure a solid image of Selena's face in my mind, a face that had been burned into emulsion a hundred thousand times. A million-dollar face with a body to match.

I hadn't seen Selena's face in years—not since People Magazine had reported her messy split with the heartthrob Livio. She had disappeared from the covers of the popular fashion magazines, so I assumed someone had finally noticed she was too tall or too fat or too large-breasted for current tastes. I imagined she had married a Roman named Rico, opened a small travel agency down the road from the Colosseum, and already had a couple of black-haired children running at her heels. Presumably, she, too, now had a last name. Welcome to the real world, my darling.

After that initial drive out to Herring Cove, things get a bit vague in my mind. My memory is not what it once was. I do know my gleaming silver thermos gave me familiar nourishment and comfort throughout the shoot. Crabby Joe's gave me similar comfort after the work day was done. I dimly recall making a pass, toward the end of the shoot, at the court stenographer. I might have succeeded, had I not mentioned her wonderful hips. I remember the director was a little Frenchman named Michel Dumont, who claimed to have worked with me years earlier. His name and face meant nothing to me, but his obnoxious cologne was vaguely familiar. And I know this for a certainty: there are altogether too many men in Nova Scotia named Bob.

Rather than rely on my faulty memory cells, I have rummaged through the stacks of mouldy boxes that clutter my loft and fill the empty spaces left by the trendy furniture I have been forced to sell, over the years, in order to pay the electricity bill. It took me several days, but I finally located the script for *Murder in Herring Cove*. (It's not as if I have more important things to do with my time.) Not only that, I made a few phone calls and discovered a video rental shop, specializing in "obscure and rare" titles, that actually carries a copy of the movie. Given the way the film was received when it was released in the theatres, back in 1987, it's easy to believe I am the first person to inquire about that "rare" title during the intervening years. If I had owned a VHS machine, I would surely exhume the tape from the dusty shelves of the video shop and revel in my final performance in a motion picture. I was the most magnificent drunk ever captured on film, if I do say so, myself.

MURDER IN HERRING COVE
SC. 144 — 145

INT. COURTROOM. DAY.

The courtroom gallery is full. People are standing against the back wall in order to witness the most sensational trial in Nova Scotia's history. After three days of medical and forensic testimony, everyone is eager to hear from the sole witness who can place the defendant, Mark STENDOR, elsewhere when the crime was committed. There is a hush in the room as District Attorney CHALMERS rises from his chair, ready to begin his cross-examination.

                  CHALMERS
Approaches the witness bench.
      Mister Gormley, you have given
      testimony here in this courtroom
      that would appear to exonerate the
      defendant, Mark Stendor.

                  GORMLEY
      Ayuh. I reckon so.

                  CHALMERS
      You might say, Mister Gormley,
      that Mister Stendor's very
      liberty rests upon your word.
      Would you agree?

                  GORMLEY
      Ayuh. I reckon so. I ain't the
      expert, though.
A chuckle from the gallery.

                  CHALMERS

Smiling.

> No, indeed. Perhaps you can tell the court what your profession is, Mister Gormley.

GORMLEY
> Forklift driver. Out on the docks.

CHALMERS

Nods.

> A forklift driver. And can you tell me, please, how long it has been since you've actually driven a forklift?

GORMLEY
> Been a while, I reckon.

CHALMERS
> Could you be more specific, sir?

GORMLEY
> In that case, I reckon it was '72, or thereabouts.

A murmur from the gallery.

CHALMERS
> Can you tell me why you have not driven a forklift since 1972?

GORMLEY
> I reckon on account of the drink.

CHALMERS
> Isn't it true, Mister Gormley, that you were fired from your

>   job at the docks, back in 1972,
>   because you were addicted to
>   alcohol? Were you not told by
>   your employer that you were
>   permitted to return to your job
>   as soon as you have overcome
>   that addiction? Is it not true
>   that you have not had gainful
>   employment of any kind for over
>   a decade because you are an
>   alcoholic, Mister Gormley?
>
>   GORMLEY
>   I may like the drink, but I
>   ain't crazy, and I ain't blind.
>   Drinkin don't make me a liar.
> A great murmur from the gallery. The
> judge strikes his gavel three times.

In the immortal words of the former bimbo, Jennifer Haimes: *Shakespeare it ain't.*

Kelly complained of sore knees.

"It's all that bloody Yoga," I said. "What do you expect when you sit cross-legged for hours on end?"

"Pinderjit says my mulabandha is coming along nicely," she said. "He says I'm developing core strength."

"And bum knees."

"Your scepticism isn't going to help me get pregnant, Billy," said Kelly. "A positive atmosphere is important. You're spoiling my vedanta."

"You were the one complaining about sore knees."

She burst into tears. Some things never change. "I'm doing this all for you, Billy," she said, between sobs. "All this is for us."

I held her in my arms. "I know, darling. Listen, you know that position where you get down on all fours?"

"Uh huh."

"I'll give you a little spanking, if you think it will help enlighten you."

"No," she sniffed. "I'm past all that, now."
Rats.

Chapter 15

Beep..."Hello, Jackie. This is Billy Fox. A voice from the past. I know it's been a few years, but I was thinking about you, and thought I'd touch base, see how things are going. I've been busy, myself. I just got back from the coast. Another feature film. I heard about *Heritage Creek*. I'm sorry. It was a good show. I hope you're not taking it too hard. Anyway, I'm doing a little thing in the Fringe Festival next month, and I was hoping you might come out to see it. It's an experimental piece, exploring the underlying correlation between Shakespeare's use of occultism in *Hamlet* and the twentieth century Wicca movement. There's a lot of subtext, you know, pretty cerebral stuff. Makes you really think. It's important that we develop new plays, instead of dredging up the same old fare, time after time. Well, I won't drone on any longer. Give me a call when you get a chance, and maybe we can have lunch. Ciao."

I bought a lottery ticket and called Herb.

"I'm doing the best I can for you, Billy."

"I know, Herb. Just do your best."

"That's the spirit."

Shortly after that, I sold the Corvette. I could no longer afford to keep it on the road. I got less for it than it was worth. There were too many used Corvettes for sale. Apparently, I wasn't the only has-been who had hit rock bottom. I used some of the money from the sale to purchase bicycles for Kelly and me.

"Just remember," said Kelly, "you make them go with your feet." She was teasing me, again.

"Chalk up another one for the good guys," said Dan Boyce, when he heard I'd traded in my gas-guzzling V8 for a bike. "We've got to teach those greedy oil barons who has the real power. Did I ever tell you about the time Dawn and I chained ourselves to the—"

Dean was so ecstatic over my news, his tail clubbed the tumbler of scotch right out of my hand.

"Good boy," said Dan. "Honey! Bring a cloth when you come!"

When we arrived home, Les Dodd was waiting outside the loft.

More accurately, Les Dodd was passed out, outside the loft. By the time I dragged him to the sofa, he was beginning to come round.

"Ack!" he said.

"Don't try to speak, Les. Save your strength." I was experiencing déjà vu. I resisted a sudden urge to rub his chest. Kelly brought a damp washcloth for his face.

A half hour later, Les was coherent, sitting up, drinking tea. "I don't know what happened, Billy. One minute I'm standing next to Woody Allen on Columbus Avenue, the next I'm climbing out the window of a rehab clinic in Arizona with a three-day beard and no shoes."

"Jesus."

"I really thought I'd made it, you know?"

I sipped my bourbon and nodded. "It just so happens I know exactly what you mean."

"I was living with Jackie Knowlton, for Christ's sake!"

"Good for you, Les."

"You know, Billy, every time we made love, all I could think about was that you had been there first."

"I'm not sure you should be telling me that," I said.

"All I ever wanted was to be just like you."

"Congratulations. You got what you wanted. Welcome to rock bottom."

But for the moment, Les had no sense of humour. "I'm a damned good actor."

There was no sense mincing words. Les was in need of some straight talk. "You're a druggie."

"So what? You're a drunk."

"No, Les. I'm a drinker, not a drunk. It's an important distinction."

"You're kidding yourself, Billy. Your name is on the shit list, right above mine."

"I'm not the one who passed out on your doorstep, Les. Think about that. What's next? Face down in a gutter with your pockets turned out? A fast ambulance ride, five thousand volts to the chest, and then a touching eulogy over your pale corpse?"

Les pondered the scenario. "Maybe that wouldn't be so bad. Maybe the only way to become a legend is to make a quick exit right at the peak. Look at James Dean. Look at Monroe. They didn't have the opportunity to lose their edge. We didn't get to witness their slow decline into obscurity."

"Clean up and get your career back on track, Les. That's my advice. In a few years, once you get over this dark period, you'll look back and thank me. Self-pity won't get you out of the shit hole, and taking a nosedive off a skyscraper won't guarantee you posterity. As long as your heart continues to beat, you have a chance to make it. You did it once, you can do it again. But staying alive is crucial to that plan." (In my experience, it is always easier to shell out sage advice than it is to follow it.)

"It just seems so hard. I don't know if I have it in me to go through it all, again."

"I'll tell you something. You have a big advantage over me. You started at the bottom and worked your way up. Now that you're back at the bottom, it's familiar territory. But me, I was plucked out of theatre school and placed gently at the top of the heap. I don't have the skills that you have to cope with the bottom. This is new territory for me, and, I have to say, I'm out of my element here. I need the wealth and the power and the spotlight. I need the pushing mobs and the fancy trailers. I need a personal assistant and a director who will coddle me through the process. That's what I'm comfortable with. I'll never get used to auditioning for a bunch of pot-bellied slobs who can't even read my name properly from the paper in front of them. I'll never be able to look at summer stock theatre as an opportunity. I haven't had to wait tables in order to make ends meet, but I'm faced with that prospect, and it scares me. I'm giving serious consideration to enrolling in Dentistry College."

That got a chuckle out of Les. I was glad to see him cheering up, and I didn't relish the thought of him slitting his wrists on my leather sofa. He stayed the night, and his father came in the morning to collect him.

"Thanks for everything, Billy," Les said, as he was leaving.

"Don't give up, Les."

In an act of financial desperation, Kelly took a job at a local school as an administrative assistant. She answered the phones and herded delinquent students into the principal's office.

"I like being around the children all day," she said. "It can only help prepare me for the day when we have children of our own. Just don't tell my father about the job."

"No kidding."

My days were an even mix of auditioning and drinking. Neither activity appeared to be getting me anywhere. Herb could no longer put me up for leading roles, thanks in large part to the prominent bald spot that was spreading across my scalp like ragweed. My helpful agent suggested I might acquire a toupee, to mask the offensive area, and I had to remind him that it had never been successfully done before. I did pick up the odd day in the episodic shows that increasingly clogged the downtown streets of Toronto (cheap fare that fed the voracious, undiscerning foreign markets). I sat alone at the Epicure Café. Even Dave Small had since moved several rungs up the ladder of success, and would give me nothing more than a nod in passing. He had mounted several original plays, to wide critical acclaim. He sat with a tight group of his cerebral cronies and discussed subtext over pints of ale. He no longer had real estate advice to give me. Jackie Knowlton recovered from the cancellation of *Heritage Creek*. She moved to Los Angeles and launched an Emmy award-winning sitcom.

There isn't room at the top for everyone.

I never would have believed that things could get worse.

It was March break, so Kelly was home. I was an unemployed actor, so I, too, was home. Kelly had spent most of the morning upstairs, standing on her head. After nearly an hour of this inversion, she fell into a Lotus position and began her daily meditations. I registered these rituals peripherally. I had learned to ignore the humming, in the same way I had learned, over the years, to ignore the rattling steam pipes that ran through the loft. At lunchtime, I heard her get up and begin to move around.

I was on the sofa, reading the paper. I heard Kelly mumble something. "What?" I called out.

"I feel a little dizzy," she said.

I looked up, just in time to witness Kelly tumbling down the stairs. A professional stuntwoman couldn't have executed a more convincing fall, complete with the eerie sound effect to emphasize the breaking neck. Jackie Knowlton's death pose in that dark alley, so many years earlier, seemed amateur compared to Kelly's crumpled shape at the base of the stairs.

In super-slow-motion, I ran to where she lay. There was no fleeing thug to blame, this time, there was no "Ack!", no "Graghh!", no poignant last words at all, save the ones she had uttered at the top of the steps: "I feel a little dizzy." There was no blood, so my pants were in no danger of being sullied as I cradled Kelly's head in my lap. I waited for someone to call, "Cut!", longed to hear the chirp of walkie-talkies, the murmur of key grips. I needed to talk to Rollie about the scene, see if they had me in close-up, to capture the full impact of my disappointment. I looked around to see if Donald Duke was lurking in the background, talking on the telephone. "Makeup!", I shouted. Kelly was looking too pale. On television you have to err on the side of *living*, otherwise the glamour is lost. No one came.

"Help!" I shouted. Again, no one came.

I buried my wife, my number one fan, a week before our tenth wedding anniversary. Dan, Dawn and Dean Jr. were in attendance, as were a clutch of sombre representatives of the school where Kelly worked. There were even a handful of young boys—some of the more troublesome students, apparently, who had spent a great deal of time waiting outside the principal's office, where they were given a few comforting words from Mrs. Fox, before receiving stricture from a higher authority. I heard one of the boys whisper to his friend, "I can't believe Missus Foxy is dead." I knew how he felt.

Herb was there, offering his own brand of support. "Even with a last name, she was a terrific little woman, Billy. You can be grateful for the time you had together."

My mother was at my side, as well, prim and tidy. She was shrinking into old age with a quiet elegance that she never possessed while my father was alive. "It's an outrage," said my mother. Evidently, Jane and Cliff had finally got to her, purged her fatalistic leanings and replaced them with reborn Christian zeal.

Death by natural cause, I thought, but did not say.

The autopsy showed that Kelly was five weeks pregnant.

I couldn't rouse myself from the sofa for a week, except to retrieve a fresh bottle of bourbon from the kitchen cupboard.

Beep..."Billy, I know this is a hard time, but I'm concerned about you. You haven't picked up the phone for days, and I know you're just sitting around that dingy warehouse, feeling sorry for yourself, probably halfway to drinking yourself to death. Listen to me, Billy, you're never going to get over this until you get back out in the real world. Let me help you. I have a little job that could help take your mind off things. It's a fairly small part...well, don't think of it as *small*...it's just...anyway, it won't be too demanding, and it's out of town. It'll be good for you to get away from home for a few weeks. I'm willing to come by your place and drop off the script, if that's what you'd like. If you don't think you're ready for this, that's okay with me, but please let me know as soon as possible. Call me. If I don't hear from you by the end of the day, I'm going to call the police."

I let most of the day pass before I found the strength to lift myself off the sofa. I knew that I could take Herb at his word, and I wasn't keen on having my front door kicked in, again. I got halfway to the telephone before my heart decided it had had enough. I clutched myself and fell to the floor. As always, I felt better on the floor. I recall wondering, as I lay dying (so I thought), why we humans grew so tall when we clearly thrived when we were as close to the ground as possible. How long do snakes live, I wondered?

Although the scorching pain in my chest diminished after several long minutes into a dull ache, I instinctively knew, without making the attempt, that I could not move. My face was turned to the left, which gave me an unobstructed, low-angle view of the spot at the foot of the stairs where my wife had so recently performed her exquisite, final stunt. As I faded slowly into unconsciousness, I dreamed that Kelly was reborn, this time as a snake. I wanted her to be happier next time around, and I was certain she had no idea what she had been missing, breathing the air at five-and-a-half feet. Do snakes have babies, I wondered?

I awoke in the hospital. A full day had passed since my ticker gave a giant hint of looming trouble. Herb was there, and so was my prim and withering mother—who had only barely had time to recover from Kelly's funeral when she was suddenly called away again. She was losing some of her Nazarene sheen. "I seem destined to live long enough to see everyone I love die."

"We got to you just in time," said Herb. He was beginning to shrink, too. He was only a few years younger than my mother. "I sent some boys around this morning to re-hang your front door."

"Thanks, Herb."

"It took three cops to shoulder that damned thing open." He rubbed his own shoulder in sympathy. "I'll tell you, Billy, when I saw you lying there on the floor, I thought you were a goner." His eyes were glazing.

"You're the best friend I've got, Herb."

"I'm just looking after your best interest. As usual."

"You're the only friend I've got left."

My mother's eyes sparked. "Don't talk like a fool, Billy. We haven't picked out your coffin, yet. You had a heart attack, that's all. After what happened to Senior, you should have known better. Herb told me all about your drinking. He told me it's been a problem for a long time."

I had been wondering what was taking her so long to start in on me.

"It's just like you to ignore good advice, Billy. I've been trying to tell you for years that you could—"

I tuned her out. Soon afterward, a nurse gave me a pill. Before I fell into a pharmacological haze, I asked, "Do snakes have babies?" I was out before I got my answer.

On the day of my release from the hospital, I caught a glimpse of myself reflected in the foyer glass. Herb was pushing my wheelchair, while my mother shuffled alongside. During my weeklong stay in the hospital, what was left of my hair had turned completely white. Hunched in the chair, I looked my mother's age. I have no doubt those who witnessed our solemn exit believed I was my mother's husband. But it may have just been the distortion of the large glass panes that gave me that impression. In my lap, as I rolled into the sunlight, were two Get Well cards, one from Les Dodd and the other from my friend, the writer. I was not completely alone in this world, after all.

Chapter 16

Everything after Kelly's death feels like epilogue. In this tale, this true Hollywood story, there are no simple answers to explain what began the inexorable decline of my glorious and brief interlude of fame. God or Fate? Bad luck? A random succession of unfortunate events? Would it make any difference if I knew?

The difference between learning something and knowing something is that one calls for action while the other does not. For a long time, I knew I had a drinking problem, but it was during my epilogue began that I *learned* I had a drinking problem. Two months after Herb wheeled me out of the hospital, I attended my first Alcoholics Anonymous meeting—better late than never, as my mother was fond of reminding me. Yes, one Wednesday evening, I found myself sitting at the back of a classroom, in the same school where Kelly had worked. I was part of a group of about thirty, and we sat behind wooden desks, arranged in neat rows, as if we were students awaiting a lesson. As I looked around the room at the other "students of life" assembled, I noticed that most of the members of this secret club were men. Most, like me, were in their middle age, and most, like me, looked older than they were. And just when I thought I could never be surprised again: at the podium, chairing the meeting of the local chapter of A.A., was my old comrade Neville Fallingstock.

"Welcome," he said, in his great actor's voice. He waited for the murmurs to fade, and then he said, "My name is Neville Fallingstock, and I am an alcoholic." There was a polite round of applause, during which he scanned the room, seemingly pleased by the turnout. "I'm grateful to see some new faces here tonight. A few more lucky souls have chosen to live." He looked toward the back of the room, knowing that that was where most of the new faces would be sitting. His eyes stopped when they met mine. "Please stand up and tell us your name," he said.

I stood up. I must have looked as terrified as I felt, for I received dozens of sympathetic nods from all directions. I looked at Neville. Whatever enmity there may have been between us had long gone. "My name is Billy," I said. "Billy Fox."

"Is there anything you want to tell us, Billy?"

I thought about it for a long time. I knew my line. I had read the script. Acting is easy, life is hard. "I am an alcoholic," I said. There was not an actor for miles around.

After the meeting ended, I had a rather fond reunion with Goober. We shared a few laughs over the old days, on *Captain Binky's Ship of Fun*. So many years had passed, even Neville could find some humour in my final performance on that show. And while we reminisced about those days, I was approached by one of the few women in my new club. She must have been sitting at the far corner of the room, because I didn't recall seeing her earlier. I could tell that she was once a beautiful girl. She still had a figure. If she hadn't been beaten down by life—and booze—she would have been a head-turner. Her blue eyes fixed on me. "I imagine you don't remember me," she said, "but I sure remember you, Captain."

"How are the twins?" I asked.

She laughed. "Still giving me grief." She put a hand on my arm. "Maybe you should drop by, sometime."

Neville sidled away discreetly.

"My wife died recently," I told her. I was just beginning to accustom myself to saying the words, and it was hard to say them without lodging a small stone of grief in my throat. But I was in control of those powerful emotions, pushing them back down into the compartment in my heart where they belonged.

"I'm sorry," she said.

Advice to men: Don't ever let an opportunity slip away. Always leave the door open a crack, in case you change your mind later. In a Random Universe, there is no guarantee that another one will come along in this lifetime. Take them as they come, and appreciate them while you've got them.

"Maybe you can wait a little while, give me a chance to grow a moustache."

"Sure. I'm not going anywhere."

I walked her to her rusty Volvo, and she kissed me lightly before she climbed in.

"See you later, Billy."

I waved. I had no idea what her name was, but there was plenty of time to find out.

Herb did his best, but I did not work much after my heart attack. Fortunately, I was no longer drinking what little money I had. Now and then, I coached young acting students. Like Rusty Kirkwood, I could no longer do it very well, but I was able to teach it with relative competency. I conducted my private coaching sessions from the comfort of my leather sofa, in the love loft. All of my students said the same thing, the first time they entered my spacious, run-down home: "Wow. This place has a lot of potential." By then, lofts were all the rage. I recommended to my male students that they get themselves a loft, if they wished to further their budding careers by living with a model. "But don't let them fool you," I'd say. "If they admit to having a last name, they're not the real thing." The young men would nod.

When I did act, I often travelled. I saw many parts of the continent I wouldn't have seen otherwise. Over the years I found myself in such far-flung places as Coeur d'Alene and Orillia and Tottenham and Red Deer. I did my best, in these places, to do justice to Agatha Christie and Neil Simon. They deserve it.

Thanks to my white hair and slow step, I was most often cast as the grandfather. I was pleased to be the doddering old man. I didn't get to kiss the leading lady, but the audiences loved me. No longer did I get to chase the thug, but I made the crowds laugh. In Sackville, New Brunswick, I blew them away with my portrayal of Henry Drummond in *Inherit the Wind*. Nowadays, I look good in suspenders.

But I have not been on a stage in over a year. My last paying gig was in Wolfville. I played a waiter. I needed a bit more practice to be a convincing waiter, but I had a couple of funny lines that made up for it. I suppose it was portentous, making my final curtain call as a bumbling waiter, since I am currently in training for the real thing. I move slowly as I navigate the narrow space in the Rosedale Diner, but my tray is as steady as a rock. I think my customers are impressed by me, so far. I can remember their orders perfectly, without writing anything down on paper. If they wish to chat with me about the weather, or whatever, I am only too happy to comply. Otherwise, I serve them with minimal interference. And those important customers can have absolute confidence that I will not ever beg them for work. I think they appreciate that the most about me. When famous people come into the restaurant, I pretend I do not recognize them. It isn't that I am ashamed of my own mean circumstances, but I wish all my customers to be permitted privacy and discretion. In fact, just the other day I sat a beautiful young couple in the window booth. I had seen his face on the television many times. And it was evident to my discerning eye that his companion was a model who most assuredly had only one name. Shortly after I delivered their drinks, the young man spluttered a mouthful of mineral water across the table, and began to cough and choke. I didn't overhear what the model had said to him to cause such a reaction, but I can make an educated guess. I have no doubt he will soon be trading in his two-seater sports car for a family van.

Now that I once again have an income, I have decided to save up for a car. Nothing too flashy, just something to get around town in.

Beep..."Billy, I need to talk to you. Can you come into the office tomorrow? Give me a call and let me know."

Hester made me sit. Mrs. Semple had trained her well. A few years ago, Mrs. Semple decided that she was through with show business, so she hired Hester (a pretty young thing whom I might have hit on, had I not been a wreck) and went home for good.

"I'm in no hurry," I said to Hester. I wanted her to like me. It's always good to have a friend in the front office.

Twenty minutes later, I was settled into Herb's newly decorated office.

"Jesus, Herb. You're living in the past," I said. "The English Pub thing went out of fashion in 1982."

Herb looked smug and tipped the fourth packet of Sweet & Low into his coffee mug. "We need to talk, Billy." He sipped his coffee and winced.

"We are talking."

"Serious talk."

"I think I'm getting gout," I said, seriously.

"Not that sort of serious."

"It's hereditary, you know. My father had it. He had to take a pill for it, every day of his life. Until he died."

"That's all very interesting, Billy, but I want to talk about our relationship."

"Our relationship?"

"Our business relationship."

I watched him gulp his coffee. I winced for him. "You're dropping me, aren't you?"

"This is a difficult business, Billy. You and I know that. We've experienced both ends of the spectrum. It's up and down."

"Hot and cold."

"Precisely. It may appear to be related to the business of acting, but it is really the business of fashion. As an actor, you are in fashion this season, out of fashion the next. Up and down, as I've said."

"Hot and cold."

"Precisely. Now look, we've been together for many years—"

"Twenty-five."

"Right you are, Billy. Twenty-five years. At a certain point, I have to make decisions that are difficult. I can only carry so many clients at once. If my roster gets too big, I can't serve anyone properly. So, there are times when I'm force to..." He searched for the word.

"Prune?"

He nodded. "Good word. Prune."

"I'm being pruned."

"Yes. I'm sorry." I thought I saw a tear in his eye, but I realized it was only a reaction to the massive overdose of sugar substitute he had consumed.

"Aren't we friends, Herb? I mean, we've been through a lot of things together. Not just business things. You saved my life. Remember that?"

"Yes. I remember. Of course we're friends."

"Well," I said, "I can't ask for much more than that. To be honest, at this point in my life, I need a friend more than I need an agent."

"That's the spirit, Billy."

"Would you mind if I came around, once in a while, just to talk? I don't mind sitting outside your office. That new girl, Hester, is really something."

"That would be fine."

We quietly regarded each other for a moment.

"Do me a favour, Herb."

"Sure, Billy."

"Call me Bill."

He gave me a long look, and then dumped his coffee cup in the waste basket.

I smiled at this small victory. "We all have to grow up, sometime."